South from
Hell-fer-Sartin

South from Hell-fer-Sartin

KENTUCKY MOUNTAIN FOLK TALES

Leonard W. Roberts

THE UNIVERSITY PRESS OF KENTUCKY

Contents

Introduction

South from Hell-fer-Sartin Creek lies one of the most isolated sections in the Kentucky hills. There I found and recorded the stories in this collection. The first seventy-five or eighty
of them—and perhaps several others—have come from the far
corners of the world, passed down orally through many generations. These stories would seem to lack both home and func-
tion if I did not describe the land where they were found and
its people. What I saw and heard on one collecting trip will
show some ways of the hill people.

Bill McDaniel was a student in the Berea Foundation School
when I was a teacher and story collector there. From time to
time he told me tales he had heard from his grandmother and
his great-grandmother, the latter recently dead. It was not
long before his stories prompted me to plan a visit to his home,
far back on a branch of Big Leatherwood Creek in Perry
County. A twenty-year-old senior, Bill still was pleased to get
home to see his folk. Many a student, younger or older than
Bill, has run away from the school, overcome by gnawing
homesickness.

From Berea we motored into the upland region. Here in eastern Kentucky half a million people build their houses along the tops of the eroded ridges and descend into the ravines to till the land, pasture their cattle, or work in the mines. Where the hills rise higher and higher and sharpen at their peaks, and the valleys get narrower, the houses come down from the crests and perch on the slopes or occupy the small level patches along the valley floors. Just a few old log houses are left. Now there are sawed lumber or frame, weatherboarded structures with not a few simple boxed cabins. Occasionally some man has remembered the comfort and protection of the old log dwelling and has built himself a new and better one, with good window light and even perhaps furnace or gas heat.

Bill talks and points out more and more familiar objects. He tells me that often the very road we are on has been scattered with kegs of tacks; all the trucks have had flats and the traffic has ground to a halt. The cause? Well, organizers have been sent in, or small groups of local miners have got together and tried to form a union. But there are too many small operators and too many men who own all or a part of the mines where they work. Occasionally their trucks are fired upon, or a barricade thrown across the road, or a bridge blown out. But they do not want a union and have never been organized.

Through this hilly country we hear odd place names, odd until one thinks of them and realizes how they reflect the light imagination and the humor of the early settlers. Out of Manchester we drive along Goose Creek and by the mouth of Bull Creek. Over the way from Hyden is Thousandsticks Creek, and we see the modest weekly newssheet in Hyden is called *Thousandsticks*. Ten miles down from the county seat is the mouth of Hell-for-Certain ("Hell-fer-Sartin") Creek, and a few miles farther the mouth of Cutshin Creek. Kingdom Come is over in Letcher County and Troublesome Creek in Perry County.

We are soon picking our way through the one-way, vehicle-clogged streets of the crowded town of Hazard, the seat of Perry County. It is made up of strings of buildings extending along the river and up the ravines and coves. The old court-house here was once taken over by one feuding faction and barricaded in defense against the other faction stationed behind trees and houses and in ditches. For a few weeks a company of state militia camped on the courthouse square to restore order. But the story of mountain feuding is too long and complex to tell here.

On the black-top along the left bank of the North Fork several miles above Hazard we come to a very thinly settled region. The hills tower higher and the river valley takes on a more canyon-like appearance. At last we reach the mouth of Big Leatherwood Creek and turn off onto its graveled road. Bill directs the way with free and easy comment. He is animated, even excited, to be back in the old familiar valley. He has also opened up his hoard of stories and has told me three or four long tales, the one about Jack and the Giant's tasks and another about an enchanted cat, and the one about the girl in the robbers' cave. I have asked him to be sure to remember them when the recorder is set up and when his folk hesitate to tell their stories.

Although the mouth of Big Leatherwood is narrow, the creek is about fifteen miles long and thickly populated. Perhaps three hundred families live along the banks of this one stream. The upper eight miles of the road along the bank are hard-topped because of the large mine of the Blue Diamond Coal Company in the very head of Clover Fork. Here too is one of the largest sawmill sets in the region, choking the valley with its field of lumber stacks and large camp village.

Bill is from a broken home. He had gone to the settlement school at Buckhorn for three years. His brother John, too young to be accepted at boarding schools, lived around with his kin, and the youngest brother had been staying with an elderly couple over on Cutshin. Bill has me stop in a lonely place on the road as he points to a shack down in a field by the creek bank. "My dad lives down there by hisself," he says. I wait while he goes down there. A home in the mountains without a mother is the saddest situation in all creation. If the

After Bill and I had toasted our shins and had made ourselves at home, Bill told them more about my work and about the recorder and how it would "take down their voices." The adults were as curious as the children to see the machine and how it worked. I brought in the machine and a suitcase of accessories and like a peddler opening his pack set it up and plugged it into the dropcord in the middle of the room. The adults watched every motion, and the little ones put their hands on the reels and covered the electric eye to X-ray their fingers. After Bill told two of his stories, Delbert, though hesitant, gave out with two or three of the many "Arshman" jokes that he knew. To my surprise grandma agreed to tell a story that Bill and I brought to her mind. She let me hold the microphone in front of her while she told that curious legend, "The Origin of Man" (No. 79). Bill asked the young mother to tell one of hers that he had often heard from her. She shook her head bashfully and said she didn't want to. But later she called Bill into the kitchen and he returned and told for her an excellent Irish folk tale, "Jack and the Bull's Horns" (No. 20b).

Delbert's wife announced, "Supper's ready," and Delbert, with the usual mountain hospitality, urged, "Le's get ready to have a little bite, boys." He carried chairs to the long table and then gave us more attention by pouring water and standing back for us to wash. Bill did not need to be urged or coaxed. Granny came to the table and took a place that no one had touched. "Eat right over there," said Delbert, pointing out a choice place for me. The smaller child hung back and looked to its mother, while the older one got ready to climb into its daddy's lap. So he did when we were all seated. "Now just reach, Bill, you fellers, and take what you can and what you can't, why holler for." Delbert gave directions in this vein as we passed the soup beans, scalloped potatoes, fried meat, and piping hot coffee. The mother fed the baby on a side table, but she did not eat a bite herself until we had left the table, a pioneer custom that persists in the hills to this day. The women serve strangers and visitors and wait for "the second table." Even if a courting young man is in the home, his sweetheart will wait the table while he eats with the men.

When supper was over, it was pitch dark outside, a time when few people stir in the hills. Bill had mentioned Charles Halcomb, his cousin, as the best storyteller in the country. We set out to find him, first starting to his home up on Beehive Creek. We "halloed" a house or two before we found him courting in a small frame house propped on the hillside high above the road. There he sat in one corner, behind a large heating stove, with a girl beside him and children and old folk in a circle around the stove. He showed interest in storytelling after we had warmed and had explained our business. Chairs were set for us. The man of the house said to him, "Yeow, Charles, tell 'em that un about goin' a-huntin'."

Charles started out, stopped to clear his voice, grinned good-naturedly from the edge of his sofa, and then went through the story "Coon Skin Huntin'" (No. 78a). This was the first time I had heard the minstrel-like piece, and I was taken with it. But not so much as were those around the stove. They laughed at the clever turns and encouraged Charles to make it funny. Later he told me that he had heard it on a "talking machine" record when he was a boy. He also told me how he had been with a troupe on the local radio station to tell a humorous story between songs. For the part he had dubbed himself "Chad McCuul." He made friends so easily and entertained so gladly that I consider him perhaps the best performer in my collecting. His voice was high and mirthful, his manner shy but affable. He had every trait of the offhand country boy.

We prevailed upon him to go with us to the electric current back at the old home place, where we recorded stories, off and on, from about ten o'clock until three-thirty. Grandma stated that she could not sleep until late and stayed with us until she had told a number of legends and "Arshman" anecdotes. The high moment came when Charles thought of a delightfully humorous (and very rare) obscene *Märchen*. Grandma held herself as best she could but had to snicker with the rest of us.

on tape, which I transcribed as faithfully as possible, preserving the irregularities of colloquial form and attempting to reproduce the dialect phonetically without making the text unintelligible.

Thirty-five years ago most of eastern Kentucky could be reached only on horseback or on foot. For more than a hundred years the settlers on the hillsides and creek bottoms had been isolated from the rest of the nation. They became self-sufficient because they had to, tilling and distilling their own corn, working for the lumber companies until the best timber had floated down the creeks and rivers and then for the coal operators who brought in a new economy on narrow-gauge tracks. A man raised a large family in the home valley, and in their turn his children raised large families, so that a man like Joseph Bach, a cousin of the composer, who came to the area in 1798, might have thousands of descendants today. Related families formed clans, and after the Civil War a simple incident like the theft of a pig could so enflame animosities already kindled in the recent strife that they would flare up into feuds, the most famous of which was the Hatfield-McCoy war that killed almost a hundred men and women in ten years and involved the governors of Kentucky and West Virginia in an epistolary duel.

If violence did break out now and then, by and large the hill folk lived peacefully with each other. They worked long and hard, but they relaxed and played, too, and the result for us today has been a rich heritage of song, game, and story. The reputation of a particular storyteller would spread from valley to valley until others wishing to demonstrate the quality of their stories would attribute them to such "big liars" as Sol Shell, who unwittingly was repeating the eighteenth-century adventures of Baron Münchausen. A grateful "stranger" would repay his host's hospitality with a story or two, and if he should happen to be a schoolteacher without a background of folk tales, he might relate a Greek myth or a fairy story from Grimm which, retold in the idiom of the hill people, quickly passed into the oral tradition. Then as now, court days were occasions for gathering at the county seat. After the necessary business was transacted, the men would meet to talk, and sooner or later they would exchange anecdotes and jokes, laughing at the latest obscene story—one which might have been written on papyrus in Egypt two thousand years earlier.

After World War I the way of life in the Kentucky hills quickly changed. The growing industrial demand for coal coupled with the improvement of the automobile brought more and better roads. With the highways came the electric lines, and with electricity came the radio. In boom times thousands of men and women traveled over the new roads to the industrial centers; laid off in slack times, these homesick people came back to their valleys with new ideas of how to live. Another direct result of highway building—school buses—promises a cultural revolution within a generation. But even the illiterate listen to the radio and pattern their lives after the notions of men living in the steel and concrete mountains of Manhattan.

The significance of these changes for the folklorist is tremendous. The old ways of entertainment have been almost forgotten. The haunting tunes of the folk songs have given way to whining hillbilly music, and the barn dance has replaced party games. People no longer gather for an evening of storytelling. Only the timeless obscene story travels from person to person, the one form of folk tale that survives in even the most sophisticated of societies.

Along the creeks of the Pine Mountain watershed I discovered probably the most isolated settlements in eastern Kentucky, where the folk tales were still remembered, if not told. I was able to drive almost all the way by jeep; I had little difficulty in finding an electrical outlet for my tape recorder. In another ten years this area, too, will have lost its distinctive folk culture.

Most of the mountain folk are Scotch-Irish. It is natural, therefore, that the tales they tell should be largely of Irish origin. Indeed, an analysis of the racial stocks in the Cumberland Plateau gives a good indication of the sources of the folk tales. Only about half of these supposedly pure Anglo-Saxon people came from England. Another 35 per cent migrated from Ireland and Scotland, and 15 per cent came from Germany. These rounded figures do not take account of the splinter groups, of which the most significant is French. My own examination of the parallels to the stories in this collection tends to bear out the conclusion that the principal source for the tales is the British Isles, with a strong inclination toward Ireland. The second most important source is Germany. Although I found more parallels from the Baltic states than from France, they seem to me unlikely as a direct source, and I would place France third in this list.

Here, then, are folk tales of eastern Kentucky. The student to whom the paraphernalia of scholarship are important will find detailed notes at the back of the book, where I have summarized minor texts not printed here and assigned type and motif numbers as I could. If the general reader finds pleasure in these old stories and from them gains some insight into a way of life that is now vanishing from our country, I shall feel amply repaid for collecting them.

Animal Tales

I have divided this collection of stories according to the classification of folk tale types set up by Antti Aarne and enlarged
by Stith Thompson. Under animal tales, the first major category of the Aarne-Thompson index, fall those stories in which
the principal actors are nonhuman but behave in a human
manner. Reynard the Fox, Br'er Rabbit, and the Three Little
Pigs are five such quadruped folk heroes. The title of the
section is somewhat misleading, for the actors may be inani-
mate objects, such as straw and lumps of coal, as well as living
creatures. The first tale in this collection, for example, has a
parallel version, current throughout the Orient, in which sticks
and beans go on a journey; they hide in the house of an old
woman during her absence and on her return attack her in
their characteristic ways.

When I sorted my texts, I found only one story that I could
place under animal tales. The scarcity of this type of folk tale
is not, I believe, typical only of eastern Kentucky. Apparently
not many stories with animal actors have entered the British-
American tradition. (The Uncle Remus stories and other similar collections of animal tales made in this country are in the
American Negro tradition.)

1   *The Animals and the Robbers*

ONE TIME THEY'S a donkey, and an old woman and old man owned it. They said it was gettin' too old to work and they's goin' to kill it. So it heard 'em and it went and broke the stable door down and started down the road. And it met a rooster. That rooster was crowin', and he said, "Rooster, why do you crow?"

He said, "Well, they said they's goin' to kill me, said I was too old to keep around on the farm."

He said, "Well, come with me and they won't kill ye."

So they went on and they met a cat. And that cat was meawin'. And they said, "Cat, why do you meaw?"

He said, "Well, they said they's goin' to kill me, I was too old to catch mice."

He said, "Well, come and go with me and they won't kill ye."

They went on and they met a dog, and that dog was barkin'. They said, "Dog, what makes you bark?"

He said, "Well, they said they's goin' to kill me, said I was too old to watch cows."

They said, "Come and go with me and they won't kill ye."

They went. And they laid down by a big tree when it come dark. The rooster flew up in the tree and the rest of them laid down there. That rooster looked way off and seed three lights. And he hollered and said, "Well," said, "I see three robbers way yonder, countin' their money," said, "le's go and get us somethin' to eat."

They all got up and went there and that donkey put his feet on the winder, the dog got on that donkey's back, and the chicken got on the dog's back, and the cat got on the rooster's back. And they all started makin' noise. The donkey was brayin', and the dog was barkin' and the cat was meawin' and the rooster crowin'. They run them robbers out. And they all went in there, and the cat got under the stove and the dog got behind the door and the rooster flew up in a tree and that donkey got under the floor.

One of them men said he was goin' to go back in the house and see what it was. He got in the house and started to punch the fire up and that cat scratched him. He started to run out the door and the dog bit him. Got out there and the donkey kicked him in the road. The rooster was up in the tree sayin', "Cock-a-doodle-do."

He went back and told them, said they's a witch under the stove scratched him, and said they's a giant grabbed him and pinched him, and said they's somethin' kicked him in the road, and said they's somethin' else sayin':

Cock-a-doodle-do
Let me kick him too!

Well, it come Jack's time the third day. And he says, "I'll shore not be tricked by him." Says, "I'll fix him up good and proper." So he goes out and splits him a log open and puts some gluts in it, to hold it apart. He goes in and gets dinner—gets it about ready and this man comes in and he says, "How long is it till dinner?"

"Oh," he says, "I just like goin' out and pickin' up a load of chips." Says, "You got to go with me."

They argue around for a long time, and finally this old man goes with him. Well, this old man would pick up around the log, and Jack he's a-easing up around this log where them gluts was in there holding the log apart. This old Dirtybeard gets his beard in there and Jack he pulls them gluts out of the log and catches him. Then he tugs around while Jack goes on and gets dinner. He tugs around and gets loose. The boys come home for dinner. They eat and talk about it and say, "Well, we're goin' to follow him." Well, they saw the blood in the snow. They went a long ways and finally they come to the ending and they was a big hole in the ground there. And Jack says, "I'll go down first."

And they say, "O.K.,"—the boys did.

He goes down and there sets that old beardy man with a razor. He says, "I'm goin' to cut your head off."

And Jack says, "Well, I don't want to be killed with no dull razor. Let me look at your razor. I want to make shore it's sharp."

And he says, "O.K."

He hands him the razor and he cuts *his* head off, down in this hole, and he hollers to Tom and Bill up above and says, "Come on down."

They come down. They's all kinds of meat and things, and all kinds of good stuff to eat down there. And three pretty girls down in there too. He says, "Well, we'll take these girls back when we go."

And Tom and Bill they got out. They climb up on Jack's shoulders and get out. And Jack, he can't get out, he is left down in there. They get his girl out and take her on back home with them. Well, he stayed down in there, and they's a hawk flew down in there, and he asked him, says, "Can you fly out with me?" and he says, "I'll give you all the meat you can eat if you can."

And he eat so much meat that he couldn't fly out with him. And he says, "Well, I just can't do it."

And Jack stayed a day or two longer, and they's a big eagle flew in. And he says, "I'll give you all the meat you can eat."

Well, this time he eat the meat afterwards. So he flew out with Jack, and he gave him all the meat he could eat. He hit out for home. When he got there Tom and Bill had picked out two of the purtiest girls and married them. So Jack had to take what was left over. And he got married too, and they settled down and lived happy ever after.

Alice and Ben 3a

ONCE UPON A TIME there was a little boy and a little girl; the boy's name was Ben and the girl's name was Alice. They lived with their mother and father in the forest. There was nothing but trees around their house, and they were very poor.

One day while Alice and Ben were playing out behind the house under a big clift whore they had a playhouse, the wind was blowing very hard, black clouds were coming over, and it was getting dark because it was coming up a big storm.

Ben said to Alice, "I am going in the house to get me a drink. I will be back in just a minute." So he went in the house. And while he was gone, a big bear jumped out from behind the rock and got Alice on his back and carried her off.

In a few minutes Ben come back but he couldn't find Alice any place. He ran back in the house and told his mother, so they all started looking for her, but no one was able to find her. So it passed on for two or three weeks. Still Alice had never been found. Everyone thought the wind had blown her away.

The two old witches come to the house and asked for some bread, and Jack gave them some. Jack said to his mother, "Mother, they have hands like dogs."

Jack's mother said, "That is the way all naughty people look."

Then Jack said to his mother, "Mother, they ate that bread like a dog."

Jack's mother said, "That's the way all naughty people eat."

Then the two old witches asked Jack to show them the way to another road. Jack didn't want to, but he finally did show them the way. But first he set a basin of water on the porch and stuck a willow switch in the basin and said to his mother, "When the water turns to blood and the limb shakes, turn my dogs loose."

Then Jack started out to show the women the way. When he had got about a quarter of a mile he looked back and saw they were down on their knees following him like a dog. Then he begin to run, and they come faster. Then he climbed a tree, and they turned their tails into axes and begin to chop. They nearly had the tree chopped down when Jack dropped an egg which he had found in a hen's nest before he had gone to show them the way. He dropped an egg and said, "Fill up!" and the tree became normal. Then they begin to chop harder. Then the tree was nearly down when he dropped another egg and said, "Fill up!" And they begin to chop harder, and Jack had one more egg in his pocket.

Jack's mother had went out on the porch where she saw the willow limb shaking and the water had turned to blood. Then she turned the dogs loose and they started after Jack's trail.

When the dogs had reached Jack the tree was nearly falling. Then Jack saw the dogs. Jack said to the dogs, "Drag them around and around for one mile!" Then he said, "Drag them around for three miles!"

Then the two old witches was dead and Jack was safe.

Jack Outwits the Giants 4

ONCE THERE WAS two boys. The mother and father was moving. They was out on the road and it was getting late. They decided to make camp. So after they eat supper Bill said he would take the first watch. So while watching that night he walked off in the woods and he saw a deer. So he shot at it and missed. Jack told him not to shoot, liable to cause the king to come. So Jack took the rifle, and Bill went back to go to bed.

Jack went out and climbed up a tree. And it was nearly morning when he looked over on the hill and he saw a big far and kittle, and three big giants. Looked like they was cooking cows. They had forks big as hay forks, and spoons like shovels. And they was eating, and Jack took aim and he fared at one. The fork jobbed in his chin. And that giant said to the next one, "Did you shove that fork in my chin?"

He said, "No."

The next giant he started to take a bite, and Jack fared. The fork jobbed in his chin. He said to the other giant, "Did you job that fork in my chin?"

The other giant said, "No."

The third giant started to take a bite, and Jack fared. The fork jobbed in his chin. He said, "Who jobbed that fork in my chin?"

The two giants said, "I don't know."

The giants was all mad and about ready to fight one another. And they decided they'd find out what was going on. So they went out and looking around and they saw a boy up in a tree. They walked up to him. Said, "Was you the one causing us to stick those forks in our chin!"

He said, "Yeow," said, "I was shooting this rifle."

They pulled him down and said, "We orght to kill you for that."

big tower and when she wanted to go up to her she would say, "Reptensil, Reptensil, let down your long hair." And she'd let down her long hair and this old witch would climb up her hair.

One day they's a prince passing by and he heard the old witch say, "Reptensil, Reptensil, let down your long hair." He went over. After the witch had gone down he said, "Reptensil, Reptensil, let down your long hair."

She thought it was the witch and she let down her long hair. And this prince climbed up her hair. And when he got up there, she said, "Who are you?"

He said, "I'm a prince."

And this girl said, "Do you know of any way you can get me out of here?"

He said, "No." They talked a while and he went back down her hair.

And he'd come back once a day for a month. And one time he was up there and the old witch had left her black hat up in the tower, and she came back to get it. And this prince was up there. She said, "What are you doing up here?"

He said, "I come up here to see Reptensil."

And she said, "I'm going to scratch your eyes out and throw you down in the briars." And she scratched his eyes out and threw him down in the briars. She said, "Reptensil, I'm going to take you out of here."

She took her out, and Reptensil jerked away from her when they got down on the ground, and she run over to that prince. And this old witch had made Reptensil's tears if they hit his eyes he could see again. She made him blind when she scratched his eyes out. So her tears hit his eyelids and he could see again. And Reptensil started running after that old witch, and she went and run over a clift. And Reptensil and the prince went to get Reptensil's mother and father and took them to his castle and they lived happy ever after.

The Little Blue Ball 6a

ONCE UPON A TIME there was a woman and she had three daughters. One day one of them was out in the yard sweepin' and a little blue ball come rollin' down the hill, and she begged her mother to let her go and get the little blue ball.

She said, "No, I'm afraid you'll foller it into the giant's den."

She said, "No, I won't, mommy. I'll come back."

She took off after the little blue ball and she follered it into the giant's den. The giant said:

> Wash my dishes, feed my cat and dog,
> Make up my bed, sweep my house,
> And I'll give you a hundred dollars
> And a buggy and let you go home.

Well, the giant went off, and that night when he come back he said, "You didn't feed my dog, did you?" The dog was out a-barkin' and jumpin' up on him.

She said, "No, I'll go feed it."

He said, "No, I'll feed it myself."

He cut her head off, hung it up in the closet, and went and fed his dog.

The next day the other little girl was out in the yard sweepin' and the little blue ball went rollin' down the hill. She said, "Mommy, I want to go get that little blue ball."

She said, "No, I'm afraid you'll foller it into the giant's den like the other little sister did."

She said, "No, I won't."

She took off after it and she follered it into the giant's den. The old giant said:

> Wash my dishes, feed my cat and dog,
> Make up my bed, sweep my house,

"I'll test you some more. If you have one speck of blood on you when I get back I'll hang you up in the Bloody House with your brother."

So Clever stayed there and he saw the same bird and he was trying to catch it when he fell and cut his knee. It bled and run down his leg. The bird said, "Give me some bread and butter and I'll lick every bit of that blood off of you."

So he pitched the bird some bread and butter and the bird licked every bit of the blood off of him. He saw the man coming. When he got there he told Clever to stick out his right arm. It didn't have any blood on it. "Stick out your right leg." It didn't have any blood on it. "Stick out your left arm." It didn't have any blood on it. "Stick out your left leg." It didn't have any blood on it.

So the man who ran this Bloody House gave little Clever two big white horses, plenty of clothes, and a lot of money. And the last time I was down there the boy was doing fine.

7 C   *The Golden Ball*

THE NAME OF this story is "The Golden Ball," and Johnny plays in it. One day he was playing with this golden ball and it rolled down the hill. Well, he went down the hill after it, because he knowed if he lost it he wouldn't get another one, because his father told him if he lost it he wouldn't get another one. So he went down there to get it and it rolled in a hole. He started down this hole to get it and he'd go down and he'd see the ball but he couldn't reach it. He just kept going and going until he come to some steps. He got to these steps and he started down these steps and he seed a light. He could still see his ball. He would get just about to it and it would roll on. He'd go again and he'd get almost to it and it would roll on. And it went on down and he got down in there and he seed a house. And this ball rolled right on the porch of this house.

And he went in and when he got on the porch the door opened. The ball rolled on in the door. He went in the door and there hung dead people all around in the house. He looked at them but he wasn't paying any attention to them. He went on after his ball, and it went in another room. He went in this room and they wasn't anything in that room but coffins and dead people. It rolled on into this other room and he went in and they wa'n't nobody in there but an old man, a giant setting there. And he asked him what he was doing there and he told him he was after his ball. And he said, "Well, I have your ball," and said, "I'm going to kill you."

He told him not to kill him.

And he said, "Well, if you'll stay down here with me I won't kill you." And said, "They's a woman killed me and buried me here," and said, "I've killed all these people and brought them down here," and said, "if you will stay here with me I won't kill you."

One day he told him he was going out for a while and for him not bother nothing. And he put this ball in a casket with a dead woman. And he went to this casket where this dead woman was and spoke to this woman and she told him to go and get her head and that she would give him the ball. And he went to try to get her head and he got the wrong head. About that time the old man come in and he told him if he ever caught him with another one of them dead people's heads he'd kill him.

Well, the next day he went off and told him not to bother anything and that he would be back. Well, he had been gone about an hour and he come in where this woman was and the woman told him to go and get her head—that her hair was blond. He went in there and every one of the heads in there had blond hair. Well, he didn't know which one to get. He brought one and it was the wrong one. The old giant caught him this time and tied him up and kept him tied about a week.

He turned him loose and told him one day that he was going out to cut wood, for him not to bother anything. He went out to cut wood and he had been gone and gone. And this little boy went in and was talking to this woman, and this woman told him to go hunt her another head and see if he could find the right one. He went in this other room to get this head and he got the wrong one that time. The old man come back in and caught him and tied him down for a while. And then he turned him loose, and he stayed around there for about a week. And this old man had to go out and he told him he had to go out and told him he would be gone for two or three nights, for him not to bother anything.

Well the old giant had been gone about an hour that day, and this little boy went on and got another head and brought it in and it was the wrong one this time. And they was a man upon the left. He spoke to him—the man that was hanging up—and told him to go and get his head and his little baby's head. That was his wife a-laying there, and they would help him out with his ball and take him back home.

He went and got the man's head but he never did get the other's head. They started to hunting, and they got all the heads, and the man helped him.

So they started off and they got about half way up the stairs and this old giant started after them and run up the stairs and caught 'em and brought 'em back and cut their heads off, and took Johnny back in and told him he never would go off and leave him any more, because every time he went off he got into something.

Well, Johnny decided that day that there wasn't any hope for him to get out. So that next day that old man told him he would be gone for a week. This man that was hanging up there told him to bring his head and his baby's head and his wife's head and that they would get out.

So they started out about dark and they got almost up to the top of the steps where they started out the top of the ground and they seed this old giant running after them. He run 'em out the top of the ground. And finally they's a man killed him.

32

Jack and the Giant's Tasks 8

ONCE UPON A TIME there was an orphan boy and he started out to seek his fortune. And he went and went and finally he came to a house. And he stopped at this house and a woman came to the door and asked him what he wanted. And he said he would like to work for her and stay with her. This woman said, "My husband is a giant and you can stay if you want to and if you will do what he says."

So the boy he went in and the woman give him something to eat. And she sent him to get some water. And he went and got the water and brought it back to the house. And here at this house there was also a little girl. She was a very good looking girl and this boy he fell in love with her. And when the old giant come in that evening he was pleased to find out that he had somebody to do his work. So when he left the next morning he said, "You have Jack—" that was the boy's name—"Jack to clean out the barn." And said, "If he hasn't got it cleaned out by the afternoon I'm going to kill him and eat him tonight," says, "I'll kill him and eat him."

So the woman sent Jack out to clean out the barn. And Jack he started out shoveling out the barn. And every time he'd shovel out a shovelful of the manure why two more would jump back in. This went on till along in the evening. And this little girl she was at the house and she asked this woman, says, "How about me taking Jackie something to eat?"

And she said, "No, don't you take him anything to eat," said, "let him hurry and clean out the barn and," said, "if he don't," said, "he will be killed and eaten tonight."

So she waited, and finally Jack—he just kept on working but he couldn't get anywhere with his work. And this little girl went out where Jackie was at and he was setting down and crying. And she said, "Well, you just set here and put your head in my lap and let me look in your head."

And he did. And he fell asleep while she was looking in his head. And when he woke up the girl was gone and the barn was cleaned out. And that night when the old giant come in he told him that the next day he said for Jack to pick enough feathers off some birds which the giant had killed that day to cover a barn.

And Jackie next morning he started out to pick these feathers. He picked and just as fast as he pulled one feather off, why two more would jump back on these birds. He done this till about all day, till along in the evening and he was becoming disgusted, and he set down and started crying. This little girl come out and she told Jack to put his head in her lap and let her look in his head. And he fell asleep. And when he woke up why the feathers were off the birds and the barn was covered.

This little girl told Jackie, says, "Le's leave now," says, "le's leave this place."

And so they got ready to leave, and they struck out. And this old giant when he returned that evening why he found out that they were gone and he became very angry. And he had a nine-mile pair of boots. And he got this nine-mile pair of boots and started out—went and got a big bull and started riding this bull. As he was going along he was about to catch up with this little girl and little boy. And finally this little girl wished the mountains would come up, big mountains, so that he couldn't get across. So he got down and he started jumping with these big boots. He started walking and he could step across this mountain. And this little girl she wished that a big lake of water would come up so he would fall in it and drown. So they was. And this old giant fell in it and was drowned. And this little girl and boy they went on and lived happy ever after.

THIS BOY ONE DAY decided he'd go out into the world to see if he would see anything to be afraid of. Well, he started out one day and walked all day. He was tired and hot. And that night he come and seen a big white house—purty too—up on the side of the bank. He hollered and said, "Hello." Nobody didn't answer. "Well," he said, "I think I'll just go up there and see if anybody lives up there."

He went up there and they wa'n't nobody in there. He opened the door and they's a little bed back in the corner. And he said, "I can't understand why nobody lives here. This is an awful purty house." Says, "I believe I'll just go on down the road."

He went on down about a half mile and saw a little hut on the side of a hill. It was getting dusty dark. He said, "Hello." And they's an old man come to the door. He said, "I'd like to get to stay all night here."

And the old man says, "O.K."

And he went up and eat supper and he says, "Why ain't they nobody lives up there in that big white house about a half a mile up the road?"

He said, "Oh, that place is hainted." Says, "Won't nobody live up there."

He said, "How much will you give me to go up there and stay in that house tonight?"

He said, "I'll give you twenty gold guineas."

And he says, "O.K."

And he went up there. They's a little bed in there and he had him a quilt. He laid down, and about the time he laid down in walked two big bears. And he said, "Whoops-ye-see, I wished I had me two big bulldogs."

About that time open flew the door and in they walked. They went to fighting. The bears were trying to get him and

The next morning the old man come up there and said, "Hey, are you dead, are you dead?"

And he jumped up and run to the door and said, "Dead! Man, you orght to come in here and look what I got."

He said, "Man, I wouldn't come in there for nothing."

"Well, I'll bring it out and show it to you." And he brought it out and showed him his chest full of gold. And he says, "That ghost told me to give you a part of this." Said, "Here, how much do you want?"

He says, "Gee! I wouldn't take none of that for nothing in this world."

He said, "Well, I'll take it."

He then took it and throwed it back under his bed, and went down and eat breakfast. Then he fooled around there and he was rich and everything. Finally he got married and lived happy ever after.

9b *Johnny That Never Seen a Fraid*

ONCE UPON A TIME there was a boy who was named Johnny and he was so mean his father couldn't do nothing with him. His daddy had been building houses and had a Nigger working for him. His name was Rastus. Rastus took sick and died. The man thought he would scare his boy by standing Rastus up in his workshop. He put the hammer and handsaw and square in his hand and left him standing there. Then he sent Johnny up to the workshop to get the tools for him. Johnny come up there to the shop and saw Rastus there. He said, "Hey, Rastus! What are you doin' up here, trying to steal my father's tools? My daddy sent me up here after the hammer and handsaw and square."

Rastus never said a word.

He said, "Give me the hammer and handsaw and square!"

Rastus still never said anything.

Johnny said, "If you don't give me that hammer and handsaw and square I'm goin' to pick up one of these two-by-fours and knock you down."

Rastus never said anything.

Johnny picked up one of them two-by-fours and knocked him down. His daddy asked him what he seen. Johnny said, "I never seen nothing but Rastus up there tryin' to steal your tools."

His father give him some money and told him to go and do whatever he wanted to with it. He went down the road and went to a house and asked if he could stay all night. They told him they was a house over across the river that he could have if he would stay in it. Said, "I want something to eat."

They told him to get him a goose. He went over there and started roasting his goose. Two girls come up and spit on it.

Said, "Quit spittin' on Johnny's goose!"

The girls went back out and he started eatin' his goose. Two cats come up and was meawing for it. He said, "You ain't gettin' none of Johnny's goose."

The cats went out. He went to bed.

The two girls come back, started seesawing the cover. He cut the cover in two and said, "You take this half and you take this half and don't come back no more."

They took it out and come back again, started seesawing the cover. He cut that'n in two and said, "You take this half and you take this half and don't come back no more."

They went out and come back in again, started seesawing the cover. He cut it and said, "This is the last I got, you don't need to come back no more."

About the time he laid down again the house started rockling. He jumped out of bed and said, "I guess they want me to come and help turn the house over." He run out there and started helping turn it over and it just set still, wouldn't move.

When he got back in the house a big wagon rolled in with a coffin on it and a hammer laying on the coffin. He said, "I guess they want me to open the coffin up." He opened the coffin up and a man with no head jumped out. He took after Johnny. Johnny run out the door, jumped the fence and into the hills. He got so tard he couldn't go. He come to a big log and was so tard he couldn't get over it. Man without no head on caught up and said, "Boy, we are havin' a race!"

Johnny said, "Yeow, and we'll have another'n if you'll let me rest so I can get over this log."

Johnny got over the log. The man was so stiff he couldn't get over it, and Johnny got away from him then.

9h *The Hainted House*

ONE TIME THERE was an an old man and woman traveling and it was getting dark and they didn't have any place to sleep. They commenced looking for a place and come upon an old house, a mansion. They went up and knocked. Nobody answered, so they just went in and started getting ready to stay there. They didn't have any matches. It was back in the days when people used candles and lanterns and things like that. So this old woman sent the man down to the store to get some matches. This old man went down to the store and the store-keeper told the man that this house was hainted, for him not to go back. He was afraid to go back so he just stayed down there.

This old woman didn't have any matches or light and so she hunted for a place to sleep and she went to bed. About the middle of the night she heard a clump, clump, clump coming up the stairs and in walked a man. He was just the shadow of a man and she couldn't see his head. This man motioned for her to get up and follow him. She wasn't so much afraid and she got up and started following him. They went out and down the stairs and out beside the house and around to the back and out back of the barn. Then he handed her a mattock and motioned for her to start digging. And she started digging. She'd dig a while and he'd dig a while; he'd dig a while and she'd dig a while. Finally they hit this chest

40

and he got it out and gave it to her because she was the only person that had never been afraid of him.

She went back in the house and slept all night. Next morning the old man come and told her the house was hainted. She told him to go away, she didn't have no use for him, he was afraid to come back, and there wasn't any use for her to have him around.

The Boy That Couldn't Shiver and Shake 9n

ONE DAY THERE was a little boy. He lived with his mother. She'd scare him and everything to try to get him to shiver and shake, but he couldn't shiver and shake a-tall. There was a man lived down the road a little piece from 'em. He said, "I got a house up there in the holler a little piece." Said, "You come down here and stay in this house tonight and you'll shore learn how to shiver and shake."

So that night that little boy went down there and went up there to that house, got in the bed. Laying there trying to go to sleep and the door opened and men started coming in, snakes and everything, bloody men, men with their heads cut off, and snakes started crawling all over him. And he set up and started yelling at 'em telling 'em to git out. They turned around and walked out. He turned over and went back to sleep, and next morning he went back down there and he still didn't know how to shiver and shake.

That man said, "I got another house on up there a little further." Said, "You go up there and you'll shore learn how to shiver and shake."

That night he went up there and got in the bed, laying there trying to go to sleep. Ever' kind of animal you could think of started coming in. They started crawling all round, all over him. They looked awful scary but he still couldn't shiver and shake. He was telling them to git out too. They just walked out and closed the door behind them. He turned back over and went back to sleep.

Well, he went down there next morning and he still couldn't shiver and shake. That man said, "I got another house on up here in the holler." Said, "You go up there and stay all night and if you don't learn how to shiver and shake," said, "you can't be learnt how."

So the next night he went up there to that house to stay all night. Went up there and got in the bed, and these animals started coming in bothering him again. He set up and started telling them to get out. And they shuck a bucket of fish down out of the loft and it fell down in the bed with him. And the next morning when he went down there he could shiver and shake.

10a *Merrywise*

ONCE UPON A TIME there was a little boy and he had two brothers, Tom and Bill, and his name was Merrywise. And they lived in a little town, and their mother died. They didn't have nowhere to go and had no one to stay with. Their neighbor was a very kind woman and she asked Merrywise to stay with her while they went out to seek their fortune, but he wouldn't stay. So they were bound to take him with them. He went, and after they started they came to a house. They traveled for a long time and then they came to this house and knocked on the door. An old woman came to the door who had long hair. She had a long nose and she was real ugly. And he says, "May we stay all night here?"

And she said, "Yes, little boy. You're so cute I believe I'll let you be my little grandson."

And he said, "All right, granny."

So they went into the house and it came night. They got ready to lie down. And this old woman happened to be a witch. And she loved to kill people and she was going to kill

Tom and Bill. So she put red caps on Tom and Bill and she had two boys, and she put white caps on her boys. And she told Merrywise he must sleep with her. So Merrywise and her laid down in the bed, and the boys laid down in the floor with their red caps and white caps on. Tom and Bill fell sound asleep and Merrywise did too. But in the middle of the night he woke up. Something was bothering him and he looked up and saw the old woman sitting on the edge of the bed. She was mumbling in a low voice, "I'll get up and whet my knife. I'll get up and whet my knife."

And then after he heard this he said, "I'll get up with you, granny."

She said, "No, you go back to bed."

And he said, "No, I'm not sleepy."

And she said, "I'll go with you."

And so they laid back down, and soon he heard her snore. He knew she was asleep. So he got up and kicked his brothers and woke them up, and changed the caps, and said, "You be ready to go when I wake you up, now."

So he went back to bed and started to snore, too, to pretend like he was asleep. And the old woman, which he called granny, woke up and set on the edge of the bed and begin to say, "I'll get up and whet my knife. I'll get up and whet my knife." He heard her, but really he pretended like he was asleep. So she thought he was asleep and she went over and looked at the boys which had the red caps on, and cut their heads off. She really thought it was Tom and Bill, but it was her boys. She went back to bed pleased and contented and laid down and went to sleep.

Merrywise got up just as soon as he heard her snore once more and kicked his brothers and they got up and went out. And as they came through the chicken yard Tom picked up a egg. As they came out the gate Bill picked up a rock, and as they got down the path Merrywise picked up a hickory nut. And they came on and traveled and traveled until it was almost the middle of the next day. But the woman had not found out until then that it was her boys she had killed and not Tom

43

and went about her work. Well, meanwhile, the old giant come in. He come in and said:

Fee, fie, foe, fum,
I smell the blood of an Englishman,
Let her be dead or alive
I'll suck her blood with my bread tonight.

Well, he eat supper and went back out to get some more men. The little girl went back up there and got her mother and they started out for home just as fast as they could go. Well, the old giant he come in and he found out they was missing and he took out after 'em just as fast as he could go. Well, he's about to catch up with 'em. They run in the house and just as she started in the house he swiped her dresstail off with his sword.

They barred the door up and he couldn't get in. And he wanted a drink of water. Said, "Bring me a drink of water to the winder."

They said, "No, we can't do it." Said, "You'll have to go up the holler. They's a spring up there that you can drink out of."

Well, he went up the holler and he laid down and he drunk so much water that he busted. Next morning the old woman got up and went up there and seen what had happened. She sent for some men with some oxen to pull him off and bury him somewhere.

11a *Nippy*

ONE TIME THEY was three boys and they'd started to seek their fortune. And the two bigger boys their mother had baked them some cornbread and put it in a black sack. And they started off. And Nippy he follered them and they whupped him and run him back once. And he went back a little piece and follered 'em again. They whupped him again and run him back. Well, it still didn't do no good. They whupped him

46

again and told him if he'd go back and make his mother bake him some cornbread and put it in a black sack that he could go with 'em. Well, he went back to the house and she said if he would go to the spring and pack 'im some water in a rid-dle—bucket—that she'd bake it for 'im. Well, he went and he was at the spring and that riddle wouldn't hold water. He said, "Daub it with moss and slick it with clay—" to make it hold water. Well, he packed the water back to the house and she baked his bread and he went to seek his fortune. He caught up with them.

Well, the first night they went to a giant's house and asked him to stay all night with him, and he said, "Yeow." Well, he went in. They asked them what they'd druther have for supper to drink—blood or water. Well, they went and chose water. And that night he went and asked 'em what they'd druther have to sleep on—a feather bed or a hot arn bed. They told 'im a feather bed.

And they went upstairs, and they shut the door on 'em. And he had three daughters and he put a gold staff against them three daughters' door and he put gold lockets around the three daughters' necks—he was going to the boys that night and kill 'em. Well, Nippy he never slept none that night, and his broth-ers slept. It was dark, and he took them three lockets off them girls' necks and put one on his and one on each of his two brothers. The giant come and he went and killed his three daughters that night.

And he went and got up the next morning and he was about to kill 'em over it. That night they was makin' hominy and they all went to bed and Nippy slipped up on top of the house and poured salt down through the chimley so it cracked in the far. The old giant he told his wife to get up, the hominy was on far. She got up and went in there and said, "No, it wa'n't neither." And they went back to bed.

Nippy he got him an old organ and he got under the bed and he was playin' that organ. And they jumped up and looked under the bed. His two brothers had gone back home, and they looked ever'where and couldn't find Nippy nowhere.

Well, he was goin' to kill Nippy anyhow if he could catch 'im.

That next night Nippy still played that organ and they couldn't find him nowhere. Well, he said, "There's only one place we ain't looked and that's under the bed." He went and looked under there and Nippy was layin' in under there playin'. Well, he caught Nippy and put 'im up and he come to feed 'im one morning—he was goin' to make 'im fat and then eat 'im—he started to feed 'im and then he jumped out and run off.

And the next time he come back he come and told the old man that an old woman was sick and wanted him to go get the doctor. He had steers and was plowin' 'em. Well, he went and Nippy got his steers and took 'em back to a man's house and he paid him so much. He didn't never know it till he come back and he was mad over his steers.

The man said he had some fine big horses and if he'd go get them horses he'd pay him a big lot more money. Well, Nippy went. And they went to bed that night and Nippy stold the old man's horses and brought 'em back to that other man and he paid him a big lot.

The man said, "If you get that organ for me I'll pay you a big lot more money."

Well, Nippy he went to try to get that organ and that old man caught him again. He put 'im up and tied 'im with a chain and locked it around 'im. He couldn't get it off. And the next morning he come to feed him—he fed 'im eggs—that was all he fed 'im. And they brought 'im water to drink. And he didn't get much fat.

Well, it come on. His two brothers had gone back home. He got out another day and he come up there and he unlocked that lock and got out of there and got the organ and went across the creek with it and took it back to the old man. And he paid him a big lot more.

And that old man said, "There is one thing that old giant has—" and if he would get it for him he would pay 'im good. He asked what it was. And he said, "It's the moonlight," said, "that they see by—" and told 'im how much he'd pay 'im and ever'thing.

48

Nippy decided he'd go and get it. When he got there the old giant was gone and the old woman was gone to the spring to get water. Well, he went to the old woman and said, "Granny, do you want me to pack your water for you, back to the house?"

Well, he started back, and she'd hid the moonlight out there when she saw 'im comin'. Well, he said he'd pack it and he started back with it. And he shoved the old woman over the hill and throwed that water on her. Well, he run off with the moonlight and took it back to that old man's house.

Then he went back home, and he was rich and his other brothers wa'n't.

The Old Woman Who Loved Mush   11 c

ONE TIME THERE was an old lady and she was a real stingy old lady. And this little boy stayed with her and he was very lazy in a way. And this old lady just loved mush. She told this little boy she would cook him a real good dinner if he would go and cut some stovewood. But the little boy knew that it would be mush. It was cold, it had been raining and was cold, and she told the little boy, said, "You go and cut some stovewood and I'll cook us a real good dinner." So the little boy he ran up in the loft away from her. So she said, "I'll go and get me some chips and make me some mush and you won't get a bite of it."

So she put her on a pot of water and put a little salt in it, and went out to pick her up a load of chips. And the little boy he was up in the loft, and he knew where the salt was kept and got an idea and he went and got a whole big handful of salt. And he opened the little scuttlehole over the fireplace where the pot was, and poured this salt down in it. And when the old lady came back she tasted of her water before she put her meal in it, and it was just brine. So she poured it out and went back and got her some water and put just a tiny bit of salt in it and went back out. And the little boy put still more salt in it from down out of the loft. Well, when the old lady came back in and tasted of it she knew something was wrong. So she poured it out and didn't put any salt at all in it this time and goes back out. And the little boy put still more salt from the loft down in the pot. And when the old lady came back in she tasted of it and she knew something was wrong. And the little boy giggled about that time. So she knew he did it. So she went up in the loft and got him and drug him down and got this big coffee sack and put him in it and said, "I'm going to beat you to death this time."

And so she tied the sack up and went up the branch to cut her a club. While she was gone the little boy managed to get out. And he goes in and gets her beautiful cream pitcher which she never did use, but she kept cream in it, and all of her real nice dishes, and her old gander and put 'em in the bag and tied it up and climbed up on the roof and peeped over where he can watch her.

So she comes back with the club, just as mad as she could be. So she hit the bag two or three times and the dishes went to cracking, which she thought was the little boy. She said, "I'll make your bones pop!" So she hit it three or four more times and this yaller cream came out and she said, "I'll make your blood turn yaller!" and hit harder. And the old gander went to quocking, and she said, "I'll make you quock!" So she hit seven or eight more big licks and she said, "I guess I've finished you now!"

She drug the old sack down to the river and went to pour it out. And instead of the little boy coming out, out come her cream pitcher broke to pieces and her old gander all beat up.

She was so mad she ran back to the house and grabbed the gun, which the little boy had put dirt in and overloaded it, and took off down the holler. So she shot the way the little boy had run, and the gun backfired and got her face all black and kicked her down. When she got up she never would have any more mush around the place because that was what got her in all that mess.

The Golden Arm **12**a

BACK UP IN the mountains of West Virginia near the forks of the Big Sandy lived two brothers, Jim and Ted. Now Ted had one peculiar thing about him. He had a golden arm. He had been born with it. Several times men had beset him and tried to cut off his golden arm, but each time he had managed to get away. A real cold winter in '65 came and Ted was taken down with double pneumonia. Before he died he called Jim to him and said, "Jim, bury me beside ma and pa on the hill."

"Sure, Ted," said Jim.

So Ted died and Jim was faithful to his word. He drug him feet first up the hill, dug a hole and dumped him in it. Halfway down the hill Jim began to study and think about that golden arm. "That thing is worth a lot of money. I'll just sneak back up there some night after dark and get it."

Some time later he sneaked back up there and dug, dug, dug till he uncovered old Ted, who was beginning to rot by that time. He cut off the golden arm and carried it to the house and put it under his pillow and went to bed. As the clock struck—bong—bong—bong—twelve times Jim awoke suddenly and an icy feeling went over him. Feeling that something was wrong he ran out of the house and up the hill to Ted's grave. All was still as a tomb and after seeing that everything was all right he started back down the hill. And then he heard a moaning voice say, "I want my golden arm back."

He began to run down the hill and halfway down he slowed down and then he heard again, "Where's my golden arm?"

At the bottom of the hill he heard, "Where's my golden arm?"

And on the porch, "Where's my golden arm?"

He flew into his bedroom and locked the door and felt himself safe from the thing that was pursuing him. Then he looked around and beheld the golden arm moving from the bed toward him. It came on and on. He seized his old shotgun and shot at it but still it came on.

It had him around the neck. It locked him up against the window and began to crush him and with a crash he went to the floor stone dead.

The next morning the sheriff of the county was making his rounds and he saw an odd sight. He saw a woman hauling a man by his heels up the hill, saw her dig a hole and dump the man in it. He spurred his horse that way but when he got there the woman was gone. She had left some marks scrawled in blood upon the grave. The sheriff was never around there again.

12c *Big Black Toe*

ONCE UPON A TIME there was an old man and an old woman, a little boy and a little girl. They all lived in a little house way out in the country. One day the old man was plowing out in the garden, which was right close to the house. While plowing he plowed up a big black toe.

The old man said, "Little girl, you take this big black toe in the house and have the old woman to make soup on it for supper."

The little girl did as her father had said. The old woman she made soup on the big black toe. And after the man had got done plowing he went in and they eat supper.

Along about six o'clock why they went to bed. The old man he dozed off to sleep, and about the time he got to sleep he was awakened by a noise on the outside of the house. He heard something say, "I want my big black toe, I want my big black toe!"

He said, "Get up, old woman, and go see what that is."

The old woman she got up and she looked all around the house and she couldn't find anything. She come back in and said, "Old man, you must've been dreaming." Said, "I didn't see anything."

Well, he said, "I know dad-blasted that I did!" He dozed off to sleep. 'Rectly he was awakened again by something, saying, "I want my big black toe, I want my big black toe!"

He said, "Get up, little girl, and go see what that is."

The little girl, being very afraid, she got up and went out and run all around the house and come back in and said, "Dad," said, "I didn't see anything."

The old man he was already about asleep. And he dozed off, and took a little nap. The little girl she laid back down in the bed. 'Rectly the old man heard something, "I want my big black toe, I want my big black toe!"

Said, "Get up, little boy, and go see what that is."

The little boy got up and he looked all around the house. And he went out to the chicken house and looked in there also. He come back and said, "Dad," said, "I didn't see anything out there."

He said, "Little boy, you got to stay right up until you find out what that is."

The little boy he begin crying. The old man he begin dozing. Finally the old man he dozed off to sleep. The little boy, seeing his father was asleep, he laid down in the bed. The little boy hadn't more than got in the bed until he heard something also. Said, "I want my big black toe, I want my big black toe!"

The old woman about this time was awakened also. The old woman said, "Old man?"

The old man he was awakened by this time. He said "What?"

She said, "If you want to know what that is you go see for yourself."

The old man said, "Dad-blasted," said, "I can." He got up and he looked around the house and looked in all the houses and come back in. He looked all around in the house. He couldn't find anything. Finally he got to peeping around and

53

he looked up in the chimney. And right up in the chimney he saw a big black thing. He said, "What've you got them big eyes for?"

It said, "To see you with!"

Said, "What've you got them big claws for?"

"To claw you with!"

"What you got that big black tail for?"

That big black thing said, "To sweep your grave with."

Says, "What've you got that big nose for?"

"To smell you with!"

Said, "What've you got them big teeth for?"

"To eat you up!"

The old man had some kindling laying right by the fireplace, and it was very dry. He grabbed some of this kindling and throwed it in the fire and poured kerosene on it and set it on fire. The big flames shot up the chimney and the old big black thing fell down in it and burnt up. The old man then turned around and went and got in bed and had a good night's sleep.

13ª *Rawhead and Bloodybones*

ONCE UPON A TIME there was a woman and she'd married a man that had a daughter, and she had a daughter. Her daughter was real ugly, hateful and everything that she shouldn't have been. And his daughter was real beautiful, sweet, kind and nice, and everyone loved her. And everyone hated the other woman's daughter and she was jealous. So she went to a witch, a friend witch of hers, and asked her what to do to get rid of the pretty girl. She said, "I have an idea." Said, "You tell your daughter to get in the bed and tell the other girl that your daughter won't live unless she goes to the end of the world for a bottle of water for her."

So she said, "Then what will I do?"

"Give her some little old food and I'll take care of the rest of it."

But the woman said, "I'm not pleased. I want to know what you're going to do."

She says, "I'm going to have a gang of horses run over her, and if she gets by that some way I will have a gate and every time it pinches her its poisonous fangs will kill her."

She said, "Well," said, "all right."

So she went back home and she told her daughter that when her stepdaughter come in from getting the water for her to lay down in the bed and to pretend she is sick. So she did, and she laid down and begin to groan, and she says, "Oh, I don't think I can live."

The other daughter come in and says, "What's the matter?"

And she said, "Oh nothing can help me except you go to the end of the world and get me a bottle of water."

She said, "Well, then, I can do that." She was kind and good and she wanted to help everybody.

So she got a bottle and got some cornbread and some water and started out. She set down to eat her lunch and they's an old gray-bearded man come up. He had a real long beard. He was short—looked like a elf—almost.

She says, "What do you want, sir?"

And he said, "I would like to eat dinner with you."

And she said, "All right," and she divided her food with him.

And he said, "Thank you for your kindness, and for being so good to me. I'll give you this stick, and when you go a little piece longer you'll meet a gang of horses. And you shake this stick at them and say, 'Down, horses, down' and they won't bother you."

She said, "All right." So she come a little ways longer and she saw a gang of horses and they were coming at her. And she shook the stick and said, "Down, horses, down," and they disappeared. She set down to eat her supper—it was dark—and this old gray-bearded man come up again. She said, "Well, you want some dinner this time?"

And he said, "Yes." So she gave him some. He said, "Now, you use that same stick you've got and you will come to a gate, by the well at the end of the world. You shake this stick

ain't going to do nothing. I don't want to put my hands on you. Get out of my water bucket."

And it said, "All right," and it crawled off and laid down in the sun. She drew up another and said, "I told you to get out of my water bucket and hush. I don't like you. Go off like the other one did."

And so it did. And another and another, and she talked sassy talk to them and was mean to them. She got her water and started home. And after she got through the gate the first Rawhead and Bloodybones says, "She was ugly, and I wish when she got home she'd be twice as ugly."

And the other said, "She smelt bad, and I wish when she got home she'd smell twice as bad."

And another one said, "She was mean and hateful, and you could tell she didn't get along good in this world. I hope she gets along twice as bad."

And another said, "Well, I hope that when she gets home that snakes and frogs fall out of her hair."

She got on home. She was going through the streets with a bottle of water and everybody smelled something terrible, and they opened their windows and, oooh! There was that horrible looking monster walking through the street with meanness glowing out all over her. And she looked like something from somewhere else that wasn't in this world. She got home and her mother said, "Gee!" says, "You've changed a lot since I saw you last. You look prettier than you were." She said, "Come here and let me comb your hair."

She started combing her hair and all the snakes and frogs and everything that was in the country started coming out of her hair. And they all come out and run her and her daughter off. And her stepdaughter lived happy ever after, there with her money.

Sleeping Beauty 14

ONCE UPON A TIME there was a king and queen who had a princess born to them, and they invited five fairies to come and feast with them. And after they had gotten through eating they went in where the princess lay and everyone wished that she would have good luck when she grew up. And before the last one came to make her wish, an old fairy that hadn't been invited came in the winder and said, "When you are eighteen years old you shall prick your finger on a spinnel and shall die."

The fifth fairy stood up and said, "I can't change that wish much but she won't die, she will just fall into a sleep of a hundred years."

The king and queen started crying because they thought this was much too long for their princess to sleep.

So one day when the princess was eighteen years old she thought she would go through every room in the palace. Finally she got up to the top one and she found an old woman spinning. And she said, "What are you doing?"

She said, "Spinning."

And she said, "May I try?"

This old woman got up and she set down and no sooner had she started then she pricked her finger on the spinnel and fell into a sleep. And the king and queen fell asleep and all the dogs and the guards.

And a long time after that why a prince was coming through the forest hunting for shelter and he just barely could see the castle because the weeds had grown up around it and the brushes. He cut his way through. He came to the door and asked the guard if he could stay here. And they wouldn't say anything. He shook the guards and still they wouldn't wake up. He hollered and didn't hear anything but his echo coming back.

He went on through the castle and he saw the king and

queen asleep and he went on up and saw the princess lying on the floor. And she looked so sweet that he couldn't help but kiss her. So he stooped over and kissed her and she woke up, and the king and queen woke up. The king finished writing his letters and the queen finished eating her breakfast. The mice filed out of the holes, the dogs and the watchmen woke up and started talking.

And the king and the queen gave this prince permission to marry the princess. And the wedding was held that night, and they lived happy ever after.

15a *Bully Bornes*

ONCE THERE WAS three daughters, and their dad loved them very dearly and he'd go to any expense to make them happy. One day he was rambling through an antique shop (they were rather rich) and he found a chair that had a sign over it, said, "A Wishing Chair." And he went and asked the keepers of the shop what it meant. And they said, "Well, this chair, you can sit in it and rock three times and make a wish in it and it will come true."

And he said, "Well, how much will you take for that chair?"

And they named the price. And he said, "Well, I want to buy it." So he bought it and took it home to his daughters.

And there was one of his favorite daughters named Judy and the others were Sally and Kate. He took it home to them and they were out on the porch playing with it and making fun. And Kate set down in it and she rocked three times and she said, "I wish the most handsome man in the world would come and marry me tonight."

And Sally says, "Well, I wish that the most ugly man in the world would come and marry me tonight."

And Judy she set down in it and rocked three times and said, "I wish that Bully Bornes, the prize fighter, would come and marry me tonight."

And after she had said that, why they got up and went to play somewhere else. They were just young girls. Then it got dark—about six o'clock. The maid come and told Kate that someone wanted to see her. And it was the most handsome man in the world. And she had to marry him. So she married him.

Then someone called for Sally. And it was the most ugly man in the world, and she had to marry him.

And later on in the night, well, someone came and walked up the steps, and they begin to think an earthquake had come. And he said, "I want Judy—I want to marry you."

And the father loved her better than anything. So he didn't want to give her up. So he said, "Why, here she is," and he pushed out the kitchen maid.

He said, "This ain't Judy. I want Judy." And he said, "If you don't give her to me I'll tear your house down."

So her father was afraid that he might, and he pushed her out and he married her. He was mean to her though—pretty mean to her. The first little baby he had he said, "If anything happens to this little baby and you cry I'll leave you."

And she said, "Well, I won't."

And so later on in the day a big bulldog came in and it snatched the baby out and ran out with it. And she began to cry and cry. And he came home from prize fighting and he said, "Well," he said, "I made good today. What are you crying about?"

And she said, "Well, an old bulldog came and took my baby off."

He said, "I told you not to cry." Said, "I'll give you one more chance, and if you cry," said, "I'll leave you."

She said, "Well, I won't."

And so they had another little baby (they had three children—the bulldog took the youngest off that day). And the next day the next to the oldest one was sitting out on the porch rocking in a chair, and she was out there rocking in the chair and up came that same bulldog and took it off, and she began to cry and cry. And he came home that night and said, "Well, I made good today—what are you crying about?"

She said, "A big bulldog came and took our second child off today." And said, "I'm crying over it."

And he said, "I told you that if you cried that I said I'd leave you."

And she said, "Give me one more chance," and said, "I won't cry. If anything else happens to our little baby," said, "why, I'll laugh about it if it will make you happy."

Well, that next day she was out washing her clothes and she had the baby laying on a pallet and up came that very bulldog and it snatched the baby away and it ran off with it. And she was screaming for dear life because that bulldog had took ever'one of her children off.

And he came home and he said, "Now what's the matter?"

"Well, that very same bulldog came and took our youngest child off."

"Well," he said, "I told you I's going to leave you."

So he packed his things and he left. She follered him. And she follered him until he came to his sister's house. And he went into his sister's house. And she went in, and he came out and she came out. And she follered him around that way for about two years. And then one day he was prize fighting. And he got a drop of blood on his shirt and he tried to rub it out and it wouldn't rub out. And he said, "I'll marry any woman who will get this drop of blood out."

And the line of women was a long long line, and this girl, who was his real wife, pushed her way in up front. And there was some old woman in front of her that had been trying for about two hours and she hadn't never got it done. And this girl said, "Now it's my turn," and she grabbed the shirt and began to rub it and the first rub it came out. And this other old woman grabbed it out of her hand and said, "Look here, Bully Bornes, I rubbed it out, I rubbed it out. You have to marry me."

And so he married her.

And they moved and went in their house, and she would come to see them every night—his real wife would. She asked this girl if she could come in and this woman would say, "No," said, "you can't come in." And then one night she came in and she said, "Can I see Bully Bornes?"

And she said, "Yes," says, "yes, I guess so." Because that night she had give him some sleeping powder in his coffee.

So she went in and she cried and screamed and hollered, and tried to get him to wake up, and he wouldn't wake up. And the next evening it was the same way. And the evening after that she didn't come. And there was an old man talking to Bully Bornes, and he said, "I wish that you didn't sleep so soundly. You rent that room next door to me and I hear everything that goes on in your room, and there's a woman comes there every night and cries and screams and tries to get you to wake up."

And he said, "Well," said, "I'll see about it tonight," said, "I won't drink anything or eat anything."

So he didn't drink anything or eat anything. And she gave him his coffee and he told her he didn't want it. She tried to force it down him. And he poured it down his shirt, and he didn't drink it.

And so that night he pretended like he was asleep, and this girl came in and she says, "Bully Bornes, are you awake?"

And he says, "Yes."

And she says, "I rubbed that drop of blood out."

And he says, "You did!"

So he took her and married her again and they went and got their three children and lived happy ever after.

The Enchanted Cat 15^b

ONCE UPON A TIME there was an old man and an old woman and a little girl lived out in the country. Now this woman was the little girl's stepmother, and this old woman she hated this little girl desperately. And this old woman she had a girl also. And the old woman and her girl hated her husband's girl. The woman's girl was older than the husband's girl. And every time this girl's father would go off to work why this older girl would be very mean to this little girl. She would slap her and whip her and make her do anything she wanted her to.

One day this little girl was out playing and she saw a butterfly, a very beautiful little butterfly. It went flying through the air and it went down in a big hole. This little girl she took off and she followed it. She went away down and down, kept on going down, down and come into a big dark place. And her eyes got accustomed to the dark and she found that she had come into a very beautiful room, just like a big mansion. And she got to looking around and there was two bedrooms and a dining room. She went into the dining room and stayed around for a while, and she fixed her something to eat. She stayed around until it became right late in the evening. Right late they's an old big cat came in. This big cat came in and it could talk. It asked the little girl what she was doing there. And the little girl told him about her stepmother being mean to her and that her stepsister was mean also. And the old cat said, "Well, you can stay with me."

Well, the little girl, when it came dark, she went into her bedroom, laid down and went to sleep. The old cat went in and went to sleep also.

This happened day after day. The little girl would stay here at this house every day and the old cat he would come in every night. She didn't know what to do. The old cat went out every day. She became curious, about the cat, the way it acted. One night she woke up, along about twelve o'clock. She got out of bed and she went to this old cat's bedroom and she looked in and she found out that it wasn't a cat at all. The cat's fur was laying on the floor, cat-like fur laying on the floor and in the bed lay a beautiful prince.

And she went back and laid down and went to sleep. And she never did anything. And when morning came the cat got up and left. And this little girl got up and went back home and told her stepsister what had happened, where she had been. Her stepsister, being older than her, was very jealous

64

of her. And she became very angry, because she thought maybe that this girl would marry before she would, maybe she would marry this prince.

So one day when the little girl left and went down to this big cave, why, her stepsister came up to the hole of this room, where this big hole went down in the earth, and called and asked her if she could borrow a thimble from her. This little girl, being very accustomed to sewing, why, loaned the thimble and reached it out. When she reached this thimble out, why this stepsister she had a big needle and it had poison on it and she stuck it into her stepsister's finger. And this little girl died. So ends the story.

The Gold in the Chimley 16^c

THERE WAS AN old lady had two daughters and she laid down to take her a nap of sleep. She hung her bag of gold up in the chimley and told her daughters not to look up the chimley. If they did her bag of gold would fall down. As soon as she laid down and went to sleep, one of them looked up the chimley and it fell down. She grabbed it and run out to the fence and said:

> Pray, fence, don't tell her I've been here,
> With a wig wig wag and a great big bag,
> And all the gold and silver in it
> That's been made since I've been born.

It said, "I won't if you'll lay me up."
She said, "I hain't got time."
She went on to a peartree and said:

> Pray, peartree, don't tell her I've been here,
> With a wig wig wag and a great big bag,
> And all the gold and silver in it
> That's been made since I've been born.

It said, "I won't if you'll climb me and shake the rotten pears off of me."

She said, "I hain't got time."

She went on to a horse and said:

> Pray, horse, don't tell her I've been here,
> With a wig wig wag and a great big bag,
> And all the gold and silver in it
> That's been made since I've been born.

He said, "I won't if you'll put me up and feed me."

She said, "I hain't got time."

She went on to a cow and said:

> Pray, cow, don't tell her I've been here,
> With a wig wig wag and a great big bag,
> And all the gold and silver in it
> That's been made since I've been born.

She said, "I won't if you'll milk me."

She said, "I hain't got time."

She went on to the mill and said:

> Pray, mill, don't tell her I've been here,
> With a wig wig wag and a great big bag,
> And all the gold and silver in it
> That's been made since I've been born.

It said, "I won't if you'll put me to grinding."

She said, "I hain't got time."

She got her gold back and beat that girl to death. Took her gold back and put it up in the chimley and laid back down and told the other girl not to look up the chimley. If she did her bag of gold would fall down.

She laid down and went to sleep. She went and looked up the chimley and the bag of gold fell down. She grabbed it and run out to the fence and said:

> Pray, fence, don't tell her I've been here,
> With a wig wig wag and a great big bag,

And all the gold and silver in it
That's been made since I've been born.

It said, "I won't if you'll lay me up."
And she laid it up.
She went on then to that peartree and said:

> Pray, peartree, don't tell her I've been here,
> With a wig wig wag and a great big bag,
> And all the gold and silver in it
> That's been made since I've been born.

It said, "I won't if you'll climb me and shake the rotten pears
off of me."
She clumb it and shuck the rotten pears off of it.
She went on to the horse and said:

> Pray, horse, don't tell her I've been here,
> With a wig wig wag and a great big bag,
> And all the gold and silver in it
> That's been made since I've been born.

It said, "I won't if you'll put me up and feed me."
She put him up and fed him.
Then she went on to the cow and said:

> Pray, cow, don't tell her I've been here,
> With a wig wig wag and a great big bag,
> And all the gold and silver in it
> That's been made since I've been born.

She said, "I won't if you'll milk me."
She milked her, and went on then to the mill and said:

> Pray, mill, don't tell her I've been here,
> With a wig wig wag and a great big bag,
> And all the gold and silver in it
> That's been made since I've been born.

It said, "I won't if you'll put me to grinding."
She put the mill to grinding.

The old woman got up then and went to the fence and said:

> Pray, fence, have you seen ary gal here,
> With a wig wig wag and a great big bag,
> And all the gold and silver in it
> That's been made since I've been born?

The fence fell on her and broke her leg.
She went hopping along to the peartree. She said:

> Pray, peartree, have you seen ary gal here,
> With a wig wig wag and a great big bag,
> And all the gold and silver in it
> That's been made since I've been born?

It fell on her and broke her back.
She went on then to the horse and said:

> Pray, horse, have you seen ary gal here,
> With a wig wig wag and a great big bag,
> And all the gold and silver in it
> That's been made since I've been born?

The horse kicked her brains out.
She went on and come to the cow. Said:

> Pray, cow, have you seen ary gal here,
> With a wig wig wag and a great big bag,
> And all the gold and silver in it
> That's been made since I've been born?

The old cow hooked her guts out.
She went on to the mill and said:

> Pray, mill, have you seen ary gal here,
> With a wig wig wag and a great big bag,
> And all the gold and silver in it
> That's been made since I've been born?

And the mill, hit ground her all to pieces.

John and the Wicked Princess 17

ONCE UPON A TIME there was an old woodchopper and he had a boy named John. John went out to seek his fortune one day, and that woodchopper give him five cents, said, "That's all I've got."

That boy took the money and started down the road. Met an ole bagger-man. That ole bagger-man was hungry, said, "I'm about to starve to death."

That boy said, "I'll give you my money. I'm able to work and get me some money. You're gettin' old."

He give him that money and John went on down the road and stayed all night that night in a hotel. The next mornin' that ole bagger-man changed hisself into a travelin' man and he asked John could he go along with him and seek his fortune. John told him he could and they went to the top of the hill that day. And they was a swan fell at their feet, and that ole bagger-man cut that swan's wings off. And John asked, "What do you want with a swan's wings?"

He said, "They'll come in handy."

They went on into town that night. And there was a beautiful princess comin' down the road. Everybody said that princess was wicked. They said a lot of boys had run after her to marry her had lost their heads, said she'd cut their heads off. Well, that ole bagger-man told John not to try to marry that princess or she'd cut his head off. John made up his mind he's goin' to go after her anyway. So that ole bagger-man went to the castle that night to see the princess. She come to her winder about midnight and flew off. She was a witch, and nobody didn't know it. And he went behind her by makin' hisself invisible. And they went into a castle. And she asked a man, "What must I ask John? I'm supposed to ask him three questions. If he can't answer 'em I'm goin' to cut his head off."

He said, "You ask him what you're thinkin' about and you'll

be thinkin' about your golden slippers. He won't never think about that." And she said she would.

And John come to her castle that next day and asked the princess to marry him. And she said, "What am I thinkin' about?"

And he said, "You're thinkin' about your golden slippers."

She said, "That's right. I won't cut your head off."

Well, next night that ole bagger-man done the same thing. He follered that girl and she went back to the witch's castle again and she said, "What must I ask him about this time?"

He said, "Ask him what you're thinkin' about and you be thinkin' about his beard. He won't never think about that, the stupid."

Well, that ole bagger-man come back to the hotel and he told John, said, "When she asks you what she's thinkin' about tomorrow you tell her she's thinkin' about your beard."

So she asked him what she was thinkin' about and he said, "I guess you're thinkin' about my beard."

She said, "Well, that's right, I guess I'll have to marry you." So she married John but she still didn't love him. And that ole bagger-man said, "Here's three feathers from that swan." Said, "You dip 'em in a tub of water and when you and that princess go out walkin' in the garden you dip her in the water three times and she won't be a witch no more."

He dipped her in the water and she changed into a good girl and they lived happy ever after.

18   *The Princess in the Donkey Skin*

ONCE THERE WAS a king and he had a beautiful daughter, and he was going to marry her to this other king in Faraway Land. And she didn't want to marry him because he was so ugly. They begin to make ready for her to marry him and she said she wasn't going to marry him. She said she would rather live in a donkey's skin as to marry him.

They said, "Very well, make you live in a donkey's skin."

They went out and killed this old donkey and put her in it and she couldn't get out. And they said, "Now you can just leave the palace."

And she left. She wandered around in the hills for a long time. Finally she came to a little hut. And she went up to this hut and they was an old woman standing in the door. And she said, "Can I stay here?"

She said, "Yes, if you'll feed my chickens and take care of my garden, clean the house, do my washing and ironing and cooking, I'll let you stay."

She said, "O.K., then I'll stay."

And she stayed there a long time and worked and worked. And finally one day the king from Faraway Land was going to come and hunt some with the prince. And this woman said, "Now you cook dinner and do it the best you can."

She said, "I will."

And she cooked a real good dinner, and she forgot there had been a diamond on her finger, and it slipped off and went into some soup. And that day she slipped upstairs while this king and his boy were eating. Well, the prince he was eating this soup and he found this ring. And he just put it down in his pocket and didn't think much more about it and didn't let the people know anything about that he had this ring.

And while they were eating dinner this girl was upstairs crying and crying, so she could get out of this donkey's skin, but she could not. Finally something whispered, said, "If you'll be real good," said, "I'll change you into a purty girl. You can just stay changed about thirty minutes."

She said, "O.K.," said, "I will."

She said, "Well, you go out on the balcony now, and when this prince comes out in the garden he'll see you up there and will fall in love with you."

And she said, "Very well." And she said, "Put diamonds in my hair and make me the most beautiful dress in the world."

And this fairy godmother said, "Very well then, since you are such a good girl I will."

Downstairs the prince said, "Well," said, "I'm going to go out in the garden and look at your flowers." And while he was out there he saw this real beautiful girl up in the balcony and he fell in love with her at first sight.

And she said, "I've got to go now. When the moon is over," said, "I've got to leave." She just told him that, telling a lie. And she said, "I've got to go now." And she left.

He come back and he told 'em about it and he said he was in love, that he couldn't live without her.

They went back to their palace. And he come back. And the fairy godmother come to her and said she could stay that way thirty minutes again. And she went out there and he asked her to marry. And she told him she couldn't—the moon's about to come over now and she'd have to go back. She went back.

Well, he went all over the world to see if he could find whose finger this ring would fit. He thought that the ring he had found was hers. He went all over the world and he couldn't find nobody that it would fit.

Finally he come in and he wanted to put it on this girl in the donkey skin, and she wouldn't let him. And they just got her down and she was crying and everything. And they went and slipped that ring on her finger and it fit. And she changed back into that girl that he had fell in love with. They were married and lived happily ever after.

19b *The Three Sisters*

ONCE UPON A TIME there was an old man and woman. They had three girls. The oldest was Polly, the next was Mary, and the youngest was Alice. The old man and woman didn't like Mary because she had only one arm and wasn't pretty like the others.

The old woman made Mary go out to the pasture every day and watch Alice's and Polly's goats. Every evening when she came in from the pasture the girls didn't want her to have any supper. So she wouldn't get anything to eat. She began to get so poor she was nearly starved to death. One day she said to herself, "I would give anything for some dinner."

All at once a little goat came to her and placed a little table of all sorts of food before her. She ate all she wanted but still had plenty left. When she finished the little goat said, "Every day when you are hungry just say this:

> Beat, my little goat, I pray,
> Bring the table again today.

So she promised she would.

That night when she went home she didn't care much about eating anything. So they suspected she was getting food some way. Her mother said, "Mary, tomorrow we are going to send Polly with you."

The next day Polly went. Mary began to sing pretty songs and Polly fell asleep. Then the little girl said:

> Beat, my little goat, I pray,
> Bring the table again today.

Then the little goat came with all sorts of things for Mary to eat. Polly never did know anything about it. That night when they went home their mother asked, "Polly, did you learn anything?"

Polly said, "No, not a thing happened."

"Well, tomorrow we will send Alice and see what she can do."

The next day Alice went. When Mary began to sing, Alice went to sleep with one eye shut and one eye open. Then Mary said:

> Beat, my little goat, I pray,
> Bring the table again today.

The little goat brought the table and Alice saw her eating from it. So that night when they went home, Alice told her mother the whole story. She said, "Tomorrow we will kill that goat."

The next day they killed the little goat, and Mary said, "Would you give me the goat's heart?"

So they did. Mary took the heart where they couldn't see her and she swallowed it. The next morning when she awoke under her pillow she found a piece of gold money. She slipped out behind the house and buried the money in a hole under the ground. She kept doing this every day until she had a great load of money.

One night when she lay in her bed she figured out a plan. "I believe I will leave this old house," she thought. So that very night while they were all sound asleep she slipped out of bed and packed what clothes she had and took her money and slipped out of the house quietly. The next morning when her parents awoke they found she had gone. Then they all laughed and said, "Let her go, old One Arm!"

20ᵇ *Jack and the Bull's Horns*

ONCE UPON A TIME 'way out in the country there lived an old man, an old woman and a little boy. The little boy's name was Jack. The old man had been married twice, living with his second wife at this time. And by his first wife he had this little boy. Jack he was very badly mistreated by his stepmother. His stepmother would whip him and make him carry water and work real hard, while her husband was gone to work. But when her husband come in she acted like she was good to Jack.

So one day Jack he was out going out to the barn around in the farmyard, and he was crying. He was crying awful bad, Jack was. He was feeling awful bad. The old red bull, a big red bull saw him and said, "Jack," says, "what's wrong?"

Jack says, "Well," says, "my stepmother just whipped me and I haven't eaten anything for two or three days."

Well, the old bull was sorry for Jack and he said, "Jack, I'll tell you what for you to do." Said, "You take off my right horn, and in my right horn you will find all kinds of food, chicken, dumplings, beans—just anything you want to eat. Just take it off."

Jack took the horn off and he eat and eat and eat. Now this did Jack much good and he went around happy, singing, and the old woman, she saw him. She suspected something. She got around and she was watching Jack. When it come time to eat that noontime meal she was watching Jack and saw him take this right bull's horn off and begin eating. So that night when her husband come in to eat she says, "Old man," said, "you know, I think the old red bull ought to be killed so we can have something to eat. You know he's got some fat on him," says, "it's about time that you killed him."

The old man says, "Well, Jack, I'll tell you what to do," says, "you stay around tomorrow and be ready," says, "day after tomorrow we're going to kill the old big red bull." Says, "I have to work tomorrow."

This made Jack feel awful bad. That night he cried and went on and couldn't sleep. Next morning just as quick as he woke up—his father had gone to work early—he got up and went out to the barn and saw the big red bull. He said, "Old red bull," says, "my father is going to kill you tomorrow," and says, "they are fixing to make beef out of you."

Well, the red bull says, "Well, Jack, there's not but one thing for us to do." Jack asked him what it was. He says, "Being as we are both mistreated and can't get much to eat around here and we're both going to lose our lives," says, "looks like you and I better leave."

Jack said, "Well."

The old red bull got Jack upon his back and they took off. They went down the road. They went and they went and they went. It became dark and they laid down and went to sleep. They woke up the next morning and the old bull said, "Jack, I had a bad dream last night."

Jack said, "What was it?"

The old red bull said, "I dreamt that I met up with another bull. I thought we fought and we fit and we fought, but I thought I killed the other bull." Says, "Now, Jack, I'll tell you what to do." Said, "Now if I don't kill this other bull you remember to do this." Jack asked him what it was. Says, "You take off my left horn and in my left horn you will find a bright sword," and says, "you take this sword and from this time on anything you strike with it you will kill it."

Jack said he would.

They went on the next day. They was going along. And they went and they went and they went. Along about noon why they heard something, a big roaring noise. It shook the ground around them, seemed like. And it was a big bull, mad bull. It come right straight toward the red bull, and into it they went. They fit and they fought and they fit and they fought. The red bull killed the other'n.

The red bull got Jack upon his back and they took off. They went and they went and they went. They eat and they slept another night. After another night's sleep the old red bull waked up next morning and said, "Jack, I had another bad dream last night."

Jack says, "What was it?"

He said, "You know, I dreamt that we met up with a big panther and I dreamt that we fit and we fought and we fit and we fought. But I killed the panther. But just in case that I don't kill it, this is what I want you to do." Jack asked him what was it. He said, "You take off my left horn and you will find a cord, a leather cord. You take that and anything that you bind with it," says, "you will be able to capture it."

Jack said that he would.

Well, they went and they went the next day. They was going along and they heard a noise, something screamed right big. And they looked out and they's a big panther gave a big jump. Jack jumped back off the bull and they went into it. They fit and they fought, and the panther wounded the bull very very badly, but the bull finally killed the panther.

The bull got Jack upon his back and they went on. They

went and they went. Come dark and they slept another night. Woke up the next morning and the old bull said, "Jack, I had another real bad dream last night."

Jack said, "What was it?"

Said, "This time I thought I met up with a big lion, and I thought we fit and we fought and we fit and we fought, but the lion killed me." Said, "Now you remember what I've told you and you'll be safe from now on."

Jack said, "Well." Jack was feeling awful bad about this. He was dishearted. He got upon the bull's back and they took off. They was going along and heard a big roar. Unnn, the bushes seemed like they shook. Jack knew what was coming, so he jumped off the bull. The bull run out and they went into it. They fit and they fought and they fit and they fought. The bull gave a big long slam and hit him and they went into it. But both became wounded. The bull fell down dead and so did the lion. He killed the lion, gored him with his horns. They both were dead.

So Jack he went down and he pulled off the bull's left horn, and from it he took the sword, and he took the leather cord and went on.

Jack was going along and he looked and he seen some men, some soldiers going along and seen that they was packing some signs. He went and he looked at these signs and it said that the princess from the realm was going to pick someone to marry, and the king had said that anyone who proved worthy to marry her, why he could marry her. So Jack he went and he come to the king's palace and he told them his mission. He said he believed he could do anything. The king said, "You're the very one that I need." Says, "Away off from here my people are being killed by this giant. He's got two big heads," and says, "if you can kill him, you can have the princess."

So Jack said, "I can."

And so Jack got ready. He put on his armor and he went. And when he got where this giant was at the giant let out a big roar and come right at him with his two big heads. Jack

77

up with this cord and threw it around one of this giant's heads, jumped to one side, whacked one of them off. He pulled the cord and got out of the way. This old giant was slinging the stub of that head where it had been cut off—blood a-flying. Jack he up with the cord again, threw it around the other one, whacked it off.

After he did this he come back, the king gave him the princess, they married and lived happy ever after.

20d *Jack and the Bull Stripe*

ONCE UPON A TIME there was a little boy—he wasn't very little, he was in his teens—and he had a bull. He had it ever since he had been a little baby. It had just practically grown up with him and he didn't know what he would do without it. He loved it very dearly. It would always go with him in the evening to get his grain and it would help him to pull his things, and everything, and it was just a great company to him, because his father had died and his mother and him were very poor and they lived alone in a little log hut.

Well, one day as they were going after some grain the bull said, "Well, I'm afraid, Jack, after we make this load, that I have to lay down and die, because I have served you for a long time and I know you love me, and I love you too." And said, "I want to do something for you after I die 'cause I think I've helped you a lot now. If I do die you might not live so good."

So this bull laid down and died—was getting ready to die—and he said, "You take the stripe of white that runs from the tip of my nose to the end of my tail, and every time you make a wish on it the wish will come true. And you say, 'Bull Stripe, make it come true,' and it will come true."

So Jack hated to see his bull die, but he knew it would help their financial business a lot and everything like that. So the

78

bull died and he buried it and cried a little bit. And then the next day—after they'd had the funeral—he wished that he had a beautiful house and everything in it was beautiful. And his mother had beautiful clothes and he had beautiful clothes, and they had a beautiful carriage. And he wished for finery and everything. And he said, "Bull Stripe, make it come true." And so it came true. Their house changed entirely. The people didn't know what to think that lived around there in that community.

This boy, Jack, was going with a real pretty girl. Her family were real rich, and when they were poor they wanted to get married, but her mother wouldn't let her marry him, because he was poor and she knew he couldn't take care of her. So this girl's mother wanted her to marry another man that was rich, and she thought he could take care of her. So Jack just kept on fighting and fighting, he wanted her so bad, and he made this wish. And when he went to the church the next Sunday he went in his big fine carriage and his mother had on her big fine clothes, and he had on his big fine clothes. They pulled up in front of the church, and they got out, and went in and nobody knew them. They thought they were some new people. So at the church that day the mother of the girl that he wanted to marry got up and announced that her daughter's church wedding was going to be there, not very long from then. So he kinda hated to hear that, and he knew if it was beyond his wishes that she would marry this boy. So he never said anything about it. And the next day was the day of the wedding and he went to this girl's house and knocked on the door. They let him come in. And when her mother saw him she knew who he was. Because he was dressed pretty good, but she thought maybe he had on his best suit. But it wasn't the best he had, but she thought it was, and said, "Throw him down in the dungeon where we have the bears." For the wedding they were going to have bear for supper, and they had it down in the dungeon fattening it up. And they put Jack down in the dungeon with the bear. And he said, "Bull Stripe, make it come true that you will wrap around this bear's neck and choke it to death." And it wrapped around the bear—the Bull Stripe did—the bear's neck and choked it to death. And Jack decided he would stay down there until that evening. Well, that evening—they fed the bear about three times a day, and the bear had two more meals to go. So they sent the platter down full of food for the bear and Jack ate it all up. And then he set down and rested and it came time for the bear's other meal. And the man that let the bear's platter down was nearsighted or farsighted one, anyway he couldn't see too good. When they let the platter down Jack emptied all the food out, and tied the rope around his waist, and the nearsighted man drew him up. He got out and ran just as hard as he could run to the girl's room—to her window, rather. He knocked on the window and she let him in. He says, "I got my horse and carriage waiting outside, and I'll get a ladder and come and get you down and we will run away. And they won't have anything to say after we are already married." And she said, "No, I have a better idea. Why don't we just tie up the man that I'm supposed to marry, and lock him somewhere, and you walk up the aisle in his place and no one will notice until it is already over with."

So they agreed on that idea. Jack got the bridegroom, called him out in the hall, and told him he wanted to tell him something. After he got him out there he knocked him in the head, tied him, and put him in the storage room. Then he went up the aisle with the girl, and no one knew the difference. After they were married, Jack took his mother-in-law and her to his house, that he was going to let the girl live in, and showed her around. She was thrilled to death and happy to have a son-in-law who had all these riches. And they found out then that the man that her mother wanted her to marry was a phony, a complete phony, and had nothing in the world and was only marrying her for her money.

Jack and this girl lived happy ever after.

Big-Foot Town 21

ONCE UPON A TIME they was a town, back in the olden days, and everybody had big feet. And they called it Big-Foot Town. One day they heard a great shout and music was playing, and a girl ran out in the street. And they was a big horse coming down the road and a chariot wagging along behind it. And a big woman stepped out and she had great big long feet. And they called her the queen of Big-Foot Town, because she had bigger feet than any of the girls in town. And every child that her and her husband had they had big feet, but her last one. He had real little feet and she didn't like him. So she put him out to tend to the sheep. And they called him the shepherd boy.

And one day he was out tending to the sheep, and he thought he'd run away. He started out through the woods, and he came to a little house. And he went in and a little red fairy was sitting there and he asked him his name. And he said they called him the shepherd boy. He asked him where he was going, and he said he was running away from home because they didn't like him, and his mother made him tend to the sheep all the time.

This man in the little red suit he took him on through the woods to a place where a lot of little people were setting around in boots and things like that, and they were having a big dance. And he went and introduced him to another little fairy with a green suit on. He went and told him about a princess of their town where she'd stuck her foot in a stream and her foot had become bigger than her other one. And he was out in the woods one day and he heard someone crying and he started walking towards the voice and he came to a princess sitting beside the waters. He asked her what was wrong, and she told him her story. And he told her that the only way he could help her was to get some water from his father's fountain.

He went and took her and went to his father's walls, and he went and come to a hole big enough for him to crawl through. And he crawled through and helped this princess through. And she went and stood by the wall while he got a glass and got some of this water. And he came back and bathed her foot in it. And her foot ever since then one was bigger than the other, because she bathed her foot in this water.

22 Soldier of the Blue Light

ONE TIME THEY was a soldier and the old king treated that soldier awful bad, and made him work for several years for him and wouldn't give him a penny of money nor nothing. Turned him out without any money or anything. He went to a place and asked to stay all night, and he asked that woman could he stay all night. That woman said, "Yes, if you will work for me all day you can stay all night."

He says, "All right, I'll stay."

He stayed and got up the next morning and went to work. And he worked and it was dark when he quit and he couldn't get home very good. It was dark—didn't have no light. And he said, "Well, can I get to stay all night again tonight?"

She said, "Yes, if you will work for me tomorrow you can stay all night."

He said, "Well."

He stayed all night and next morning he got up and she says, "Now I'll tell you what I want you to do. I want you to go down in a well and get a blue light." Says, "They's a little blue light down in the bottom there," and says, "I want you to bring it back up and give it to me."

He says, "All right."

He clomb down in the well. He got the blue light, started

back up with it. When he got back up purt near the top, why she said, "Hand it to me."

And he says, "No, wait till I get out and then I'll give it to you."

And she said, "No, give it to me now."

And he said, "No, just wait till I get out."

And it made her mad because he wouldn't give it to her then, and she just dropped him back down in the well to starve to death. He couldn't get out no way. And he studied how he could get out. He started rubbing his hands and that rubbed that little blue light, you know, and they's a little man appeared to him. That little man said, "What do you want?"

He said, "Well," said, "I want out of this well." And says, "I want that there old lady put down in here where I's at."

And the little man said, "Well, light up your pipe."

And he said, "All right."

He lit up his pipe and the smoke went coming up through the well and that smoke just drawed him right up out of the well and he got out up to the top. And he dropped his light and broke it about the time he got up to the top. He got to the top and he said, "Well, I don't guess I'll have any more luck now." But they put the woman down in the well right where he's at.

He went home then, and he went to see about something, I forget what it was. And the old king heared about him, what he had done. And he wanted that blue light, you know, and he sent down after that light. And he said he didn't have it, sent back word that he didn't have it. And the old king sent back word that he was going to put him to death over it.

And he said, "Well. But they's one thing that I want to do before I die. I want to smoke my pipe."

And the old king says, "Well, you can smoke your pipe."

He went to smoke his pipe and blue smoke come up and a little man appeared to him again and said, "What do you want this time?"

And he said, "Well, I want you to kill all these men that's

around here. Have them put to death and," says, "I want you to cut the king in three pieces and give him to me."

And he killed all of them men then and started to cut the old king up. And the king went to begging so pitiful that he couldn't hardly do that.

The king told him, says, "Well, you can have my daughter and all I own here, if you will spare my life."

That soldier said, "Well."

And he went home then and he owned all the king's property and everything, and he lived happy ever after.

23a *The Magic Bag*

THIS STORY I'M going to tell you is about two old poor people who lived together, a man and a woman. This man all he would do was go out and trap, and his old woman would just put him out of the house when he come in without anything.

And one day he went out to his trap and they's a bird in there. This bird told him if he would turn him loose he could have anything he wanted. Well, he turned him loose, and this little bird flew by and dropped a bag. He told him to say, "Two out of the bag, and two in the bag," and when he said, "Two out of the bag," they'd be a table come out with anything on it he wanted to eat.

And so he said, "Two out of the bag," and they's a table come out and he eat all he wanted. He said, "Two in the bag," and it went back in.

He went on to an old man's house and he stopped and showed this old man what he had. The old man said, "Well, le's go out in the garden and see what a fine garden I have."

He took him out in the garden and he was all around over the garden so long. And so this man's daughter was in the house making a bag just like his'n. They made a bag and put it down in the place of his'n and took his bag.

He come back in and took his bag and went on home and

told his woman to come there and see what he had. He said, "Two out of the bag," and nothing come out.

And she said, "You old crazy thing," said, "you know better'n to bring something like that in here." Said, "That hain't reasonable sense."

He said, "Well, maybe it hain't."

The next day he went back to his trap and this little bird flew over and dropped him another bag and told him to say, "Two out of the bag and two in the bag."

He said, "Two out of the bag," and they's two men come out just beating him to death. They beat him for about an hour just as hard as they could beat him. This little bird flew over and told him if he would say, "Two in the bag," they would go back in and if he'd take this bag and get his other bag back that he would tell the men to go back in and quit beating him. So it said, "Two in the bag," and those men went back in.

So he took this bag and went on to this old man's house and stopped. He said, "I've still got a better bag now than what I had before."

He said, "Have you?"

He said, "Yes, I've got a whole lot better one than what I had before." So he set it down.

And this old man said, "Come go look what fine hogs I have out here."

These girls they said, "Two out of the bag," and these two men come out just beating these girls to death. They beat them for about an hour, and this man heard his girls hollering. He went back in the house and asked this man to make 'em quit.

And he said, "I'll make 'em quit," said, "if you'll make 'em give me that good bag back."

And he said, "I'll get it."

And he said, "Two in the bag," and the little men went back in and they went and give him his good bag.

And he took his bags on home and went in and told his woman, said, "I've got my good bag now," said, "come and see." He said, "Two out of the bag," and this table come out with good things on it. They set around the table and eat.

And one day he was out in the garden and was plowing. This old woman she decided she'd see what he had in this other bag. She said, "Two out of the bag," and these two men come out and they's just beating her to death. And he come in and she said, "I want you to make 'em quit."

And he said, "I will if you'll always be good to me and never say another bad word to me," said, "I'll make 'em go back in."

He made 'em go back and she was good to him, and they lived happy ever after.

24 *Jack and the Miller's Daughter*

ONCE UPON A TIME there was an old woman who had three sons, Will, Tom and Jack. Now Will and Tom, being the oldest, considered Jack no good. Jack wasn't very handsome like his brothers.

It had been raining for several days, when the news reached the boys that the river was flooded and there were no bridges, and that the rich miller, whom everybody knew, had said that the first one to cross the river could have his daughter. The three brothers were talking about it when their mother said to Will, "My oldest son, take this sieve and go to the spring and fetch back a sieve full of water and I will make you a poke full of sweetbread for your journey."

So the oldest son Will went to the spring. As he would dip up a sieve full it would pour out. A little bird flew over and said to him:

> Stick it with clay and daub it with moss
> And you will carry away a sieve full of water.

Now this made Will angry. He rocked the bird away and called it a little fool. He finally carried away a little water in the rim of the sieve and his mother baked him a very little sweetbread. So he left for the river.

So Tom's mother sent him to the spring for his sieve full of water. When he reached the spring the little bird came again and called out:

> Stick it with clay and daub it with moss
> And you will carry away a sieve full of water.

But he also rocked it off and carried away only what was held in the rim of the sieve. So his mother baked him a small amount of sweetbread and he also started for the river.

So it was Jack's turn. He took the sieve and went to the spring and was dipping up a sieve full of water and it was pouring out, when the little bird flew down and said:

> Stick it with clay and daub it with moss
> And you will carry away a sieve full of water.

So Jack stuck the sieve with clay and daubed it with moss and carried away a sieve full of water. So his mother said, "Well done, my youngest," and she baked him a big poke full of sweetbread and he left for the river.

Will reached the river and worked all day trying to get across, when the same little bird came again. When Will saw it he didn't give it time to say anything before he rocked it off. The next morning Tom arrived and he also rocked the little bird away when it came. They worked and worked, and when the fifth day passed the river ran down some and they finally crossed the river and went to the miller's house and knocked on the door. Will said, "I bet Jack met some poor dumb creature and fed all his sweetbread to it and had to go back."

At the thought of this they both laughed, when the door opened and there stood Jack dressed in the finest clothes you ever saw. Will asked him what he was doing there and he said, "This is my house now! You see, I came to the river and there was a little bird whom I fed and in return it gave me several wing feathers and told me to get some little rocks and put them under my arms and fly across. So that was what I did."

At this Will and Tom turned and ran from the house because they couldn't stand to think that they had been beaten by their youngest brother whom they had called a fool.

25 *The Rather Unusual Frog*

ONCE UPON A TIME there was a little girl in my neighborhood whose mother was a widow and didn't want the little girl, but she couldn't think of any way to get rid of her unless the neighbors would know about it. Now the little girl was like all little girls—she didn't like to work. So one morning she forgot to do her sweeping before she went to school. So the mother had to do it and while she was sweeping she found a flea. This flea was the biggest flea I ever did see. The widow had to use a twenty-pound sledge hammer to kill it. After she killed it she skun the skin and hung it behind the door. She decided that she would give her daughter to anyone who could guess what kind of skin she had. She told the neighbors she would give them three guesses each day for three days, and if one guessed it they could have her daughter. Several people tried but no one could guess it. Now there was one little boy who had come every morning to take his guesses. So on the third morning he came in so sure that he would be right that he came prepared to take the little girl home. He asked the widow,

"Is it a buffalo skin?"

She said, "Nope."

"Is it a bear skin?"

"Nope."

Having only one more guess he stopped to think a minute. Now behind the door lived a rather unusual frog that understood everything that was said. He had lived behind the door for some time, but no one knew it. And when the widow came around that morning to look at the flea skin she didn't think of anyone being there so she said, "Now Mr. Flea, someone had better guess you this morning." So Mr. Frog decided he needed him a wife. Out from behind the door he hopped and said to the widow and the little boy,

"It is a flea skin!"

At this the boy and the widow were shocked out of their senses, and when they recovered, the frog and the little girl were gone. The widow was not very sad, but I am sure the little boy went home broken-hearted.

The little girl was frightened and was crying as Mr. Frog hurried her along to his real home. They passed a fine house and the little girl asked him, "Is that your house?"

And the frog said, "Nope, my house is finer than any you ever saw." So finally they came to a creek which was the only road in our neighborhood. He took her back on the creek bank a piece and stopped and said, "This is my house."

Now there was only a big log with a piece of bark laid up against it for a cover. It was pouring the rain. The little girl refused to go in, and the frog set to pulling and tugging at her, when a kind old farmer came by and heard the noises. When he saw the little girl he came up where she was and asked her what she was doing, and she told him. So he told her he would take her home to his wife for her daughter. But Mr. Frog refused to let go of her until the farmer finally had to take out his whip and cut the frog in two. He took the little girl home. They were good to her and she became a beautiful woman. She didn't like any of the boys who came to see her although they were rich. Then one day a stranger came to the farm and she fell in love and married him in a few days. The farmer and his wife wondered why she married this stranger whom she knew only a short time, when several of the rich young men had asked her to marry them.

She told the farmer and his wife good-by and left with the stranger. He had sent word to his mother that he was bringing his wife home with him, and for her to prepare a wedding supper for them. She had supper ready for them and it was the finest supper you ever saw. The girl was enjoying her supper very much until someone said,

"These are the finest frog legs I ever ate."

Now the girl had seen only one frog in her life, so when she learned that she was eating frog meat she fainted. That scared all the family stiff, except her husband, who had had his love stolen from him by a rather unusual frog when he was little, and he knew what was wrong.

26 *The Skillful Brothers*

ME AND ONE OF MY brothers oncet we started out to take a mechanic course, ye see. He asked me if I thought it was best for us to go to the same school. I told him I didn't think it was—that we wouldn't pull against one another so much if we went to different schools, ye see.

So I went to one school and he went to another about ninety miles apart.

So one day I went to the post office and got a letter. I opened the letter up and looked in it. It was a letter from my brother, ye see. He said, "I want to show you how I'm improving with my course." Said, "I've made you a needle here." Said, "It's very small. You may have to have a magnifying glass before you can see it." He said, "But, anyway, I've put an eye in it. I want you to look at it," said, "just to show you how I'm improving."

So I picked the needle up. It was very small. It had an eye in it. I took it in my shop and drilled a hole in it from one end to the other'n and run a thread through it and sent it back—to show him how I'd improved. Well, he didn't like that. So he quit his mechanic course and said, "I'll just make a carpenter."

He went out and got a contract building a house for a man for five hundred dollars. He built the house. The man said, "Now, is it possible to paint this house air color?"

He said, "I think it is."

He went ahead and painted it air color. The man come in that evening from work and couldn't find his house. He went and hunted up my brother and said, "I'll give you five hundred dollars more if you'll take me to the house and paint a black ring around it so I can find it when I come in at night."

And so he made purty good at that job. And I guess that's about all, boys.

The Silver Tree 27a

ONCE THERE WAS an old man, an old woman, and three little girls. The old man went out and killed a rabbit and brought it in and told the old woman to cook it.

The old woman cooked it and it smelled so good, she decided to taste it. It tasted so good she tasted it, and tasted it, and tasted it all away.

She didn't know what to do. Her little girl was up on the hill playing. She called to her and said, "Hey, little girl, come down here."

She said, "No, I'm afraid you want to cut my head off."

She said, "No, I just want to look on your head."

So she came and she cut her head off and cooked her by the time the old man came in to dinner. He started to eat, and forked out a piece and said, "Old woman, this looks like my poor little girl's hand."

"Ah, eat on, you old fool; that's just a rabbit's fore paw."

He ate on and after a while he took out another piece and said, "Old woman, this looks like my poor little girl's foot."

She said, "Now, eat on, you old fool. That's just a rabbit's hind paw."

91

After a while a little bird flew up over the door and hollered:

> My mamma killed me, my daddy ate me,
> My two little sisters sitting under the table
>   catching my bones,
> Washing them in milk, wrapping them in silk,
> And burying them between two marble stones.

The old woman says, "Little girls, go out there and see what that little bird says."

The little girls went out there and says, "Say that again, little bird."

And the bird said:

> My mamma killed me, my daddy ate me,
> My two little sisters sitting under the table
>   catching my bones,
> Washing them in milk, wrapping them in silk,
> And burying them between two marble stones.

And the bird dropped them down a great big bag of gold. After a while the bird flew up in the tree again and said:

> My mamma killed me, my daddy ate me,
> My two little sisters sitting under the table
>   catching my bones,
> Washing them in milk, wrapping them in silk,
> And burying them between two marble stones.

The old woman said, "Old man, go out there and see what that bird said."

The old man went out there and said, "Say that again, little bird."

And the bird said:

> My mamma killed me, my daddy ate me,
> My two little sisters sitting under the table
>   catching my bones,
> Washing them in milk, wrapping them in silk,
> And burying them between two marble stones.

92

And the bird dropped him down a silver tree saddle of some kind, and they went back in.

After a while the little bird flew up over the door again and said:

> My mamma killed me, my daddy ate me,
> My two little sisters sitting under the table
>   catching my bones,
> Washing them in milk, wrapping them in silk,
> And burying them between two marble stones.

The old woman says, "I'm going out to see what that little bird says myself." She went out there and says, "Say that again little bird."

The little bird says:

> My mamma killed me, my daddy ate me,
> My two little sisters sitting under the table
>   catching my bones,
> Washing them in milk, wrapping them in silk,
> And burying them between two marble stones.

The little bird dropped a millstone on her, and squushed her.

The Dumb Supper 28a

ONCE UPON A TIME there was a family in the mountains and in this family there were three pretty young girls. So they decided to set what was known as a dumb supper. Everything they did was to be done backwards. So they got ready and one put a fire in the stove backwards, one cut a little wood backwards. They peeled the potatoes backwards and then set the table backwards. After they had done all this hard work they got to make a wish that was supposed to come true.

The youngest girl made her wish. First she wished for a nice young man. Soon the wind began to blow. It kept blowing till the door came open and here came a nice young man in and he went over and set down by the youngest girl. Then the next youngest girl, who set her things in the middle of the table, got her stuff ready and backed over and put a big long-bladed knife by her plate. She made her wish and wished for a nice young man. And the wind started blowing and in a few minutes the door opened and in came a coffin. The girl quickly made another wish and by the time she had made it the coffin vanished and there stood the young man she had wished for. He went and set down by the young lady and he picked up the knife and looked at it and he gave it back to her. He told her to keep it till he called for it.

Now it was the third girl's time to make her wish, so she wished for a young man. And soon the wind began to blowing and in came a young man and he took a seat by the third girl. And they all eat supper and had a good time eating and talking.

A few weeks went by and they all got married and owned their own homes. After they had been married for several years the girl who had taken the knife to her plate went to the bottom of her trunk where she had hid it and saw it. She told her man she had something to show him. She brought it and when he saw it he took it and then ordered the girl to go and stand up against the wall. When she did this the husband throwed the knife and stuck it through the girl's heart. She was soon dead. The man was tried and was hanged for the crime. The girl was buried in a coffin just like the one she saw that night. The other two girls lived happily with their husbands.

29   *Jack and the Hidden Valley*

ONE DAY AS Jack was setting in his favorite corner by the chimbly smoking his cob pipe, he said, "Daddy, I think I'll take a little walk."

It was long about noon when he started out down the road. He had walked a right smart piece when he noticed one of the hollers all strewed with roses. Now Jack always wanted to know everything, and being his cur'osity was up he walked up this road and after a while he come to the top of the hill. He looked down and saw what looked like a party doings, and beings as how his cur'osity was up a right smart more he ambled down to see what was coming off.

He seed men and women dancing the Virginia Reel, and right up on the corner of the platform he saw what looked like the King and his daughter. So he walks up and says, "Howdy, King."

The King said, "Howdy, son."

"Do you mind if I set a while?" said Jack.

"Course not. Set down," grumbled the King.

Well, Jack he got him a chair and placed it right down by the King's daughter. No sooner had he got settled when he heard a furious bellering down the valley.

"What's that?" gulped Jack.

"Oh, just Daddy's soldiers," said the King's daughter.

At that moment a whole passel of big unicorns all keeping time with their feet rounded the corner. When they stepped them up in front of the King they all bellered a mighty blast.

Well, after dancing a right smart, Jack got to wanting the King's daughter for his wife. So he walks up to the King and says, "King, I'm bound to marry your daughter."

"Well," the King said, "you ain't going to do no such a thing, Jack. Now le's not hear no more of this talk or me and you will fight."

Jack shut up, but he waited and waited and along at six-thirty when everyone was a-drinking and a-getting drunk, Jack scooted himself over to the King's daughter.

"How about marrying me, Honey?" he said.

"Sure, Jack," said the King's daughter.

"All right, Honey," Jack said. "Wait till I say, 'Go,' and then you run like thunder."

Well, Jack waited till he seed they was all drunk and then he whispered, "Go on, Honey."

The daughter took out with Jack on her heels. They run

elin' around. He bought him a little old bull. And he got with these fellers with these horses. Two fellers with fine horses, and Dirty Jack had the little bull. So they's goin' along in a big way, and these here horses they'd just bounce around good. And they come to a big mud ditch and these horses they just jumped right on over that ditch. And so this here bull started to jump it and he fell down and broke his neck right there in the ditch. And Dirty Jack he just down and skinned his bull and—you know, cow hides is mighty good and bring a good price, or did then anyway.

And so they went on, and they seen Dirty Jack a few days later and he had money rattlin' around, and said to him, said, "Dirty Jack, where'd you get all that money? You never had no money before."

He said, "Why," said, "I sold that bull hide, man," said, "it brought some money and I got rich."

They said, "Reckon if we killed our horses and sold their hides, reckon it'd bring us any money?"

"Yeow," said, "you'd get plumb rich," said, "just throw the meat away. It's no good, and just take the hides."

So they killed their horses and skinned 'em out and they went down to town. They thought they had to be a salesman in town and went right through town hollerin', "Horse hides for sale, horse hides for sale."

A policeman come up to 'em directly and said, "You better get outten town here," said, "we'll lock you up, put you in jail right now."

Run 'em outten town and they come back and they decided they'd kill Dirty Jack. And that night—they knowed where he'd sleep at, you know—the room. And so he found out about this and he put his grandmother in the bed where he's supposed to sleep—he swapped beds with her.

And so that night they went in and cut his granny's head off. Well, the next morning he went down and took his grandmother, and said he had to take her to the doctor. And he took her down to his neighbor's house and he called for his grandmother a drink of water, said he believed she was thirsty.

He stuck her head back on and they didn't know the difference. And the neighbors come out there to try and give her a drink of water. And so they hit her in the mouth with the dipper there and her head fell off. And he accused his neighbors a-killin' his granny. Well, he knowed how to work 'em, a course, and they said, "We'll give you a lot of money if you won't tell this on us for that." Said, "We didn't mean to do that."

Well, he went back. And a day or two later he saw these rich fellers and they said, "I thought we killed you!"

Said, "No, you killed my granny, but," said, "I skinned her out and sold her hide and got rich—sold her hide and got rich."

Said, "Well, if we kill our granny and sell her hide," said, "would we get rich?"

"Law," said, "you'd be the richest men ever was, if you'll do that."

"Well," said, "we'll do that."

So they went and killed their granny and skinned her out and so they went down through town hollerin', "Granny hides for sale, granny hides for sale."

Said, "Get that granny hide back outten town. If you don't we're goin' to lock you up right now." The police, you know, got angry about that. They had brought their horse hides in there and went back and brought their granny's hide.

Well, they went back and they saw Dirty Jack in a day or two atterwards, and they told him, "We are goin' to work on you, Dirty Jack." So they slipped around to two women, told 'em, said, "We can't do a thing with Dirty Jack." Said, "If you'll only kill him we'll pay you a good price."

Well, they agreed to do that, and they took him out and caught him and put him in a sheet and wrapped him up right nice. And they tied him up and went out in the woods to get 'em some clubs. And while they was gone he kept kickin' and scramblin' around. Finally he kicked out. And an old sheep come along. He tied that old sheep up in there, you know. When he tied that sheep up in there he got behind a tree to watch when they come back to see what was goin' on. And they begin to beat and that old sheep went, "Baa, baa." And they said, "We'll make you baa." And they said, "We're goin' to wind you up."

Well, they beat that old sheep to death, you know, and rolled him over the river bank into the river. And they just thought shore they's rid of Dirty Jack. Well, they saw him a day or two atterwards and they said, "Dirty Jack, we thought we killed you and put you in the river."

Said, "You did."

Said, "What happened?"

"Why," he said, "I just washed to heaben and got rich and come back."

They said, "Reckon," said, "if you put us in the river we would wash to heaben and get rich and come back?"

"Yeow," said, "you'd be the richest women on earth."

And they said, "Well, we'll let you tie us up and beat us."

Well, they got a sheet, and he took that sheet and he rolled 'em up right good and he got him a good club and he beat 'em to death and he rolled 'em overboard. And when he got 'em rolled out in the river they wa'n't no coming back because they's done and dead. He played pranks on 'em all the time.

And so he seed these fellers a few days atterwards, and they said, "Why, Dirty Jack," said, "we hired two women to kill you."

He said, "Yeow," said, "that's all right," said, "I'm all right." Said, "I got rich and come back."

32a *Rich Tom of Ireland*

ONCE UPON A TIME there was a young man who had a wife and six children. He was a very poor man and didn't have any kind of income. So he pulled out one day looking for a job of work. After he had traveled a long ways he come to an old farmer's house and asked if he could get a job there. The farmer told him to come in and he fixed him some victuals and a place to sleep. The next morning the young man went to work and the farmer liked his work fine. Soon the young man had worked a year and he said, "I would like to go back home to my wife and children," and the young man went on to say, "Now I would like my pay."

The old farmer said, "I am going to give you an advice that will be worth more to you than your year's work."

The young man said, "I want to know what that could be."

The farmer said, "When you are out traveling if anyone meets you at the crossroad and tells you it will be closter to your home if you take the left, you must never do that. Just keep going the way you were headed."

So the young man decided to work another year. He stayed and worked another one, and at the end of the second year the farmer said, "I have another advice that will be worth more to you than your year's work."

"Well, what could this be?" asked the young man.

The old farmer told him, "When you are out traveling never stay at a house where there is an old man and a young woman."

So the young man took the advice without any pay and went on and worked another year. Now the young man made up his mind to go home to his wife and children. The old man gave him another good advice. The farmer told him, "Always think three times before you speak or act once."

Well, the young man traveled on his way. The farmer gave him a big cake and a lot of small cakes to eat on his way home. Pretty soon after he had left the farm he came to a crossroad. He saw three men sitting above the road. After he got up to where the three men were they said, "If you are traveling a long ways today you can cut off several miles if you will take that road going left."

"Well, I sure need to save a lot of time," he said, and took the road to the left till the men got out of sight. Then the man turned and went the road that he had started out on. After traveling a little ways he met up with some people. He asked if the road he had just passed was a nigh cut. They told him that everybody went on that road was robbed and killed.

The boy was glad he took the old farmer's advice. He had traveled till it was getting about dark. He came to a house and asked to stay all night. Here come a young lady to the door, and said, "Sure, come in."

He went in and set down. It wasn't very long till here come an old man in and set down. Soon they eat supper and while they were eating this boy begin to study about what that old farmer had told him. After supper was finished the young man told them that he had decided to go a ways further. They tried to get him to stay but he went on. He saw an old barn standing down below the house, so he decided to go and sleep in this barn. He entered the barn lot and begin looking for a place to sleep. He got into the bottom of the fodder rack and soon went to sleep. Long about twelve o'clock this man heard a noise. He laid right still and he could hear them talking, the young woman among them. They were helping her kill the old man. One of the men throwed his coat over on the fodder rack where Tom was and while they were killing the man, Tom reached out with his knife and cut a square block out of it. After they had killed him the woman took her company back to the house. Soon as they left Tom got out and made his getaway for home.

He traveled for several days until he reached his house in the night. He went up to the window and looked in, saw wife and children lying in the floor. There was a man sitting beyond the children. Tom thought he would kill the man. Then he remembered the advice of the old farmer, so he went in and found out that the man was his brother and that he had brought some food for the starving family to eat.

Tom broke open the big cake the farmer had given him. When he broke it open there was ten thousand dollars inside the cake. They ate it up and the family got well.

In a few days there was a murder case to be tried and had a twenty-thousand-dollar reward if anyone could fit the piece of coat back in the hole. Tom took his piece of coat and he matched it in the hole and told how the murder was done. Ever since, he was called Rich Tom of Ireland.

The Man and His Three Sons 33

THIS IS THE STORY of a man who had three sons, and he give 'em an equal amount of money, give 'em seventy-five dollars each, told 'em, says, "Boys," said, "I'm goin' to give you three weeks to see which one can make the best of it."

And the first boy took his seventy-five dollars and he went out and he bought it up in whiskey and had a big time. And the next boy went out and he done the same thing.

The third boy went out and he traveled all day till late one evening and he looked and seen a sign on a door said, "Give any man seventy-five dollars to stay here all night." Said, "It's a hainted house."

Well, this boy decided he'd stay. He went in and he had a newspaper there and set down and went to readin' his newspaper. While he was a-readin', why, he heared a little knock on the door. He said, "Come in."

They's a haint come in, set down beside him. He said, "Set down over there. I'll talk with you when I get through readin' my paper."

He read on a while and atter while another sound knocked on the door. He said, "Come in." Said, "I'll talk to you atter I get through readin' my paper." Another haint set down.

Well, he read a while and in come another haint. He said, "Set down. I'll be through with my paper atter while and I'll talk with you."

He read his paper on a while and atter he got his paper read, he got up and said, "Now," said, "what do you want?"

He said, "Well," says, "I's killed one time and buried over yander under a tree," said, "foller me and I'll give you something that'll be worth a lot to you."

He follered him over there and he give him a five-dollar gold piece. Said, "Now you can spend this gold piece anywhere you want to and it'll become right back to your pocket."

Well, he come back and he talked to the other one, and she was a girl. "Well," she said, "I'm goin' to give you a handkerchief," said, "anywhere you use this handkerchief," said, "you are welcome."

And he come back and he talked to the other'n. He said, "Well," said, "I's killed one time and," said, "you're the only one's ever talked to me," and said, "I'm goin' to give you this walkin' cane." Said, "Anything you put that walkin' cane on, it'll talk."

Well, he went on the next day, started on and got hungry about twelve and stopped and asked about gettin' dinner. They said, "Well," said, "we never do keep no strangers." And he just wiped that handkerchief over his nose, and they said, "Yes," said, "come on in. I guess we can keep you."

Went on in there, talked around a while. And the old man said to him, "Son, you're a purty intelligent looking man," said, "I've got three girls," said, "I'd like for you to marry one of my daughters."

"Well," he said, "if you will send them in one at a time," said, "I'll see how they talk and whether I love 'em or not."

Sent one in and he talked with her a while and he said to her, "Well," said, "are you purty hard to get along with?"

She wouldn't answer him. He just laid the walkin' cane over there, said, "Are you purty hard to get along with?"

She said, "Yeow," said, "I am," said, "I have a lot of trouble with my parents."

"Well," said, "I don't want you."

Sent in the other one, said, "What is your name?" She told him. Said, "Are you a older girl than the other'n?"

Said, "No, I'm younger than the other'n."

"Well," he said, "Are you purty hard to get along with?"

Said, "No," said, "I'm very easy to get along with."

Said, "Why, you go back in and send the other'n." Said, "I'll talk to you later."

Sent the other'n in. Said, "Well, what's your name?" She told him. Said, "Well, are you hard to get along with?"

She wouldn't answer him. So he laid his walkin' cane on

her. She said, "Yes," said, "I have a lot of trouble with my parents."

Said, "I don't want you."

Well, he took this other girl and went on, and that's the end of it.

Jack and His Master 34

ONE TIME THERE was two men and they killed people when there was cotton pickin'. Well, cotton was ripe and they invited people there and killed them. Well, they invited a girl named Mary. She didn't tell her mother where she was goin' and she got on her horse and rode off. And every little rock and twig and tree would say:

> O fair maiden, don't be so bold,
> Your own heart's blood will soon turn cold.

She didn't pay any attention to it. When she got there she saw Jack and his master coming down the hill pulling an old woman by the hair of the head. And she went and hid her horse in the rushes where they couldn't see it, and she went to find her a place to hide: it was a big blood-hole. She crawled back in it where she didn't think anybody could see her. They couldn't see her way back in there. They saw a ring on this old woman's finger. And they went and killed her. They tried to get it off and they said, "Well, we're going to clean out the blood-hole tomorrow and we'll just cut her whole finger off, and throw it back in there when we get it."

And so they cut her finger off and threw it back in there and it hit in Mary's lap and she picked it up and put it in her pocket. Well, after they got her cut up and put her in the blood-hole they said, "I wonder why Mary is not here." And Jack said, "Well, I guess she will be here, because it takes a woman a long time to come some place on a horse." Said, "Well, we'll go upstairs and sleep a while."

When she heard them snoring she went down to the creek to wash off her ridin' skirt. She got on her horse. She didn't tell anybody where she'd been. Her mother's cotton begin to get ripe and she said, "Mother, why don't we have a cotton pickin' and invite Jack and his master?"

She said, "Well."

They all did their work and they set by the fire after they done all their work and told riddles and rhymes and stories, and she said she was going to tell her dream, and she said, "I don't want anyone to come out or come in." So she said, "I dreamed I was going to Jack and his master's house and come on the road and every little rock and twig and tree would say:

O fair maiden, don't be so bold,
Your own heart's blood will soon turn cold.

She said, "I dreamed that I didn't pay any attention to it. And I come and saw Jack and his master coming down the hill pullin' an old woman by the hair of her head. She was beggin' them to turn her loose, but they wouldn't. I dreamed that I hid my horse in the rushes where they couldn't see it, and I went and got in a big blood-hole where nobody couldn't see me. And they went and drug that old woman there and killed her and they saw a ring on her finger. And they couldn't get it off so they threw it in the blood-hole and it hit in my lap." And she said, "Here is the ring and the finger to prove it so." So everybody took Jack and his master out and killed them.

35a *The Witch Store Robber*

ONCE THERE WAS a store out in the country and things had been gone from it. These men would set around on the bags and wonder how it was getting out, and they said it was a witch coming through the keyhole, coming through the keyhole and taking the things out. And it would always write on the winder in the dust and fog and say, "I'll see you later."

Well, this little boy he was down there that day and he heard them saying that tonight was the night the witch was supposed to come back in. And so this little boy he wondered about it and he went back home, and was setting out on the steps that night and he was wishing that a witch would come along and take him with it, or something. Along come this old woman and she was wearing a long black cloak and a broomstick and asked him to go along with her.

So they went along, through the field and the cuckleburs, and the little boy asked her was they going to walk all the way there. And she told him they was a bunch of little calves there and they were going to turn them into horses. So they walked up to this little bunch of calves and she told the boy what to say into their years. And he whispered in their years and they turned into horses. There they had two fine horses. They rode down through the field. And when they come to these big wide ditches the horses would jump 'em. (The old witch had told the little boy what to whisper in its year to praise it.)

So they went on and she told him what to whisper to go through the keyhole. So they went through the keyhole and got what they wanted. And when they got ready to leave she wrote upon the winder in the dust and fog, saying, "I'll see you again." So they come back out through the keyhole and rode home through the field and left the little boy.

So the next day the little boy didn't go anywhere. He stayed at home, and he wondered that he didn't get anything except what he eat and he couldn't remember much about that. So when night come, the night they was supposed to go again, he was setting out on the steps and along come the old witch and took him with her to the same bunch of calves and whispered the same thing in their years and they turned into horses. So they went on and crossed the same bridges and he whispered the same words of praise to his year, and they went on and went through the keyhole.

Then they got all that they wanted and the old witch looked

all around and when she was ready to leave she wrote up on the winder, said, "That's all folks!"

And so they went out through the keyhole. And the little boy begin to wonder if he wasn't doing something wrong. So he wondered and come to this ditch and the horse jumped it. And he forgot what to say. And the old witch was in ahead of him. So he said, "That was a mighty good jump for a little lousy calf like you."

And so the horse turned into a calf. And the next morning when the little boy woke up he was going around through the pasture on this little lousy calf, a-flying. And the old farmer after him. And so the old farmer drug him off the little calf and took him home and made him work three days because he had rode his little calf all night.

35b *Witch Magic*

ONCET THEY WAS a man traveling and he put up to stay all night where two witches lived. And when they fixed this man's bed he went on to bed. And they'd go back ever oncet in a while to see if he's asleep. They went back twicet and then they pronounced him asleep. And then they got out their trunk and opened it up and got their salve, witch salve, and greased under their arms and got out their blue caps and went and looked up the chimbley and said: "By the ole blue cap and out the chimbley-top we go."

And after a while this man thought he'd try it—see if he could do that. He got up and got him a cap and greased under his arms, said: "By the ole blue cap and out the chimbley-top I go."

He lit out on top of the chimbley and seen two—just like two stars. He lit out right between them women. And the next thing he lit onto a yearlin'—we call it a bull yearlin'—and it was just a-runnin' for all power. And it jumped a ditch with him. And he said, "That's a good jump for a bull yearlin'."

And it left him right there. And then he was about two days gettin' back home. Don't know how long he'd a-been if he'd went on and never said nothin'.

The Two Witches 36^b

WELL, ONE TIME they's two ole witches. And before you can be a witch you have to do somethin' mean ever' night. So these two ole witches—one lived up on the creek just a little piece above the other one and each night one would go to the other'n's house to make up what evil thing they'd do that night.

So one of these ole witches come down to the other'n's home and she was down to the barn milkin'. And she had a big tree hollered out for a hog trough. So—they was a man he'd violated the law and he'd travel by night and when daylight come he'd take up and hide somewhere and stay till it got dark again. So he had turned this hog trough down and was under there and these two witches didn't know it. So they set down on this hog trough to make up what evil thing they'd do that night. One of these ole witches had a son lived up the creek a little piece had a little baby—his wife had died and left him a little baby to care for—so she told this other'n that she's goin' up there tonight to kill that little baby. Well, this other ole witch she said, "Well, I'll kill my neighbor's three cows."

So this ole man was under there. Soon as they made up what they would do, she milked and went back home. This ole man he got from under there and went up to her son's home. And he told this man what he'd heared his mother say what she was goin' to do. She was goin' to turn herself into an ole sow and go up to his door and reach under the door and cut the little baby's head off. So this man told him that he was dodgin' the law and didn't want to be seen.

And he said, "Well, you can stay here with me. I'll hide you in the closet."

So he went and done his work up and set down by the door and took his baby on his knee, and was settin' there with the Bible—readin' the Bible. After while he heared an ole hog out at the gate, gruntin' and rooted around the gate a while, and directly she squealed and jumped over the fence. She rooted and grunted around a while and she come on up to the door. Witches, I've been told, wears rings with a spring in 'em and a long keen knife. So he held his baby on his knee and— the man told him how his mother was plannin' to do—she would reach under the door with her hand, and ever' time she would reach under a little further, tryin' to get a little closter to that baby.

Well, he set there and had his butcher knife filed real sharp. He let the sow reach under as far as he wanted her to and he hacked her hand off. And there fell a woman's hand—cut the hog's foot off and there fell a woman's hand.

Well, she squealed and squeeaaled and run round and round and round and right back out and over that fence and down the road she run a-squealin' and went back home. And he picked the hand up and put it in his pocket, went to bed, and next mornin' he got up and went down to his mother's house.

She was in bed. He said, "Well, mother, what are you doin' in bed this mornin'?"

"Oh," she said, "I happened to awful bad luck yisterday. I was out choppin' wood and cut my hand off."

He said, "No, you didn't. You was up there tryin' to kill my little baby last night." Said, "I've got your hand right here in my pocket." He took the hand out and measured it. And he said, "I'm goin' to have you hung."

She said, "No, I hain't done a thing to be hung."

Well, he took her hand out and measured it and went and got a doctor, and he said it was the same hand, belongin' to her.

So they took her out and hung her. And that was the last of the ole witch.

110

The Witch Plot 36^c

THEY WAS A MAN one time goin' off to buy him a farm. He was goin' to move. And he traveled all that day and called to stay all night, and nobody wouldn't let him stay all night. He just put up in an old waste-house. He aimed to lay out in that house. And they's a big pipe in there—some kind of old stove pipe. I don't know what they had that big pipe for. And he just crawled up in that pipe.

Well, about an hour or two atter dark they come in cattle in that house and all around, and sheeps and cats—come in some cats. And they's a-smoking and talkin'. Says, "What will we have for supper tomorrow night?" They named over this man's big fat baby. Said his wife's goin' to wash tomorrow and said when she got her clothes hung out they would come a wind and blow her clothes off and while she was hangin' up her clothes said they would get that baby.

Well, the old man he traveled and went plumb back home that night. All the way back home. And the next day he got his gun and he had it loaded and settin' with his baby in between his legs, a-lookin' for that old sow to come. And she come up. They said she'd come up like drinkin' soapsuds and while she was pickin' up her clothes she would grab that baby. And that sow come up there eatin' soapsuds, drinkin' the soapsuds where that woman had throwed her soapsuds out. The wind come and blowed her clothes off. And that sow grabbed that baby right out from between that man's legs and him with his gun layin' across his lap. And she run off a few steps and he shot her right in between the shoulders. Shot that sow. Just about killed her. It never hardly killed her. And he got his baby then and brought it back.

Then she went on home and was in the bed and just complainin' of her shoulders they was hurtin' her so bad. She didn't want to show her shoulders. Finally she showed 'em and there was a hole where she had been shot right in between the shoulders. And she was a witch and he killed her then—her man did—because she was a witch.

37 Riding the Witch

ONE TIME THEY was two boys slept together all the time. And one got so poor—a witch had been a-riding him ever' night—he got down so poor he was just about gone. This other'n said let him sleep before, said he'd ride the witch—if the witch come and slipped the bridle on him.

Well, way long in the night this witch come, slipped the bridle on him and away she went on him. Had a fine mule of him. Went and hitched him to a peach tree. And he somehow slipped that bridle—somehow or other. I guess he was part of a witch too by him knowing so much about slipping the bridle. Well, when she come back to unhitch him, why, he slipped that bridle on that woman, on that witch-woman. And he traveled two or three days. He was away out in the country and traded her off to a real horse (he went and had her shod though first before he got through traveling with her). He swapped her off to a real horse. And he told 'em not to take the bridle off of her that night—just to wait till the next morning.

Well, they sent one of the boys to feed her, and he pitched her down home hay and fodder. And she said, "I don't eat hay."

Well, that scared him then. He run back and told his father they's an old woman standing in there. They just went and turned her out. I don't know how long she was a-getting back.

When she come back she was in the bed complaining—just about to die with her hands and feet. Her husband told her he wanted to feel her pulse, to see how high the fever was on her. She didn't want to, but she finally stuck her hand out, and there it was—a horseshoe nailed on her hands and feet. And he decided then she was a real witch. He run him a silver bullet then and killed her. That's all the way they could kill a witch—just with silver.

Taking the Turkey 38a

ONE TIME THEY was a Nigger and a white man went out a possum huntin'. They was goin' up through the woods and they killed a turkey. They was a lot of turkeys at that time. That's been some years ago, I suppose. And they killed a turkey. And they went on and they got a possum. Next mornin' they decided that they'd divide their game. They had a turkey and a possum to divide. And this white man he said, "Nigger, you can have the possum and I'll take the turkey; or I'll take the turkey and you can have the possum."

Well, this old Nigger, he didn't know what to say. He stood around there and studied a while. And he said, "Why, white man, you never said turkey to me nary time!"

Taking the Big Possum 38b

THEY WAS TWO Niggers went a possum hunting one time, a big Nigger and a little Nigger. So they hunted around about all night and finally the dog treed and they shuck him out and it was a big possum. Of course the big Nigger he wanted the possum, you know. Directly the dog treed again and they shuck him out and he was a little possum. They hunted on till daylight and they got to figuring out how to divide them possums. They argued and figured around about a half an hour, and finally this big Nigger said, "Well, now, I'll just tell you how to divide 'em." He got out a pencil and started counting. He said:

An aught's an aught, and a figure's a figure,
So the big possum belongs to the big Nigger.

That little Nigger said, "Yeow, yeow, you're shore right, you're shore right, Nigger, you get the big possum."

39 *Bobtail and the Devil*

WELL, ONCET UPON a time there was two people lived in the world. Of these two people it was always questioned by other people which one was the smartest, Bobtail or the Devil. Now Bobtail he was just a Bobtail, just a-running around, and the old Devil he had other things. So one day Bobtail said, "Well, Devil," says, "we can't decide which one is the greatest. So I tell you what le's do. Le's raise a big patch of potatoes." The Devil agreed to do it.

Well, they planted 'em a big patch of potatoes. Bobtail planted him a big patch in his lot and the Devil planted him a big patch in his lot. Now Bobtail, he took and put manure on his potatoes. But the Devil he was lazy and sorry—he just run around, getting anything for nothing—and he didn't put anything on his.

Well, when digging time come Bobtail went and dug his potatoes. He had old big potatoes. The old Devil he had just little old small ones. He didn't like that much. So he—as the Devil is—he thought he had been cheated. He said, "Well, Bobtail," said, "you had your choice. Now I don't think it was fair. Le's raise some hogs."

Well, Bobtail said, "O.K., we will."

So Bobtail and the Devil got their hogs and they begin to raise hogs. They put 'em all in a lot together. Well, they fed their hogs, fed 'em corn, just anything they could feed 'em. When killing time come—when the hogs got up big enough—

114

the question come up how they was going to divide 'em. Well, Bobtail says to the Devil, says, "Devil, I'll give you the first choice," says, "you take out you a hog and then I'll take out mine and we'll divide 'em."

So the Devil he went in and he looked over the hogs. As the Devil is, he wanted to cheat him, you know. So he retch down and picked up the biggest one he could find, an old big fat one. It went, "Weeeeeeennh!" and he picked it up and throwed it over the fence. Bobtail went down and he picked up his'n. It squealed right big and he throwed it over his fence into his lot. The Devil looked around and he picked the next biggest one he could find and he throwed it over the fence. Bobtail picked up another and put it over his fence into his lot. Well, there was just one more hog left, and the Devil said to himself, "Now I've got it on Bobtail, I've got it on him—that's sure!" So he picked up this small hog and threw it over in his lot. The Devil was pleased. Bobtail he kindly scratched his head, you know, and he said to himself, "I've been cheated."

But he got to looking around directly, and the Devil he was looking around. And then the Devil hollered at Bobtail, said, "Bobtail!"

Bobtail said, "Yes, Devil, what do you want?"

"Looks like your hogs are in your lot, but I haven't got any hogs."

Bobtail said, "Why?"

Said, "I've fooled around and my fence has got holes in it and my hogs have got over in with your hogs."

Bobtail said, "Ah, that's all right. You see, when I picked up my hogs," said, "I twisted their tails," said, "I know mine."

As far as I know the Devil is still looking yet trying to find them straight hog tails.

Jokes and Anecdotes

The stories in this division have two characteristics: they are more or less humorous; they are short, having only one motif. The latter qualification does not exclude tales, such as No. 56, which are really a series of separate anecdotes told in a chain. One category of tales needs further elaboration. This collection contains seventeen stories about numskulls (Nos. 40 to 56), identified in every case except No. 48b as Irishmen. It seems logical to conclude, from an examination of the parallels, that most of these anecdotes came from England, where the numskull was frequently a Welshman. Perhaps these stories migrated to eastern Kentucky after Ireland had replaced Wales as a trouble spot for England and the identification of the numskull was changed to suit the new situation. Perhaps the large English element in eastern Kentucky chose Irishmen for their jokes because a number of their neighbors were Irish and a joke became more pointed if it struck at home. Perhaps the prototype of the Irish numskull was the Irish immigrant laborer who laid the railroads in the Cumberland Plateau.

Many of these tales have become so localized—or at least Americanized—as to hide their origin. European parallels can be found for some stories of American frontier experience.

Irishmen Squirrel Hunting 40

THEY WAS TWO more Irishmens. One was named Dick and the other Sam. And they was going along, going along, going along the road. Finally they seen a squirrel going along a fence. Well, they tried to catch it, run it down and catch it. Well, Sam says to Dick, says, "Well, you go on and catch it and while you're gone I'll go and get a skillet and grease, and we'll have a feast out of the squirrel."

Well, he went on to get the skillet and the grease, and bless goodness, don't you know, Sam he climbed the tree and the squirrel jumped from one tree to the other tree. And he said, "Huuh," says, "if a little thing as you can jump through that away," says, "I can jump just as fer as you can."

He jumped out of there, trying to jump from limb to limb, like the squirrel. He fell and killed hisself. And the other come back and says, "Don't you know, he catched that squirrel and eat it up blood raw, and now I don't need no grease ner no pan to fry it in."

Irishmen Looking for Gold 41a

ONE TIME THEY's nine Irishmens and they started out, you know, to try to get rich. And they got to hunting for money and gold and they hunted around, traveling around, you know. Finally they seen the moon shining in the river. Well, they go down, and they start figuring out a way to get it out. They thought it was a sack of gold. One of them he said he would get hold of a bush and they would take it hand by hand and go down and get it. Well, they lined up, one holding to the bush. They all lined up, hand by hand, down into the river.

117

And the first one's hands got to slipping. And he said, "Now hold tight till I spat in my hands."

When he turned loose to spit in his hands, you see, that turned 'em loose and they all went down in there. And they got out and they'd count. One he'd count, "One, two, three, four, five, six, seven, eight." One gone you see. Then another'n he'd count, and never count hisself. Well, they's a big cowpile laying there. So he said, "Le's all stick our noses in this and count the holes."

They all stuck their noses in it and then counted the holes, and they's nine holes now. "Well," he said, "fat-to-my-jassum, we're all here, le's go!"

42 Irishmen and the Red Pepper

ONE TIME THEY was two I'ishmens a-travelin' the road in a big ferrish [far-off] country. And they traveled and traveled and traveled—along and along and finally they got hungry. These two fellers, just like you two fellers, travelin' together. And one was named Pat and the other was named John. And come up to a lady's garden—garden—and he looked over in the garden and says, "What is that purty red things over there?"

And Pat said to John, says, "It looks like purty good cherries." And he said, "I believe I'll get over and see what it twis and try out a mouthful of 'em."

Well, he got over and picked him a big handful and put 'em in his mouth and went to chawin'. And he commenced a-cryin'—just bawlin' big.

And says, "Pat, what are you cryin' for?"

Said, "I'm cryin' because my father died and never got none of these here good cherries."

And he went in and John says to Pat, says, "If they're that good," says, "I'll get over and try me a bite of them cherries."

And he went on back and got over the fence and pulled off

a big handful and put 'em in his mouth. And the tears commenced to run down his face.

Well, he says, "What're you cryin' about?"

He says, "I'm cryin' because you didn't die before your father did."

Irishmen Deer Hunting 43

HERE'S A STORY about a white man and two Irishmens. They was deer hunting one day and they went up in the woods, and there was two roads led from a big deer lick back into the woods. Pat and Mike was these Irishmen's names. And this white man said, "Well, Pat, you watch this road, and Mike, you watch that one over there." Said, "Now don't let 'em pass. I'm going to roust 'em. They're licking up there. They's a deer lick up there in the mountains."

Well, they's standing there looking and watching for the deer. They never saw anything like that. Down Pat's way there come a big deer. And it was in a big hurry. And he didn't know what that was, because he had never seen one. So he just cleared the road and let it pass. He went along, tramping around there in the road a little bit. And then directly he met a big mountain toad frog, a big rusty'n. And so he just killed the frog. And this man come directly and said, "Well, where's the deer?" Said, "I thought it come down this road."

"Oh, man," said, "I've got him killed here."

Said, "Why," said, "you ain't got him. Why, that's a toad frog."

Said, "Fat-to-my-Christ," said, "it looked big enough for a deer to me."

He said, "Why a deer is a big thing. Didn't you see nothing like that come down through here?"

"Yeow, I seed something looked like the Devil with a chair on its head and I let it pass."

"Why," he said, "that was a deer."

"Ah, that wa'n't no deer to me." Said, "Fat-to-my-Christ, I just let that pass. That was the Devil with a chair on its head."

44 *Irishman Eating Dungbeetles*

THEY'S TWO OLD Irishmens out a-travelin' one time and they found a mulberry tree. Been a lot of cattle layin' out around under it. So Pat he was so lazy he wouldn't climb the tree, and Mike had to do all the work, climbin' around. So Mike he climbs the tree and was up there eatin' mulberries. And these old tumblebugs was all over the ground, you know. And so Pat he's just a-catchin' 'em and eatin' 'em just as hard as he could. And directly he looked up at Mike and he said, "Mike," said, "has mullems got laggums?"

He said, "No, mullems ain't got laggums."

He says, "Fat-to-my-jassum, if I ain't eat my belly full of spradlin' bugs."

45 *Irishmen and the Hornets' Nest*

ONE TIME THEY was an old Irishman. He's traveling along and oh, he wanted to be a bad man. He wanted to fight. And he met a feller one day and said, "Thanks to my Christ, buddy," says, "I'm just dying to fight. Do you know where I can find anything to fight?"

He said, "Yeow."

Said, "I want to whup you."

That old man said, "No, I hain't able to fight, but," said, "I'll tell you where you can get you something to fight."

And he said, "Where's that at?"

He said, "They's a little gray house hanging way down

hyonder on a beech limb." He said, "You go down there and go up to the door and call 'em out and tell 'em you want to fight and they'll come out and fight you."

Well, he went down there and he bowed up to fight and he hollered at one—hit's a big hornets' nest—and he hollered at one, and one come around, "BooOOoo." He just slapped it, says, "Thanks to my Christ," said, "get away from here. I knowed you's all cowards anyhow." And he just whaled away and hit that hornets' nest and just tore hit all to pieces and they like to killed him.

And a few days after that they's a yaller jacket come around where he's at, going, "BooOOooOOoo." He said, "Get away from here," said, "you can change your color, but you can't change your voice."

The Irishman and the Pumpkin 46

TWO IRISHMANS come along one time, and they's a farmer and he's a-gatherin' corn and pumpkins, and they asked him what they was. He told them that they was mare eggs. And the farmer had a colt. And they asked him how he got the colt. Said he raised it from them mare eggs. They asked him if he would sell them one. Said he'd give 'em one. And he told 'em how to use it—to take it out to a broomsage field where the broomsage grew and put it on the sunny side of the hill and cut a hole in it, where the sun would shine on it, and he could raise him a colt.

Well, the Irishman would go ever' morning to see about his pumpkin. One morning he went along and he saw something come out of the hole of the pumpkin. And he took after it and ran along. It was a-flyin'—it was a rabbit and it was a-flyin'. He hollered, "Wee, little colty, here's your mammy; wee, little colty, here's your mammy." And the rabbit just run off.

47 a *The Irishman and the Watch*

ONCE UPON A TIME there was an Irishman walking down the road and he saw a watch. He picked it up and heared it ticking. He said, "By faith and by Christ, here's a tick and I'm going to kill him." So he laid it down and mashed it with a rock.

Then he walked on and he met a man. This man said to him, "Have you seen a watch anywhere on the road?"

He said, "No, I've not seen anything except an old tick up there and I killed it."

This man said, "Will you go back up there and show me where this tick is?"

This Irishman went back with him and showed him. And that man said, "This is not a tick, this is a watch." Said, "The next time you find a watch you pick it up and put it in your pocket." Said, "It will tell the time of day—it is worth something."

He said, "O.K."

He went on down the road and saw a terrapin, small terrapin. He picked it up and said, "By my faith and by Christ, here's a watch and I'm going to pick it up and put it in my pocket so I can tell the time of day."

So he picked it up and put it in his pocket and went on down the road. And he met some men. And these men asked him what time it was. He got this terrapin out of his pocket and said, "By faith and by Christ, it's twelve o'clock and scratching like ninety for one."

Irishman and the Watch 47c

THEY WAS AN Irishman goin' down the road and he found a watch, and he called it a rattlesome bug. He carried it along and said, "If you don't hush your rattlesomin' I'm goin' to throw you away." And he went in a house and it kept on rattlesomin' and he said, "I'm goin' to throw you right out that winder if you don't hush, or holler out loud one."

He throwed that watch out the winder and hit a policeman in the back and that policeman hollered, "Ouch!"

He said, "I knowed you'd holler or die one d'rectly."

The Battle of the Boards 48b

ONCET UPON A TIME Daniel Boone come through Kentucky and he had built little houses about every ten miles apart, and around them little houses he would raise corn. He come to one of them little houses to stay all night there. He had a bunch of wild meat, coon and deers and rabbit and all that. And he was getting ready to fry it. He had his skillet hot and everything just about ready to put his meat in. And he went out to a little spring to get some water.

Well, he went out there and he seen the Indians a-coming. He was scared to death; he didn't know quite what to do. Well, he went back in and just kept on frying. Up overhead was a trapdoor, and up over there he had boards that he could drop out. He put his table right under there and pulled the ladder up after him.

When he got up in there he had a stick like a plow handle to put over the trap door. And all around there he put two hundred boards. And when he pulled out that stick the boards would fall. The old Indians they come in and they's hungry.

gettin' tuned up. And finally he got to sawin' his bow across the strings to see if it was in tune good.

And this Irishman got scared and he went down to another house and called to stay all night. They said, "Yeow, come on in. I thought you's goin' to stay up at the other place?"

"Well," said, "he had a thing, a big long thing," said, "he got it outten the trunk after supper and he'd twist its years and saw a stick over its back and it'd squall like a cat, and, fat-to-my-Christ, I didn't know what to think about that."

And so the man said, "You can stay all night with us."

And he went out in the apple orchard, big apple orchard, tryin' to get some apples outten the apple orchard. And so a whippoorwill come right down just in the top of an apple tree there, set there, you know, hollerin', "Whippoorwill, whippoorwill." And he never heard one of them things, never saw one before. And the lightnin' bugs just as thick as they could be all in the air and everything. And about the time, you know, they'd get to lightenin', that old whippoorwill would say, "Whippoorwill, whippoorwill." And he run off and run into a porch post when he got back to the house. And, man, he like to got killed too, but they got him in the house and said, "What's the matter?"

He said, "I don't know," said, "fat-to-my-Christ, I heard something."

Said, "What did it sound like?"

Said, "Well," said, "I don't know," said, "it was something goin' 'Whippoormythrash, Whippoormythrash' and fire was flyin' ever' lick."

53 Irishman Who Bought a Mule

THEY WAS AN Irishman traded for a mule, you know, and he didn't know nothing about a mule. Somebody saddled it up for him. He decided he'd ride across a hill to the store or mill or something or other, I don't know. But anyway he went over the hill. He rode that old mule right up the hill, you know. The way we generally do, you know, we ride up the hill and lead down the other side. But he didn't know the difference. He just rides up and down too. He was riding down the hill and it was in hot weather and them doggoned old flies bothering that old mule and he'd kick and switch his tail and jump once in a while, and finally he got his foot hung in the stirrup, you know. And that old Irishman he kept looking first one way and then the other. And so he didn't know what to think about this old mule kicking, you know, getting his foot up in the stirrup. He didn't know that they could do that, I don't guess. But he kept looking first one way, right and left, and directly he says, "Fat-to-my-Christ, if you're going to get up and ride, I'm going to get down and walk."

The Lazy Irishman 54

ONE TIME OLD PAT and Mike started out to hunt 'em a job. Mike he was purty smart and he worked and he could get a job anywheres. But old Pat he couldn't do any good, he wouldn't work and couldn't hold a job nowheres. So Mike he'd get a job and Pat'd come along and he'd give him his job. Pat'd go to work and Mike'd go on and hunt 'im another'n. He done this three or four times. And Mike he got in trouble and they got him up to hang him. So they put him up on the scaffold, and tied a rope around his neck. Had him a-hangin' up there. And Pat he come along, and he always wanted him a job they wa'n't no work to it. Mike was a lot littler than Pat. So Pat looks up at him and asks what he's doin' there. And Mike says, "Oh, this pays three dollars a day," says, "just standin' here."

He said, "That's the job I want."

So he told him to come up and untie him. And he untied

Dock pulled the trigger but his gun didn't go off. Dick pulled his trigger and shot Dock. He thought sure he had killed him and run home as fast as he could go. When he got to the house there was a clock setting on the dresser and it was saying, "Tick, tock, tick, tock," and Dick thought it was saying, "Dick shot Dock, Dick shot Dock." He said in an angry voice, "If you don't hush I'll throw you out the window and break your back."

Well, the clock kept on saying, "Tick, tock, tick, tock." He grabbed the old clock and throwed it out the window and hit an old woman in the back. She yelled out, "Oooh, my back!"

Dick said, "I told you I would throw you out the window and break your back." The old woman got scared and run away from there a-flying.

While Dock was getting over his gunshot, Dick thought he would get in plenty of wood for the winter. He hitched the old mules to the wagon and got his ax and went into the woods. He come to a big tree and said to himself, "There are enough wood in that tree to last a whole year." He got to studying how would be the easiest way to get the tree down and loaded. So he decided to put the wagon under the tree and to cut the tree on the wagon. That would be the fastest way. He cut the tree down on the wagon. It broke the wagon up and killed the best span of old mules in the country. He picked up his ax and started back home broken-hearted.

He came upon a pond full of geese and wanted some for their supper. He decided that by jumping in the pond and threading the geese on a string would be the fastest way to get roast goose for supper. That was what he did. And when he got a lot of geese threaded they rose and flew away with him. They flew way up in the air with him and stopped and stood still. Dick said to himself, "How in the world am I going to get down from here?" He took out his spudge of a knife and cut the line. He fell and wedged his head between two rocks. He couldn't get out anyway. So he cut his head off and went to the house and got a grubbing hoe and dug it out. Then he carried it to the house and sewed it back on.

When Dick and Dock got over them scrapes they thought they would go a-squirrel hunting. They got on top of the hill. Dock was standing by a big tree, when he asked Dick, "What is this tree standing on?"

Dick said, "On the ground."

Dock said, "What is the ground standing on?"

Dick said, "On a rock."

"What is the rock standing on?"

Dick said, "Giant holding it up."

"What is the giant standing on?"

"How far down do you think I've been?" asked Dick.

Well, they went on around the ridge and saw a squirrel. Dick said, "You stay here with it, Dock, while I go to the house and get a gun to kill it with."

Dick pulled out for the house. When he got gone Dock thought he would climb the tree and catch the squirrel, but the squirrel jumped out of the tree. Dock said to himself, "I can jump as far on my two big legs as that squirrel can on its four little ones." So he jumped out after it and it killed him.

The people found him before Dick got back, and dressed him up and started out of the hill with him. Soon they met Dick coming up the hill. When Dick saw him he said, "I wish I had stayed up there with the squirrel this time."

"Why?" asked a man.

"Well, he is dressed up like the President of Washington, D. C."

He didn't know that Dock was dead. So they buried Dock. Dick was still living the last time I heard from him.

The Three Sillies 58

ONCE UPON A TIME there was a young-like man traveling around and it was becoming dark and he had to have a shelter. He come to a farmer's house and they were just getting ready to have supper. And he knocked on the door and asked them if he could stay all night. And they said, "Why, of course."

And they told the girl to go down in the cellar to get some buttermilk and she went down and just about had her pitcher full when she looked up and saw a old rusty ax sticking up in the ceiling. And, oh, she just started crying and just let the buttermilk run out. After a while the mother got uneasy about her and she went down to see what was the matter. And the buttermilk was all run out over the floor, and she said, "What's the matter?"

And she said, "See that ax sticking up there in the ceiling? Supposing I come down here some day to get buttermilk and that ax should fall on me. Oh, how dreadful that would be." And the mother set down and started crying, and so did the girl.

Well, after a while the father got uneasy and he went down. He saw both of the women setting there, and he asked what was the matter. And the mother said, "See that rusty ax sticking up there. Supposing some day our daughter should come down here and the ax should fall on her—" And he went over and started setting down too.

And the stranger got worried and he went down to see what was the matter. The buttermilk was in a big barrel and he turned it off, and asked them what they's all crying over. And he said, "See—that old rusty ax up there? Supposing some day our daughter should come down here to get milk, like she was a while ago, and the ax should fall on her. Oh, how dreadful that would be."

And the stranger reached up and pulled the ax down. He said, "I've traveled many places, but," said, "you all are the three silliest I ever heard."

Well, he stayed all night and left in the morning. Before he left though he said, "I'll be back. I'm going to travel around a while and if I find any people sillier than you I'll come back and tell you."

Well, he's traveling along that morning and he come to an old woman. And she was trying to get her old cow up the ladder, upon the house to eat the green grass. But she wouldn't walk up it. And finally she tied a rope around the cow's neck and stuck it through the chimney, and she had hold of it. And the cow started to fall off the house and it jerked the woman up the chimney and left the cow hanging there.

Well, the stranger thought, "Well, there is another silly, but I don't think she is half as silly as those others." Well, he traveled on, and it was getting dark and he come to an inn. And it was all full up and they said, "Well, we can't give you a room by yourself, but we can give you one with another man."

He said, "Well, just so I get a place to sleep, it's all right."

And they put him in and they slept all right. The next morning he got up and was ready to leave. And this other old man, he said, "Oh, only one reason I just dread to get up in the morning. I have such a hard time putting my trousers on."

And the stranger said, "Why don't you just put them on the right way?"

He said, "The only way I know is to—" He had them hanging up on the bedstead trying to jump into them. And the stranger showed him how to put them on.

And he was traveling along, and that night he come to another little village and he saw some people with rakes and hoes and shovels next to a river. And he said, "What are you all doing?"

And they said, "We're trying to rake that big piece of cheese out of the river."

And he said, "Don't you know that is just the moon reflecting on the river?"

Then he started back to these three sillies' home, and he told them he had traveled a long way and that they's the three silliest he'd ever seen.

59 *The Two Woodcutters*

ONE TIME THEY's two men and they went out to cut wood. And they sot down to rest. So they got up and started on off. And they got way off and one man forgot his ax. He went back to get it and he got lost from that other man. It come dark on him and he laid down and couldn't sleep for the wild animals hollerin'. And he laid there seben days and seben nights and didn't have nothin' to eat. And one day he met a man. That man told him to go home with him and said he would give him somethin' to eat. And so they started. And that man shot at a rabbit, and blood run down the shotgun barrel and a baby cried.

So they went on and seed a big bunch of pheasants. That man raised up and shot at them. And they's a baby cried and blood run out of the shotgun barrel again. And he went on there.

He didn't have no woman, so he fixed a good supper and they sot down and eat, and so that night they went downstairs to sleep. And so they locked about seben doors goin' down through there. And so that night that man he was sleepin' next to the door, and he heared somethin' comin' down through there, said, "Let me in or I'll knock this door down."

And he runned over there and tried to wake that other man up and never could wake him up. And then he runned back over there and got back in his bed. It kept right on, "Don't let me in I'll knock this door down." Knocked that door down and ever' one of them and come down in there and come to that door right over the top of his bed, and said, "Don't let me in I'll knock this door down!"

He run back over there and tried to wake that man up and couldn't. Then he laid back down and that thing knocked that door down over top of his bed there, and said, "You come and go with me," said, "you're in dangers."

He went with that woman—hit's a woman and had her head cut off, and a little baby in her arms had hits head cut off. They went there to a big cliff and that woman said, "O.K.," said, "you raise that rock up."

That man said, "Why," said, "I can't raise that rock up."

Said, "Yeow, you can," said, "try it."

He raised it up and there's the awfulest lot of money ever was. Said, "Well, you take that money now and divide it with one of my brothers." She showed that man where her brother lived.

And he went there, and they's two men caught him, put him down in a sack. They went to a place and sent Little Black Sambo out there, told him to drown that man and feed the horses. Went out there and fed them horses and started to drown him. That man said, "Well," said, "Little Black Sambo, want to go to heabem?"

Said, "Yeow, I sho' do."

"Ye want to know how to get there?"

Said, "Yeow, how?"

Said, "Come here and open this sack and let me out and get down in here."

Opened that sack and Little Black Sambo got down in there. And when them two men come out they throwed that sack out there, and they thought it was that man and it was Little Black Sambo, and they drownded him and went on and started up the road.

And that man—the one got out of that sack—he had went and bought a big bunch o' cattle. Started down the road. And them two men said, "I thought we drownded you?"

"Well," said, "you did drown me," said, "I went to heabem and the Lord give me all these cattle and I come back." Said, "Do you want to go?"

Said, "We're goin' to get us two sacks and let you do us that way."

So that man drownded them, and he lived happy ever after.

60a *Big Fraid and Little Fraid*

ONE TIME THERE was a man and he had a pet monkey. And he also had a little boy who used to go out and get the cows every evening. And this little boy would always come in late. And the man decided he would put a stop to it. So he put a sheet over his head and started out the door. And this little monkey of his grabbed up the tablecloth and threw it over his head and started after him.

The man didn't see the monkey and didn't say anything to it. Then after they got to the graveyard, where the little boy had to pass every night, the man humped down beside of a post, and the little monkey humped down right beside of him.

And the boy came along, whistling a little tune and singing to the cows. And he looked over and saw this white thing, and he didn't scare too easy and he wasn't afraid of it. And this white thing started running after him saying, "Boo, boo."

The man saw he wasn't going to get scared, and he saw that the little boy was going to say something. And he said, "Run, big fraid, or little fraid will catch you!" Because the monkey was chasing the man.

And the man looked back and saw the monkey, and he ran all the way home and fell in the door. And he never, never tried to scare a little boy out after the cows late any more.

61 *The Graveyard Wager*

ONCE UPON A TIME there was some colored men talking about the graveyard up on the hill by the schoolhouse. And they was saying that if they went to school there they would be scared of it. And one of these colored men said he wouldn't be scared of it, said he'd go up there at midnight. And these others said they wouldn't, but he said he would. They told him that they'd give him five dollars if he would go up there at midnight. He said he would. They give him a nail to make a mark with and said, "You put this in the gate post when you go up there." He said that he would.

And so that night at twelve o'clock he went up there to the graveyard and he had on a kind of loose coat. And he drove this nail in the post and got his coat fastened on to it, and he started to run away when he got the nail in. And he couldn't and thought a ghost or something was a-hold of him. And he wrastled around there and couldn't get loose and thought something was holding him and wrastled around till he scared himself to death.

The Tailor and the Giants 62b

ONE TIME THERE was a little tailor. He had an office upstairs in a building. So he was working one day and a feller come along there selling belts. So this little tailor bought him a belt. Well, he worked on and a little later on there come a salesman selling sandwiches. And he bought him a jam sandwich. So he laid it up while he worked and flies got on it, after that sweetening, and got on the sandwich. He was working on and he noticed all at once that flies had got on it and just covered his sandwich. So he pulled off his belt and struck those flies and killed seven flies at one stroke. He wrote on his belt in big letters: KILLED SEVEN AT ONE STROKE. So he went downstairs and went on down the road. And people that saw him thought maybe that he had killed seven men at one stroke. Well, they's all afraid of him and he felt very important. He went on down the road there and finally he met a giant. He was talking to the giant and the giant said, "You're an awful little feller to be a great man like that, do great things like you have—kill seven men at one stroke."

And he said, "Oh, I can do anything."

Well, as they went along a salesman was traveling along behind him and caught up with him. They walked along behind this giant and the giant never did see 'em. And he bought a piece of cheese offen this salesman boy who was traveling through, and put it in his pocket, and went on with the giant. They went up the hill, and saw a bird beside the road. Just as it happened he got it hemmed and he slipped up and caught it and put it in his pocket and went on with the giant. They got on top of the hill there and the giant said, "Oh," said, "I can do some tricks greater than you can."

The little tailor said, "Oh, I can do anything most that you can."

Well, he picked up a rock and said, "I can squeeze the water out of this rock. Can you do that?"

The little tailor said, "Oh, that's nothing." So he just retch down and got a rock and eased this piece of cheese outten his pocket, dropped the rock and the giant never noticed. He just helt it up and squez till the water just poured out of this piece of cheese.

Well, the giant looked funny sorty and said, "Well," said, "they's something else I can do that you can't do, I bet ye."

He said, "Well, le's see you do a trick that I can't do."

He said, "Why, I can throw a rock up and you'll never see it come back."

"Oh," the tailor said to the giant, "that's nothing. I can throw a rock up and you'll never see it come back neither."

So the giant he threw that rock up, and the tailor never did see it come back at all. Well, he just eased this bird out of his pocket and tossed it up, and the giant thought it was a rock, and it just sailed up and sailed away. The giant said, "Boy, you're the powerfulest little man I ever saw in my life."

Well, they went on down the hill there in the forest. And the giant said, "Le's see if you can do this." Said, "Le's pick up a tree here in the forest, pull it up and carry it out of the forest."

The tailor said, "That's nothing for a man like me."

So they retch down, and the tailor got hold of the tree and

138

he was grunting just like he was pulling, but the giant was pulling the tree up all the time, but he didn't know the difference. The tailor said to the giant, "You carry the trunk of the tree and I'll carry the branches. They're the heaviest anyway."

So he showed the giant where to get under it, the trunk of it, so he could balance it right good. So when he started out he had his back turned to the top of the tree and the tailor he just jumped up on top of the limbs, set down there and rode on out of the forest. When they got down there he hollered, "Le's let it down."

The old giant was panting for breath, and the little tailor was rested—he'd rode out of the forest. The giant said to the tailor, "Are you tired?"

And he said, "No, not a bit."

And he said, "Boy, you're the toughest little man ever I saw," said, "man, I'm give out."

So they went on after they let the tree down there. They left the tree there, went on through the woods and started to cross another hill, and this tailor he heard something or nother popping away out ahead of him. He looked and there was three big giants. They had roasted a sheep apiece, looked like, out there and they was forking 'em up with hay forks. That was just a little fork to a big giant, you know. They went out by where they was. But this little tailor he was afraid of these giants, but he never let on. And this other giant was telling about what a great little man this was, what a great man to be so little. And these giants they got so they was afraid of him. This here tailor he was plumb scared of 'em but he never let on. So they invited them to eat with 'em, and he helped 'em eat their sheep, eat all he wanted and they went on.

Started to go to the palace of the king. They went on in there, and this princess now was struck on one of the giants, and the king didn't want his daughter to marry a giant. And it was such good news about this little feller being such a great man, as this giant thought the little tailor was, that he eased around and told it to the king. And he got a-holt of it and he eased around to the tailor and told him that if he would get rid of these giants, kill 'em all, that he would give him his daughter.

So he fixed him a trap up in a gateway, a big blade of a thing, up overhead, with a trigger to it so that when a giant come through it he could knock the trigger, and each time they come through there he would cut their heads off. And so the first giant come along, and he retch down and whacked his head off. And the other giant behind him said, "Oh," said, "you're not nervy," said, "I'll go on in."

So he stuck his head up there, and another and another until the fourth giant was killed. Well, after that the king said to the little tailor, "You shall have my daughter."

And they married and lived happy ever after.

63 The Gaping Woman

ONCE UPON A TIME there was an old woman who lived by herself and she carded and spun all the time. She'd set up and card and spin till she gaped three times and then she'd go to bed. One night three men fixed to go and rob her. One of 'em had two eyes and another had one. The man who had two eyes went to her house and clumb upon the chimley, eavesdroppin' till she went to bed so they could go in and rob her. He got up there watchin' her, and she carded and spun away, till she gaped once. She said, "Now one's come, two more to come and then I'll go to bed."

Well, he jumped off the chimley and run home and told 'em she was a witch, said she said, "Now one's come, two more to come and then I'll go to bed."

Another one of 'em who had two eyes said, "I'll go and see." He went and clumb upon the chimley and was settin' up there watchin'. She was cardin' and spinnin' away and she gaped again. She said, "Now two's come, one more to come and then I'll go to bed."

He jumped off the chimley and run home and told 'em she shore was a witch, she said, "Two's come, one more to come and then I'll go to bed."

The one-eyed one come and got up there, and she was cardin' and spinnin' away till she gaped three times. She said, "Now three's come, and I'll go to bed. Old one-eye, I'll eat you for my supper." Somebody had give her a one-eyed fish to eat.

He jumped off the chimley and run home and told 'em she shore was a witch. They were afraid to come back and rob her because they thought she was a witch.

Casting Sheep's Eyes 64

ONE TIME THERE was a young man got about old enough to court and he couldn't think of anything to say when he went to see the girls. He got to asking around what must he do. Some of them just told him to say "first one thing and then another." But his daddy told him to cast sheep's eyes at the girls. Well, he went out and killed two or three of his daddy's finest sheep and took out their eyes and went on to see his girl. He went up and he says, "Howdy! and first one thing and another." They spoke to him and he asked where the girls was, "and first one thing and another."

The girl come in the room after a while and they would got to talking and ever once in a while he'd throw one of them sheep's eyes over in her lap. And I don't know what she done about it. But in a day or two his daddy was out with his sheep and he found two or three of them gone. The boy had taken the eyes a-sparkin' with him. He had been casting sheep's eyes. I guess they scared the girl worse than if he never'd a-took them.

65 *The Soap Boy*

ONE TIME THERE was a little boy out playing. His mother started to wash and found that she didn't have any soap. So she called him and told him that he would have to go to the store and get her some soap. He starts off down the road to the store saying, "Soap it is, soap it is, soap it is."

After he has gone a little down the road, he stumps his toe and falls down. When he got up he had forgotten what his mother had told him to get when he got to the store. So he starts running around in a circle saying, "Here I lost it, there I found it; here I lost it, there I found it."

About that time an old man rode up. He heard the little boy saying, "Here I lost it, there I found it," and he says, "Hey, son, what did you lose?"

The little boy doesn't pay any attention to what the old man said. So he just kept on running around in a circle and saying, "Here I lost it, there I found it." So the old man got curious about what the little boy was looking for and said, "If you don't tell me what you're looking for I'm going to get off my horse and help you look for it anyway."

The little boy doesn't say anything to the old man. He just keeps on going around in a circle saying, "Here I lost it, there I found it." So the old man starts to get off his horse and his foot slips out of the stirrup and almost causes him to fall. So he gets a little mad and says, "Well, I'll be damned if that stirrup ain't slick as soap."

So the little boy thanked the old man for helping him find what he had lost and starts off down the road again saying, "Soap it is, soap it is, soap it is."

The Devil and the Angel 67a

ONCE UPON A TIME there were two boys who had worked for several weeks gathering walnuts. They piled them up behind a big tombstone in a lonely graveyard and left them there until they were done gathering. When they finished gathering the walnuts they started dividing and carrying them home. They worked all day and until dark dividing and carrying them. At dark there were only a few of them left so they decided to finish up. The night was peaceful and quiet. There was no sound except from the boys, who were counting and saying, "You take this one and I'll take that one."

Now just below the graveyard stood a large oak tree, and behind the tree stood Jack, known to all the children as old Roguish Jack, waiting for some one to pass that he could rob. The little boys didn't know he was there or I'm sure they wouldn't have stayed in the graveyard very long 'cause all kids were afraid of him. Now all the walnuts were divided except two, and one of them rolled under the fence close to the big oak tree. Jack thought he heard someone, so he was listening right close. He heard a voice from the graveyard say, "You take this one and I'll take the one under the fence."

Lo and behold, when Jack heard this he was scared out of his wits, because he thought it was the Devil and an Angel dividing up the dead people and he didn't know which one had chosen him. He was most sure it was the Devil. At this instant Jack started running toward home, and he made so much noise that it scared the boys and they started out in the same direction with their white sacks. Jack looked back and saw the boys with them white sacks and this scared him even more and he never looked back until he reached his shack.

People who knew him said that he never went near another graveyard until he was carried there dead and they believe that he actually trembled in his coffin when he was brought there dead, because he never did know whether it was the Angel or the Devil that had chosen him.

68   *Gabriel's Horn*

AN OLD NEGRO MAN once went out hunting, and he took his little boy along to carry the lantern and their fox horn. They hunted nearly all night, until it began to rain hard. They had no place to go in the dry. Finally they came to the old Negro church and went in and got under some sacks and boards in the back to keep warm. Sunday morning broke and the Negro people started coming in for meeting. The old preacher took the stand and started preaching. He called out, "O Lord, let Gabriel blow his horn." He kept calling on the Lord until he got in a big way preaching, and the people got to shouting and stamping the floor. Directly the old preacher called out louder than ever, "O Lord, I hear the trumpet blowing now!" The little boy thought it was time to help him out a bit so he put the fox horn to his mouth and blowed it as loud as he could. Before you could say "scat," Negroes went out of that house every way they could get out, and they broke every window out and the door down clearing out of there.

69a   *Robert and the Peachtree*

IN THE HILLS OF Kentucky once there was a man by the name of Robert Taylor. He was noted for stealing peaches. One day while walking through a man's field he saw a peachtree. Robert decided to get him off a peach or two. He climbed the tree, which was very small. He realized it was not an ordinary tree. An old deer's head had wallowed in the mud. And a peach stone had sprouted out and that was the tree Robert was in.

Robert threw a peach stone and hit the deer on the nose. The deer got all excited and began to run, so Robert held tight. The great deer was strong as a buffalo. Before Robert could get out of the tree which he was hanging onto for dear life, the deer was across the mountain in Virginia.

Then Robert decided to never steal peaches again because he had to walk all the way back to old Kentucky.

The Split Dog 69c

ONE TIME I figured I wanted to go a-hunting up North. I went up in Alaska. I had the best dog I ever owned in my life. That dog was so fast he would jump a rabbit and have it half dug out before it ever got to the hole. So one day he jumped a red fox. So I figured right there the boy had struck his match. He run into a tree and split hisself wide open. I got to him just as quick as I could. I was in a hurry, you see, and I slapped him together and I got two legs up and two legs down. Well, he would run on two legs a hundred yards and he'd run on the other'ns a hundred yards back. And he froze hisself to death a-running from one of them trees to the other just a hundred yards between 'em, you see.

Tall Hunting Tale 70

ONCE UPON A TIME I bought me a dog. I give three bushel of dried apples for him—sold the dried apples and then bought the dog. Well, the feller I bought him from said he would tree coons. So I took him a coon huntin'. He begin barkin' about ten o'clock, out on a high knob. We went up to see what the dogs was barkin' about. I looked up on a cliff about thirty feet high. The dog was lookin' up the cliff. I looked up in a tree and about ten feet above the last limb a coon was stickin', a coon on a little knot. I asked him if he couldn't climb up and catch it. And he nodded his head. So he backed off about thirty yards and clim up on another cliff about forty feet high. I asked if he could jump from one cliff to the other, and he nodded his head. He backed off about four hundred yards. He started to jump. And he got out about half way and saw he wa'n't aimin' to make it, so he turned around and come back.

Well, I thought it was smart of him, you see. He went ahead and I shot the coon and it rolled off the cliff. I picked it up and we took on off to the house. We got down to the creek, and my brother was with me. We started across the creek on the swingin' bridge and I dropped my flask of carbide down in the water, river about twenty feet deep. I told him I'd go down and get my carbide, if he'd wait for me, and he said, "No," said, "you've had a cold. I'll go down and get it," said, "it'd make you sick."

He dived down and was gone about thirty minutes. And I dived down to see what he was doing. He was settin' there on a log, stealin' my carbide, takin' it out of my flask, pourin' it in his'n. I asked him what he was doin', and he said, "Nothing, I just needed a little carbide and I was takin' it out of your flask—I seed you had plenty of it."

Well, my dog, see, I was gone about thirty minutes and my dog he got worried. So he come down to see what I was a-doin'. He run around to the end of this log where we was settin' and he begin barkin'. I looked in and saw an old boar hogfish and a gang of little shoats. I nodded my head and he went in after 'em. He shook his head. He couldn't make it. I kindled me up a far at the other end and I smoked them out. I smoked and smoked and smoked. About thirty minutes here they come. And the water run out of their eyes, I'd smoked 'em so much. My brother said, "How did you kindle a far?"

146

I said, "I jerked a few slabs off the log we was settin' on and struck me a match, and that's all there was to it."

Well, we caught the fish and come on up to the top. I had a rifle-gun, had one round of ammunition. I looked out in front of me and there laid a rattlesnake about twelve feet long. Well, I started to shoot it and about that time I heard a noise down the river. I looked and there was 5,000 wild ducks comin' up the river. Well, I didn't know which to shoot, the ducks or the rattlesnake. About the time I started to shoot the ducks I heard another noise up the river and I looked and there was 5,000 wild geese. Well, I shore didn't know what to do then. I knowed I couldn't kill the geese and the ducks, all, and the snake. So I said to myself, "I'll kill the snake and try to catch a goose as she passes." I pulled the trigger. The barrel busted. Half of it went down the river and killed 5,000 wild ducks. The other half went up the river and killed 4,999 wild geese. The gun flew all to pieces. I didn't have nothing left but the stock.

I gathered up all my ducks, killed the snake, gathered up all my geese and started across the swingin' bridge. I looked over in the corner and saw my gun locks, stickin' there on a rail, had that other goose hemmed. I walked over and picked her up and wrung her neck. Well, I had all them geese and ducks and started across that bridge, and the bridge broke with me. Down I went twenty feet deep in the water. I swimmed, I kicked, and I paddled, and when I finally got to the bank and got out I had 300 pound of fish in my hip boots. And I went on to the house and told my wife I thought I had purty good luck. And that was all of it.

71a *Jack on a Hunting Trip*

ONE TIME THEY was a boy named Jack and he decided to go out hunting one day. He called up his dogs and went up the hill and they treed a possum up a big tall tree. And he clumb up there. He got in the top of the tree and he had to hold with one hand and he had a hatchet in the other hand there. And he didn't know what to do with this hatchet he had, at first. Finally he retch up—the moon was shining bright—and he stuck his hatchet up in the moon, see, so he could hold and try to catch the possum with the other hand. Soon he heard something come fluttering through the air there, and directly a big owl come flying into the top of the tree where he was. And he retch up to get that old owl by the back, you know, or any way he could catch it, probably, and that old owl when he got hold of him, he sailed right on off with him, over the other mountain top and lit right in the top of an old holler tree.

Why, he went down in that tree there. This here tree was holler. He heard something in there and he decided to go down and see what was the matter. And he went down in there and they was three small cub bears down in there. So he decided, "I'll just take one home and make a pet out of it." He was down in there and he picked up one, and when he picked it up he didn't know what to do with it. He was down in there and couldn't get out. He couldn't climb up the tree with this bear cub in one hand. He had to brace hisself before he could get up. And he heard a noise about that time. He looked up and there come the old she bear right on down the tree. But all bears come down a tree back'ards, you know, tail first, down the tree. Well, he didn't know what to do at first. Finally he grabbed his knife out, and when the bear got right in reach of him, Jack he just retch up and got the bear by the tail, and had his knife in the other hand and he begin to job

148

the old bear with the knife and holding onto him with the other one. That old bear took out toward the top of the tree as hard as he could go. You know, he was frightened. When he got to the top of the tree he was all safe then, but he never got his cub bear though. He got on top of the tree there and he let go of the old bear. But the bear was still frightened, and he just hung onto the top of the tree and let the bear go on.

Well, he clumb down after the old bear had gone, and went back to get his hatchet, where he had left it stuck in the moon. So he clumb up there and got his hatchet and then went on.

Bears in a Holler Tree 71ᵇ

THEY WAS A MAN started out to track him up a—at first he was goin' to track him up a possum. And he got on the track of this bear in the snow. He tracked and he tracked. Kept a-trackin'. Finally he tracked this bear up to a big chestnut tree. And the chestnut tree was holler at the top. And he had him a big rope with him. And he looked down in this here holler chestnut tree, that he could look down in, and he seed they was some young bears in there. And he took a notion that he'd tie the rope at the top of the tree and go down and catch the young bears. Well, he got down to catch the young bears and tied 'em with his rope. And he thought he would just come out by the rope just like comin' out of a well. And he heared something nother on the outside. And it was this old bear. And he come up there and he come down back'ards, the bear did. They can't climb down for'ards like a squirrel—a squirrel a-tall. And then he come down till he got down close. And he had one of these big dirk knives—knives and he got the bear by the tail and went to jobbin' the bear up'ards—that away—with this here dirk knife, and made the bear climb back out the top of the tree. And when he got out he had to turn right around and climb back down the tree back'ards. Well, when he got down to the bottom of the tree—tree—he had a big .45 Colts pistol and he hauled off with this here Colts pistol and he shot the bear right square between the eyes with the Colts pistol and killed the bear. And then he drug the young'ns out at the top.

72 *Bragging Englishman*

THEY'S AN ENGLISHMAN come over from England oncet, come over to the United States, and of course the American people, ye see, figured that he might be capable of taking a crew of men and working them. They give him a job as foreman.

While his men was working he'd let a feller go out and hunt. He went out one day and killed a couple of squirrels and brought 'em in and showed 'em to one of the men and said, "I've killed us two fine squirrels today."

The man looked at 'em and said, "Ah, that ain't nothing," he said, "Oh, we've got 'em bigger than that in England."

He went out the next day and he caught a fine string of fish. The old Nigger come in and said, "Boss, I've got us a fine string of fish today."

The Englishman looked at 'em and said, "Oh," said, "that ain't nothing," said, "we catch 'em over in England and throw 'em away larger than that."

He went out one day and killed a couple of rabbits. Colored man walked in and said, "Boss, we've got us two fine hares for dinner today."

The boss looked at 'em and said, "Oh, we throw 'em away in England bigger than them."

It made the old colored boy mad, so one day he was out hunting and he found a terrapin. He picked the old terrapin up and put it in his haversack. He brought it in. And he made up the boss's bed that night and put it in his bed. He went to bed about eight o'clock. And about nine o'clock he squalled out, "Come here, come here, come here!"

So he come running in (the old colored boy) and said, "What's the matter, Boss?"

He said, "They's something a-hold of me—really a-pinching." He throwed the cover back and said, "Now tell me what it is."

He said, "Boss," said, "that's one of our bedbugs we got here in America." Said, "Have you got any in England bigger than that'n?"

Well, that same trip the old Englishman said, "Well, I'd like to drive around New York, look around at the city." Said, "I've always heard of this place and I'd like to look it over."

The feller got him in a convertible, driving him around through the city and come to a five-story building. The Englishman said, "Bud, how long does it take you all to build a building like that?"

He said, "Oh, something like six months."

He said, "Oh, we build 'em in England in two months," said, "do a turnkey job."

He said, "That's purty fast."

They drove on. Come to a fifteen-story building. He said, "How long does it take you all to build a building like this?"

He said, "Oh, we build a building like that in two months and a half."

He said, "We build 'em like that in six weeks—do a turnkey job."

Come to a thirty-story building. The Englishman said, "Bud, how long does it take you all to build this building?"

He looked it up and down, said, "Oh, I guess we can build it in a couple of months," said, "we do a turnkey job on it—"

He said, "We build 'em over in England in two weeks, do a turnkey job."

About that time they drove up to the Empire State Building. And he said, "Now, Bud, how long did it take you to build this building?"

He looked it up and down and said, "I'll be durned if I know." Said, "It wasn't there last night when I passed!"

Then one day he was married and he had some turpentine settin' upon the mantel, and his little boy climbed in the chair and spilled the turpentine off on the floor. And his house drawed up small enough to make a birdhouse out of it.

75 *My Pet Charlie*

ONE DAY MY uncle and I went fishing in an old mill pond by the creek. We hadn't been fishing long until my uncle caught a big one about two feet long, the biggest one I ever saw. We took it home with us and put it in an old tin tub till morning. The next morning we got up to have fish for breakfast, but we didn't have it. It wasn't in the tub where we put it. It was chasing the cat and dog around the house. Well, it went on with our pets that way for about a month. One day we decided to name him, so we named him Charlie. He went everywhere we went. One day a heavy snow fell, so we decided to go hunting. When we started Charlie started along behind us. You ought to have seen him wiggling along behind. Soon we come to a little creek with a small log across it. We got across it and called for Charlie. He started across and got about half way, and he started wiggling and slipped off and fell in and the rascal drowned before we could get him out.

76 *The Cats That Clawed to Heaven*

ONCE UPON A TIME there was two boys who went out on a hunt. They hunted in the woods for a long time, but they couldn't find anything. They decided to go down to the river bank. One of the boys looked around and saw a wildcat coming after them. They both cocked their guns and fired at the same time. They killed her and she rolled into the river. The two little cats came out of the woods and they caught them and put them in a sack. They got the old cat out of the water and skinned her. They started for home with a little cat apiece and one hide. They began to quarrel about who was to get the hide of the mother wildcat. At last they hit on a bargain. They would keep the little cats for six months and then meet somewhere and let them fight it out. The one whose cat won the fight would get the hide.

Six months later they met at one of the boys' houses and got ready for the fight. They put the cats on top of the smokehouse to fight. They started fighting and one couldn't outfight the other. The cats wouldn't give in nor back down the roof none at all, so the only way they could go was up. They clawed to the top of the roof, and clawed right on until they went up in the air and soon out of sight. The boys waited a long time while the fur was falling all over the place.

They went away and six months later they came back to the smokehouse again and the fur was still falling like snow. So they give the old mother hide away because the little ones could not whip one another.

The Bad Bear 77b

THERE WAS AN old log cabin set up on Boot Hill Mountain. Grandfather said his grandfather said his grandfather said the house had been there for a long time. In it lived a family— there was a girl, a woman, man, boy and a monkey.

The woman was sick one day and wanted a drink of water. So they sent the little girl after it. When she got up in a dark place in the road there stood a big tree, and she heard a voice say:

> Take a bite of honey,
> Take a bite of hay—
> Gobble you up!

It was a bad old bear and ate up the little girl.

When she did not come back they sent the little boy to look for the girl. As he come up to the big tree in the dark place he heard a voice say:

> Take a bite of honey,
> Take a bite of hay—
> Gobble you up!

And the old bear ate him up too.

Then the old man set out to see what had happened to his children. When he came to the tree he heard the voice say the same thing and he was gobbled up at one mouthful too. And the old woman set out to see where her folks had gone to. And she went down into the old bear's dark belly like the rest.

The monkey got lonesome at home and he set out to find his masters. When he came to the big tree he heard:

> Take a bite of honey,
> Take a bite of hay—
> Gobble you up!

The monkey ran off and ran up a tree. He sat down where he could see the bear. The old bear started climbing after him, but he could not make it further than the first limb. So the old bear decided to waylay the monkey. He stretched out on the limb and with his old stomach so full he was soon asleep. The monkey slipped down the tree to him and pushed him off the limb. When he hit the ground he bursted wide open. Then out come the little girl and she shouted, "Goodie, goodie, I'm out!"

The old man crawled out and said, "Goodie, goodie, I'm out!"

The boy got out and yelled, "Goodie, goodie, I'm out!"

The old woman came out and said, "Goodie, goodie, I'm out!"

Then the monkey from the tree said, "Goodie, goodie, I didn't get in to get out!"

When the old bad bear woke up he couldn't find his pieces quick enough to put hisself back together and he died. The last time I heard from the family they were getting along good.

ONE TIME THERE was a fat man and he went out in the middle of the road. An old man and old woman sent a little boy after a fat piece of meat. That fat man went to this store, and he grabbed that fat piece of meat and he said, "I'm goin' to eat you, fat piece of meat." He grabbed it and swallered it whole.

That little boy come to get that fat piece of meat. And that fat man said, "I've eat a fat piece of meat and I'm goin' to eat you." He just grabbed him and eat him up too.

That man and woman sent that little girl atter it. That fat man met her, said, "I eat a fat piece of meat and a little boy, and," said, "I'm goin' to eat you." He didn't have to chew 'em. He just swallered 'em whole.

That night, why, that old man sent that woman atter 'em. Met that man. And she was kinda fat herself. And he said, "I've eat a fat piece of meat, and a little boy and a little girl, and I'm goin' to eat you too." He had to chew her a little 'cause she's fat.

And that man come out that morning. And that fat man met him and said, "I've eat a fat piece of meat, a little boy and a little girl and an old big fat woman, and I'm goin' to eat you too." He grabbed him and just swallered him whole.

He come to a rabbit. Told that rabbit, "Eat a fat piece of meat, eat a little boy, a little girl, an old woman and an old man, and I'm goin' to eat you." Swallered him.

And met that squirrel. Said, "I've eat a fat piece of meat, eat a little boy, eat a little girl, an old woman and an old man, and I'm goin' to eat you too."

The squirrel climbed a tree. That old fat man started to climb up after him. Stepped on a rotten limb, and he fell and busted open.

That little boy said, "I'm out."

The little girl said, "I'm out."

Fat piece of meat said, "I'm out."
Old woman said, "I'm out."
Man said, "I'm out."
Rabbit said, "I'm out."
The squirrel said, "I'm out and never been in."

78a *Coon Skin Huntin'*

Now ME AND MY PAW we lives down in Moonshine Holler
about a mile, mile and a half, maybe two mile. The other day I
told paw le's go a-larrapin, terrapin coon skin huntin' if he
cared, so he asked me he didn't care. So I got out and called up
all the dogs but ole Shorty—called him up too. So we went on
down the mountain till we got on top of the hill and all the
dogs treed one but ole Shorty, and he treed it too, up a long
tall slim slick sycamore blackgum saplin', about ten feet above
the top, right out on an ole dead chestnut snag. So I told paw
I'd climb up and twist him out if he cared, so he asked me he
didn't care. I clumb up and shook and shook and shook, and
directly I heard something hit the ground. Looked around and
it was me. Every one of them doggoned ole dogs jumped on
top of me, but ole Shorty, and he jumped on top of me too.
Now when I come to my right mind I told paw to knock 'em
all off if he cared, and he asked me he didn't care. Then paw
picked up a pine knot and knocked them all off but ole Shorty—
knocked him off too.

So we decided that was enough huntin' for one day and
started back down the hill and all the dogs holded one in a
huckleberry log about two foot through at the little end. So
I told paw we'd have to cut him out to save time if he cared
and he asked me he didn't care. And paw picked up the ax,
and the first lick he cut ole Shorty's long smooth tail off right
behind his years. Just like to ruint my dog. So we started
back down the hill and paw seen all the punkins in the pig
patch and we chased them doggoned punkins all over the field

and finally I got mad and picked one up by the tail and slammed its brains out over a pig. Then paw talked to me like I was a redheaded stepchild, be gosh!

So we laid up the gate and shut the fence and then paw told me to shuck and shell 'em a bucket o' slop. So I's settin' there shuckin' and shellin' that bucket o' slop and I decided to go down to Sal's house. She lives in the Moonshine Holler on the tough of the creek and the furder you go the tougher it gits. Sal lives in the main last house. It's a big white house painted green, both front doors on the backside.

So I told paw I'd ride that day, it being kinda sunny, if he cared, and he asked me he didn't care. So I went out in the lot, put the bridle on the barn, the hoss on the saddle, led the fence up side the gate and the hoss got on. So we went ridin' along down the road, study like and all at once a stump in the corner of the hoss got scared and r'ared up and throwed me off right face fo'most, a-flat o' my back, in a gully about ten feet deep, right in a briar patch. Tore one sleeve outten my Sunday britches. So I got up and 'peared to me like I wa'n't hurt. Brushed off the hoss and went leadin' him on down the road.

Got to Sal's house and she had both front doors shut wide open and the winders nailed down. So I knowed she was glad to see me. So I hitched the fence to the hoss and went in and throwed my ole hat in the fireplace and spit on the bed and down I sit in a big armchair on a stool. So we begin to talk about pat and polly-cake and all other kind o' cake, and finally Sal 'lowed, "Bud, le's go down in the peachorchard and get some apples and make a huckleberry pie for dinner." So I asked her I didn't care. And we went down to the peachorchard, and I was just as close to Sal as I could get, me one side of the road and her on the other'n. So we got down to the peachorchard and I told Sal I'd climb up the pear tree and shake off some apples if she didn't care. And she asked me she didn't care. And I clumb up and shook and shook and shook till the limb I was standin' on broke off and throwed me right a-straddle of a barbwire fence, both feet on the same side.

79 *Origin of Man*

ONCE UPON A TIME they's a man layin' out, and he went to a cave. And he was layin' out in there and the Yeahoh come and throwed a deer in to him—something would come every day and throw a deer in to him, and leave out. One time that Yeahoh come and got down in there with him and not long after that she had a kid. Then one time he took a notion to leave her and he would go to leave and she wouldn't let him go. She'd make him come back. A-finally he got out and made her think she was going with him. And they went and he got on a ship going to cross the waters. And he got started and rode on off and left her. And she stood there and hollered and screamed after him. And when she seen he'd got away from her and she couldn't go, why she tore the baby in two and throwed one half in after him.

80 *The Giant and the Chipmunk*

ONCE UPON A TIME there was a little chipmunk and it lived with its grandmother. One day this little chipmunk went out in the mountains and it was making noise. And its grandmother told it before not to make no noise; if it did the old giant would catch it. Told it to be quiet when it went out in the mountains. Well, it didn't believe its grandmother.

One day it went out in the mountains and it was making noise and it looked down and saw a giant. That giant said, "Little ground squirrel, come down here. I've got some berries here I want to give you."

It said, "No," said, "my grandmother told me you'd eat me." And that chipmunk throwed a big branch over a cliff where the giant was. And the giant thought it was the chipmunk and it jumped on top of them trees, and the chipmunk got away. And the giant took atter it, and the little chipmunk went down in a hole. The giant took atter it and put his hand on it and it made streaks down its back.

King Richard of England 81a

ONCE UPON A TIME in England there was a king, a very good king. His name was Richard. Richard ruled his people very well, and there was peace. But he had a war with a country far, far across the ocean. The day he got ready to sail across the ocean and fight this way, why, there was a son born in his palace. They named him John.

Richard sailed off and just disappeared. The queen and the people never did hear from him. The queen thought he had been killed. She raised her son up and told him that his father was once a king, and that he must be ready to take a king's place, whenever he could do a certain task. She wouldn't tell him the task until he became eighteen years old.

The boy waited until he became eighteen. Finally that time arrived. The day that John became eighteen his mother took him out to a big stone and told him to try to lift it. He took a-hold of the stone and he couldn't lift it, could barely move it. He asked his mother to let him have another try and she wouldn't let him. She said he had to wait till next year. All that year John roamed the woods and forests and developed his muscles. He wanted to be strong enough to lift that stone. He was very curious what was on the inside of that stone.

Finally the day came when he was nineteen years old. His mother took him out again and told him to try to lift the stone. He took a-hold of it and he lifted it up. He just got it a little above the top of the ground and he dropped it. He had to wait another year.

He waited until he was twenty. He then took a-hold of the

163

stone and lifted it. He lifted it up about half way and he dropped it. He had to wait another year.

He had to wait till he was twenty-one. When he became twenty-one years of age he went out and took hold of the stone and he lifted it up. He threw it clear back. He went into this pit that was dug in the ground, and in there he found a sword. He buckled it on, and on this sword he found papers saying that when he done this task he should be king, if he so desired, and that he must sail for the country for which his father had sailed.

His mother told him that he must go. The next morning he set sail. He sailed and he sailed. Finally he arrived and he inquired for the king. The king his father had come to this country and set up a palace. He inquired after him and found the king. The king was now very old, getting along in years. And he was very worried. The reason for his worries was that he had been conquered. He was controlled and the people around him were controlled by great monisters that had a den down under the ground. There were three of these monisters and they were large, more like giants. Big. He told his son about them.

His son took his sword, which was made of very excellent steel. Very strong. He went out and he met up with one of these giants. Every giant was formed like monisters. He got into a battle with one. He killed this one.

As time went on he met up with another one. He fought with it. But he didn't kill it. He wounded it and he got wounded himself. One day while he and the king himself were at a theater amusing themselves, one of the monisters came to the palace and stole a lot of the jewelry that they had and had run down into this big cave. The son of the king, being very angry, took his sword and went down. As he went in he run into these big monisters. The first one was the one which he had wounded previously. He fought with it and killed it. But in doing so this monister had struck him over the left shoulder and wounded him. He went on in and got into a fight with this other'n. He fought and fought. Finally this monister struck him just over the heart and wounded him. In doing so John had struck hard at this monister and broke his sword. He had a dagger in his pocket. And he took the dagger and threw it and stuck it in the monister's heart. The monister died. John struggled to get on the outside of the cave. Just before he got on the outside of the cave, why, he died.

The Prince and the Monister 81ᵇ

ONCE UPON A TIME, a very long time ago in England, the king of England he set sail to a foreign country. And just before he set sail he had a son born to his palace. And he set sail to a new country in a war he was waging in this country between himself and a great monister. And this monister had an army, big army. The king went and he fought with this army and his army was destroyed and he was subject to the rule of this monister.

This monister was half bull and half man, had two heads and two large horns. This king agreed with this monister that he would each year, the best young men which he had in his kingdom he would send for this monister to eat. This monister lived down under the ocean in a cave, a big dark cave. Everyone who ever went in there never did come out alive.

Now my story goes back to the prince. The prince after many years grew up, and in these years of growing up he watched the young men march out and go to be eaten up by this monister. One day when he became of age, eighteen years old, he lined up with a line of young men to go across the ocean to be eaten by this monister. He wasn't like the rest of his companions who went with him. His companions were shuddering and crying, going on, but he had a great sword on his side, and he was very brave. He said he was going to kill the monister. His companions even laughed at him. He marched up in front. The king did not want him to go. The king by this time was very old and he had very many troubles and he was subject to the rule of this great monister. When the prince got ready to sail the king asked him, said, "Prince, will you please put out a white flag on your ship going over, and if you kill the monister, why you put a black flag on the ship on your return."

The prince promised that he would. He set sail with the white flag. He sailed and sailed and sailed. Finally he landed. When he got on land he marched straight down to this big cave. He went down to the monister in a big cave down by the sea. As he went in why this big monister made a lunge at him, fire a-flying out of his nostrils. And he stepped to the side. And this big monister when it lunged why he knocked one of its horns off against the side of the cave. The blood begin to fly and run down its head. It shook its head. And he stepped back in front of it and it made another lunge and he stepped to the other side and it knocked the other horn off. And just as it did he stepped back with his sword and whacked both of its heads off at one time.

Now just before he went into the cave he had met a very beautiful girl and he had fell in love with her. She told him to take a spool of thread and go back into the cave and she would keep one end of this thread and that as long as he was standing up, as long as he was living for him to pull it and she would know that he wasn't dead. And if he wasn't dead he would have some way to get back out of this cave. As you know, he couldn't see in this cave. When he had killed the monister he came back out of the cave, and married this girl and got ready and they had a big feast and he stayed with this girl on this land for two or three days.

When he got ready to set sail he was so excited that he did not put the black flag on the ship as he had promised. The king was very wearisome back home and he got out by the seashore and started looking over the ocean. And one day he looked and saw the ship coming. But it had the white flag on it. Being very troubled and very sorry that his son had been killed, at least he thought he had been, why he up and fell into the ocean and drowned.

When the prince landed and found that his father had drowned himself, he was very sorry and did much weeping. But he took his king's place and became king of England. And him and his queen lived happily ever after.

Indians Out of Fire 82

ALONG BACK IN olden times there weren't no houses and the people lived in caves all together. They made beds out of moss and leaves and so on, and built their fires of log heaps under the clivves. They didn't have any chimleys. They had firekeepers to watch the fires, one of a night and one of a day to watch 'em. They didn't have no matches. They sometimes had a flint and a little tow they called it, made out of an old rotten tree.

One night there come a big tide and flushed out the cave and washed everything out and put their fire out and they didn't have any fire left. Well, they had a meeting and an old man by the name of Sharpeye and a young man by the name of Strongarm decided to go to a different land and get some fire. They didn't have any and it was getting cold weather and they had to have some. They got up some provisions and took off. They went for miles and miles, traveling through the woods.

Well, they got fire and started back. They got about half way on their journey and they's a painter attackted them on the way. And so old Sharpeye couldn't climb very well, and Strongarm was very young and quick and he clumb a tree. And the old man was too slow and he got killed by the painter. And the painter kept Strongarm treed two days and nights.

Well, when the painter finally left, Strongarm got down out of the tree and dug him a hole in a sinkhole and buried the old man as best he could. He went on with his fire back to his home back at the cave and they had fire.

83 *Tommy and the Indians*

ONCE UPON A TIME there was a small family that lived way out in the open clearing about a mile from the settlement in the wilderness of Kentucky. There was only the woman and one girl and one boy. The father of these children had been killed by Indians earlier and the family had not yet got in their crops and had not found a safer place to live. The family had to be on the outlook for Indians all the time. In the log house was a little window cut out in the upper side so they could see if there were any Indians coming.

One day the mother of the children left them alone while she went out to the far field to get some corn to grit for bread. Before she left the house she told the boy to put the little girl in the stove oven if he saw any Indians coming toward the house. It wasn't very long after she left till the little boy looked out of the window and saw a large tribe of Indians sneaking out of the woods. The little boy got busy hiding his seven-year-old sister. He put her in the oven like his mother told him. After he had done this he ran and got under a kittle which set on the dirt floor about eight feet from the stove. He had just got under the heavy iron kittle when he heard a loud noise come splashing through the window. He whispered to Jane and told her to stay as quiet as she could. The Indians knocked the door in and came on into the house. They started looking under the beds and behind the stove and up in the loft, and everywhere they thought they might find something. After they had just about give up and were ready to go away, one of the Indians, coming out from behind the stove, stopped and stared at the kittle. He thought he saw it move a little bit. He didn't pay it much mind at the start, but a little later he stopped and looked at it again. He called for all the other Indians and they came out of the loft and stood looking at the black kittle for a long time. Then suddenly they all lunged

168

at it, turned it over and at last found what they had been looking for so bad.

Two of the Indians seized little Tommy and tied his hands and feet with leather strips. One of them carried him and they set out for their camp. By this time it was getting dark. They all set down by their big roaring fire and ate their supper and talked about how they were going to kill the little boy, now lying on the ground before them. They all finished supper and laughed some because they were feeling good about the day's hunt. Soon they dropped off to sleep, one by one.

After the fire had died down and they were all sound asleep the boy began to try to get loose. He keeped working his hands till finally he got them loose. Then he started working at his feet. While he was loosening them he heard an Indian turn over and groan. He quit and sat in the dark for a long time, until the Indians seemed settled down in sleep again. When he was free he turned to the side and found that he was right between two old Indians. He eased along past them and was about to reach the open place, when another one of them turned over and rolled over several times. Tommy lay just as still as a dog. Soon the Indians got anted right again. Then he started crawling away, and rose and started running just as fast as he could in the dark.

He run through the woods for about three hours and then it began to thunder and lighten. It started to rain. He remembered the Indians sleeping in the open, and he got more scared than he had ever been yet and ran his legs off taking distance from there. But it was no use. He heard noises behind him, he heard sticks a-breaking and leaves a-rattling. It was so dark and he was so tired he was ready to lay down and give up. Then he found a holler log and crawled into it. The Indians tramped nearer and nearer, looking at everything for sign of him. One big Indian stepped upon the old log he was in. The boy's heart was beating two strokes at once then. The tramping died away and he came out and couldn't see nor hear of them. There was still some lightning streaking the sky, and he stood and waited till it lightened and then

169

picked out a piece to run. He ran and fell this way till near morning. And at last he came to the river and then he knew where he was. He followed the riverside till it brought him home again. There he found his mother and sister, crying and wondering what had become of him. Soon after that they moved in to the settlement where they were safer from the Indians.

84 *Yansoo Po Shinie!*

WELL, IT ALL happened one time when they was two little girls going through the woods to their grandmother's, and on the way they met a bunch of Indians. And they asked 'em where they were going, and why their father and mother wa'n't with 'em. And they were foolish enough to tell 'em where they were going and that their father and mother weren't with 'em. So these Indians kidnaped them and took them to the village to cook and wash for 'em.

And so they stayed with the Indians and the Indians treated 'em purty good until one of them started to run away and they killed her. And so the other one stayed around waiting for a chance. And they would always go off like they was going to hunt and they would go around behind a mountain and watch this girl to see what she would do. But she was always too smart for 'em. She stayed in the village and cooked and went on about her chores, just like she was as happy as she could be.

And one day the Indians went upon the mountain, said, "She's too happy," said, "she'll never leave us." Said, "We'll hunt today."

So they went off to hunt. And when they left her there she knew she must make her escape purty soon. So she started off picking up little twigs and things like she was going to build a fire with them. And so she got out to the forest and she made a break for it. And she went on and on through the woods.

And these Indians come back. So they got their dogs and started out after her. And she heard them after her and so she went and crawled up in a big holler log. And these Indians come on through the forest after her. And they had these two little dogs, and this girl knew these two little dogs. These two dogs run back up in the holler log where she was at and she give 'em a little piece of meat. And they went back out. And an old Indian was just setting on the log chopping on it and hollering, "Yansoo po shinie!"

And so they went on and left her. And the next morning she got out and she was in the forest and she heard something rustling through the leaves. And so she went and hid again behind a big log. And this man he come through the woods and saw her and she seen it was a white man and he seen it was the long lost girl of these neighbors that lived beside of him.

And so he went and took her home, and these people gave him all the money he wanted and gave him a house, and he could marry the girl if he wanted to. So he married that girl and they all settled down and lived happy.

Lovers' Leap 85

ONE TIME THERE was a boy and a girl wanted to get married, but the girl's father didn't want them to. They kept going with each other and it looked as though they would marry up too, in spite of all the father could do. So the girl's father and brother framed the boy and made it appear that he had stolen some cattle, but the boy hadn't done it. He grieved himself sick over such a trick. At first he thought he could prove himself innocent but he wasn't sure he could. So he slipped the girl out and took her to a big high cliff and they agreed to jump off, and putting their arms around each other they leaped off and were killed.

I don't know how true this is but it was told to me for the truth by my uncle. He is known to be a pretty big blower.

171

they couldn't find their sons anywhere. And they were scared. They just knew that they had been killed. They were weeping.

The next morning those boys got up and they would go one by one to the spring to get a drink of water, and come back and get in the log. And they were quiet, for they were afraid that somebody might hear them in the woods and kill them.

An old man by the name of John came through that part of the woods a-hunting and he saw this little spring and he saw the footprints there in the mud, where those boys had been to the spring to get water. And he saw the footprints went back to this log. And he didn't go over to the log. He was afraid that if he did, whoever it was, he would frighten them and he didn't want to scare them.

So he thought that the next morning he would come back and find out who lived in the log. He would hide up above them in the woods.

The next morning he came back and he was sitting up there in the woods, and one of the boys came out to get a drink. And when he got back in the log this man saw that it was those boys that had been lost so long. And he went down to tell their father about it. And went down to the father and said, "What would you give me if I told you where your three sons were?"

And he said, "I know there isn't any use. My three sons are dead."

And he said, "No, they aren't." Said, "How much will you give me if I'll tell you where they are?"

And he said, "No," said, "I know there isn't any use." Said, "My three sons have been killed a long time."

And he said, "Well, if you will take an ax and go with me, I'll show you where your three sons are."

The old man started off with John, but he didn't think that he would find his sons, but he was going to please John. And when they came to this little spring he saw the footprints there in the mud and he knew then that someone lived in the log, and he was in good heart then. And they went over to the log and peeped in, and he saw his three sons. He talked to them and told them to come out, that he was their father. And his three sons had forgotten him and they didn't believe him, and they wouldn't come out.

He kept on talking to them and they still wouldn't come out. And him and John chopped the log open, and the chestnuts started rolling down the hill, and the boys came out. And finally they recognized that it was their father. He took his sons home and they lived happy ever after.

The Last Chase   88a

WELL, CHILDREN, I'll tell you about Aunt Meg and the panther. Aunt Meg was a good old lady. She lived by herself, as she was a widow. Her husband was killed working in timber.

Aunt Meg helped the folks around for her living. One day she was helping the Kelleys work up meat. She left for home about dust dark with a large sack of meat the Kelleys give her for her help. As Aunt Meg was going home she heard the screams of a panther. She began to hurry, as it sounded near and very angry. Aunt Meg went around a curve by an old spring, with many trees around, and a panther leaped from a near-by tree and sprang at her. Well, Aunt Meg begin to run for her life 'cause she was still a mile from home. When she begin to run the panther give chase. After she ran a little ways she saw the panther was gaining ground on her, so she had an idear strike her and she dropped a piece of meat. She would have dropped it all but it was all she had to eat but a little bread at home.

When she dropped the meat the panther stopped and eat it, so giving her a little time to get ahead. But the panther was soon so close on her she dropped another piece of meat and made the varment stop again. This kept up the mile home and just as Aunt Meg entered the gate of her front yard—that near home—the panther give a loud scream and leaped on poor Aunt Meg's back. Well, luck for her she still had the sack, with a little piece of meat still in it on her back. She dropped the meat, sack and all, and dropped with it the panther. She run in the house and closed the door tight. The panther fell on the sack of meat and ripped it open like he was starving to death. Aunt Meg caught her breath back and tore into the big house and grabbed her dead husband's old shotgun. She sneaked to the window and took aim at the panther and then after she waited for the panther to raise his head—and soon he did—then Aunt Meg shot. Well, I'll be doggoned if she didn't hit that panther right among the eyes.

If you would like to, you can go to see Cousin John and see dear old Aunt Meg's panther rug, for John still has the rug Aunt Meg had made out of the only panther she ever killed.

89 The Bear and the Baby

ONE TIME THEY'S an old woman went out to pick her a mess of greens and put her little baby in the bed while she was going out to pick her greens. Why, this bear comes in and steals her little baby and takes it off. And took it way off across the mountain. Well, they hunted three days and nights. They went up to the top of the hill one day and looked over down the hill, and hit's a-layin' in a sinkhole. And had it in with her little young cubs, you know. And they'd run up and hit the little baby with their paws, and she'd run up and then she'd knock them down—that away—knock the little cubs down. Well, she'd go off again pickin' around and here they'd come back.

And finally one day they's three men come along and they looked over down the mountain and seed the little baby layin' in the sinkhole. They wondered and wondered how they could get that little baby to keep that bear from killin' 'em. Well, they watched her pick across the p'int, across the knob again, and when she done that they run down and grabbed the little baby and run home with it.

The Untold Secret 90

GRANNY, PLEASE TELL us the story of the hainted house down by Mrs. Grundy's house.

Well children, I'll begin the evening of the quilting bee. When John and me was first married, the married women of the neighborhood all belonged to a club called the Quilting Bee. They met the first week after we's married and invited me to join the club.

Well, I went to the Quilting Bee and all met at Mrs. Shutt's, Aunt Mary as everybody called her. She lived in the house that is called the Hainted House now. This was one winter evening and Aunt Mary had a great big fire in the fireplace. We was sitting around the fire piecing quilt tops as fast as fingers could fly. The talk was flying thick and fast as fingers, or faster. Then Granny Tucker begin to talk about secrets. Granny Tucker said, "No one ever kept a secret all their lives without telling hit," and she said if one person ever knowed anything that nobody else knowed that they always told one other person, at least, before they died.

Well, Aunt Mary rose and said, "I don't believe this for I have kept a secret all of sixty-five year without telling hit."

We hushed and listened to her. Everybody knowed she was wanting to say something special.

"This," Aunt Mary went on to say, "is my secret. All you kind people remember my good husband Tom and have wondered why he left me to make a living alone. The fact is he never left me at all. He is still here—right in this house. Fact is Tom is in this very room."

At this all the women looked nervousness around. Aunt Mary never cracked a smile. She waited a second and then went on. "No, don't look, for you can't see him. He hain't alive. He is dead, for I killed him with my own hands sixty-five year ago. I have kept my secret for sixty-five year, and if it wa'n't for you—" pointing at Granny Tucker, "I wouldn't have never told it. Oh, well, it makes mighty little difference anyway. I may as well tell you the rest of it.

"Tom come in one night—the very night he disappeared—and told me he was tired of living here and wanted to move west. I didn't want to go, and then Tom told me he had a good bit of money saved. I didn't know he had. Well, he said it amounted to about a thousand dollars in all. I was already mad and I become very angry when he told me this. I decided, with the place and that money, I could do without Tom purty well, and before Tom knowed what I was doing I grabbed the poker and hit him over the head. He fell and I bent over and found he was dead.

"Tom had been working on the fireplace and I put him in the opening that was there, and I finished the fireplace, a little at a time. Some of you know I went to my sister's and stayed after I told that Tom had left me, and by slipping back and fixing a little at a time I soon had Tom sealed in. He is there now. If you don't believe me, you can open the fireplace and see for yourselves."

The tale broke up the Quilting Bee, and the women went home and sent their husbands back to find if what Aunt Mary told was true. Part of the men dug out around the fireplace and tore it down and, sure enough, there was a man's bones behind the jamb rock. The law come to take Aunt Mary away but when they begun to look for her they found she was gone, and they begun to search for her. They found her dead in the attic. She died the night she told her secret.

People tell now that you can hear Aunt Mary and Tom fussing about midnight if you will go and stand outside the house. No one will live there now, it is believed that the house is hainted.

Now you all get out of here so I can get the menfolks's supper.

Rail-Splitting Sally 91

IN ABOUT 1850 Oneida in Clay County was in the wilderness, and the people had a very hard time getting the things they needed. They arose at three o'clock in the morning and went about fifteen miles to a town to get supplies. They had to go in jolt wagons and they made hard traveling.

Now up in the hills lived Sally Helton, her husband and her nine children. Her husband didn't care too much about working, but Sally was born to work, and she did from daylight to dark. Her husband soon died and a lot of her children married off, but still Sally had to work. By this time she was getting old and wasn't very strong. Now most of her work was in splitting rails for people. She was give up to be as good as any man in the country at rail splitting. The rumor was that she had saved a lot of money. But nobody never knew, for she worked right on and was very stingy when she bought stuff. After a few years old Sally died over a log she had been splitting. She was buried and it appeared that she didn't have much. Somebody said she had money hid in an old feather tick, but it was never found among her belongings.

Last year, 1948, a lot of men were working on a road called the Crane Cliff, when one discovered a feather tick, partly rotted away, with quite a bit of money in it. The man knew someone would claim it so he made his getaway. Now Sally's daughter was still living in the neighborhood. When she heard about it she knew at once that it was her mother's, but she didn't get time to claim it. The man has never been seen since and probably never will be because he knows about Old Sally and her work splitting rails and that she had a lot of money that was never found.

begin to talk, 'I never expected to see you alive after you didn't come down last night and I had to wait so long to wake you this morning.'

"I asked him, 'Why, what's the matter with this room?' playing the goose, I was.

"He begin to say, 'About ten years ago this hotel was well known. The richer people come here, and one night two men who had struck it rich in the mines come in and I rented 'em rooms. They was big buddies. Went by the names of Jack and Bud. They had a good bit of their money with them and went to Bud's room to play some poker. Well, nobody knows just exactly what happened, but the next morning the maid found them locked in deadly combat, their arms around each other, on the bed—dead. The police was called and found Jack shot and Bud stabbed. Killed each other. The blood had run through the bed on the floor. The floor is still stained with it.' He saw how I had moved the bed and went behind it and rolled back the rug and showed me the stains.

"Then he went on. 'After that night nobody had been able to use this room, or sleep here—till you did last night.' He left me and I packed and come out of that town.

"About three months after, I was in Akeron again and just thought I'd stop there again and see what they were saying. When the clerk sees me he looks at me right funny and then he sent for the boss. He told the boss, 'Here's that man stayed in that room that time and rid it of them ghosts.'

"The boss shuck hands with me and invited me to dinner with him, and while we was eating he told me to stop there just any time I was in town, and he went on to say, 'Just any time you come around you can have a good room and your meals free.' I asked him why and he said his ho-tel wa'n't hainted any more and that business had picked up just to suit him. And of course after that I made it a point, in my travels, to go by Akeron for a good feed and lodging. I remember one time I stayed there—."

About that time the bus came and we had to run to catch it, and didn't hear him finish all of that tale.

The Mystery of the Haunted Road 93

WELL, CHILLERN, I'll tell you how Mr. Simms unwound the mystery of the killing of Jim Cook and his sons. Now it was this a-way. Jim Cook owned a big sawmill and three or four fine places with houses on them. He had money in the bank and was a man well thought of around town. Jim just had two sons and no girls, but he taken to raise his brother's boy, Joe Dale. His wife was dead and that just left the three boys and the old man to keep house for theirselves. All of the boys worked at the sawmill with a big crew of men that old man Jim bossed. Tom was the oldest one of the boys and he would be boss if and when anything happened to the old man. Then would come Jack and after him Joe Dale, if he ever got a turn at any of the property.

Well, to get on with the story—one dark night the old man Jim was riding his big fine black horse along the road just even with the graveyard. Then all at once the horse r'ared up and throwed the old man. Tom and Jack didn't know just where Joe Dale had got to so they set out hunting their paw and they found him laying in the road dying. He told them he had seen a ghost and it had spooked his horse and it had throwed him. He tried to ask where his horse was and how bad he was hurt, when he sunk back in the road dead. The horse had to be killed. They buried Jim Cook by his wife Mary and the whole neighborhood mourned his loss.

Tom took over the sawmill, and the boys divided the old man's belongings among the three of them. Everything settled down good again and the boys managed everything all right, except the lonesomeness the father left behind.

Well, one night Tom had been down to see about the mill and to check up on the watchman, and then he had to travel the same road his father had traveled when he got killed. At the same spot where his father died the horse r'ared and throwed Tom. Jack was home and got to worrying about Tom, and finally he decided to go and look for his brother. He was awful scared and troubled when he found him. He saw that Tom was dead and found the horse bad hurt. He went for help and some men helped carry Tom home and they saved the horse. The men found Joe Dale in the bed and they asked him why he had not gone with Jack. Joe Dale told them he was up the hollow after a big load of wood for the fire. They buried Tom by his paw and maw.

So Jack and Joe Dale divided up the belongings again and then Jack took over the running of the places and the mill. He had been working for about two weeks when an old friend of his father's come in and asked for a job. His name was Ray Simms. He was an old hand at the work and he helped Jack a lot.

It wasn't long until Jack had to be at the sawmill late. He was riding along home when Ray Simms run into him and he told Jack he oughtn't to pass that graveyard after dark, and begged him to come in and pass the night with him. Jack heeded his words and went in and spent the night. The next morning Jack and Ray Simms went to the mill, and not long after, Joe Dale come to work and he was pale as he could be. Ray Simms noticed this and a thought struck him like a sledge hammer, but he didn't let on a-tall.

Well sir, Jack had to stay late again in a few days. And he was fool enough to push on toward home, but he never got there. He had to be carried in on a shutter and then after a night's watch he was buried with his folks on the point. Joe had went to Mr. Simms that night late for help and told him he had waited up late and had set in to worrying about Jack, when he got out and started looking and found him by the graveyard.

Ray Simms didn't lose much time scouring around that place and, lo and behold, he found a letter that was backed to Joe Dale off in the woods there, and then he found a rope and a stake. He got some men to go with him and they questioned Joe about these things. At first Joe Dale denied it every breath, but after a while, when Ray Simms kept right after him, he broke down and confessed. He had stretched a rope across the road and then had come out in a white sheet and had frightened the horses till they wanted to run away. He had done all these crimes because he wanted all of his uncle's property. He claimed he was bad in debt and the people were pressing him for their pay. So he just set out to kill them off one by one to get the property. Joe Dale was about the first and might nigh the only man ever hung in this county.

The place went to Mary Cook's sister's sons and they paid off Joe Dale's debts and they didn't have to sell anything to clear the debts either. You know the sawmill that John Black owns? Well, that is the old sawmill belonged to Jim Cook. John Black is the Cook's cousin on their mother's side.

Run out and play now, I want to talk to your mother a while.

The Headless Ghost 94

WHEN I WAS a little girl my mother told me this story of a house she lived in when she was a young girl.

"Well, Mamie, you know the old white iron bed you sleep in is the one Uncle Tom died in. My cousin Earl and the men who boarded with us never would sleep in that bed or even the room after Uncle Tom was murdered. Course Uncle Tom wa'n't really my uncle but all of we young ones called him uncle out of respect for him. He just boarded at our house.

"Well, to get on with the story, Uncle Tom went to work in the mines one morning and, though he didn't think a breath about it, that would be his last day of work. Rock fell on Uncle Tom and cut him up pretty badly. The men brought him home and put him to bed. Uncle Tom didn't rest all night nor the next day. He talked all day about something awful going to happen but he couldn't make out what it was, he would say. Now the second night after the rock fell in the mines we woke up at the oncoming of a funny sound coming from Uncle Tom's room. My daddy and one of the boarders went in to see about him and found that pore man in the bed with his head cut off!

"There wa'n't nothing else to do but bury him and then all went well until we had a new boarder to come and ask for a room. This man was Joe Brown. He was given Uncle Tom's old room and the first night he was there he stayed up all night—I could hear him moving around like he was looking for something.

"He went to work the next morning as if he was worried about something. This went on for a few days, and then one day Jim Davis come and asked for a room. Earl moved in with Joe so Jim could have his bed. The very first night Earl slept in the room with Joe, he woke Earl up and told him to look at Uncle Tom's ghost. But at first Earl couldn't see a thing. Then he did see something, which moved acrost the room. He said he could see the hands, arms, feet and legs, but he couldn't see the head. Earl moved out, but Joe said he wa'n't afeared. Lo and behold, in a few days Joe moved out and left.

"One of the other boarders moved in the room but didn't stay but one night. This went on for about three weeks, and I begged mommie to let me sleep in Uncle Tom's room so I could see the ghost. My sister Hattie had to move with me and she didn't like it a bit. I stayed awake a-looking at the window but couldn't see anything. I went asleep and while I was asleep I turned over so I was looking at the opposite end of the room. Well, I saw a white object with no legs nor arms. I made a light and found it wa'n't a thing but a chair of white clothes mommie had ironed that day. I never saw any ghost that night—or any other night. It tickled my mommie and daddy because I stayed in the room when the boarders wouldn't. I shamed the boarders because we slept in the room.

"After we had been sleeping in the room about two weeks, Joe Brown died and just before he died he made a confession. This is what he told. He had rigged up a sheet and fixed it so it would pass through the room to scare whoever was in there. He had killed Uncle Tom for his money. Uncle Tom had told Joe he had hid some money in his room at our house. Joe took his room to find it but he never found any money.

"Soon after Joe died our house burnt down and we saved the bed and a few other things. As I was putting the bed up in the house we moved to, the roller come out and I found Uncle Tom's money. My daddy sent the money—I forget how much it was—to Uncle Tom's sister in Virginia. After that nobody saw any headless ghosts floating around in our rooms. When I got married mommie and daddy give me the bed.

"Well, I guess you had better go to bed—your sister will be home any minute now."

The Falling Bars 95

MY MOTHER USED to tell me a story that happened to her when she was a little girl about fourteen years old. She said, "My mother kept telling us a story about ghosts being in our barn lot. The lot had an old barbed wire fence around it, with five wooden bars for the entrance and every night about 10:30 you could hear the five bars fall one by one.

"One night I was coming home from school. I had to ride in an old hack for about six miles and then walk two and a half miles home. The hack was late that night and I was 10:30 getting in home. As I come past the barn I heard the bars falling and so I counted them as they fell. I was sure they were all down and the lot was open, so I went to see for sure. Then I heard footsteps walking down through the lot. So I decided to follow them to see where they went. I followed them down through the lot and then all of a sudden they stopped, and so I stuck a stick I was carrying in the ground right where they had stopped. Then I ran to the house and told mother what had happened. Then she said,

"'About forty years ago there were some men robbed a bank. The sheriff had been looking for them for about a week, when one night about this time of night they were coming through our barnyard and the sheriff got up with them. Just as the sheriff and his deputy started through the bars these men shot and killed them and then hightailed it down the river, but they were caught and were hung. But when they were caught they didn't have a cent on them. Some people thought maybe they gambled it all away, and then others thought they hid the money somewhere. But nobody never found it.'

"That night I went to bed and got a pretty good night's sleep. The next morning I eat breakfast and done my work. Then I slipped out of the house and went to the barn and got me a mattock and started digging where I had stuck the stick. I dug away down in the ground when I come to a flat rock. I dug it out and then looked in the hole and I saw an old money bag about rotten. It was bedded in around rocks. I lifted it out carefully and ran into the barn to count it. I forget how much it was but I know when I got married it was enough to buy a good home for us. I don't think anybody ever found out where I got the money or where it went."

96 The Returning Wife

ONCE THERE WAS an old woman and she was supposed to have been a witch, and she died and then she would come down to the house where she lived. Her husband had married another lady. And so this poor old witch she would come down to the house ever' night and set around with them. They would talk to her but she wouldn't talk back. They would try to get her to shake hands with them but she wouldn't shake hands.

So this old man's brother said to him, said, "I'll tell you what I'll do," said, "I'll shake hands with that lady if I'm ever there when she comes."

And so he got his brother and brought him up there and said, "Now I have a cue this old lady'll be down."

And so the brother went out and planned with another guy to dress up like this old lady and come in first. And so when the old witch come in, he thought it was this other boy that he had dressed up. And so this old witch beat him in first. And this man said, "I'll show you how to jump up and shake hands."

And right up he jumped and ran and met her in the door and said, "Oh, how are you getting along?" and run and shook hands with her. Off come his arm up to his elbow. So you see how he got messed up at his own tricks. Cards must have stacked against him.

The Jealous Wife 97

THEY WAS A LADY and a man. They was having trouble between each other. And she had a little baby. And she killed this little baby. They lived in a little log cabin. And when her husband come in from work he saw her sitting there. And ever' time she would look around she would see this little baby in the cracks in the logs because she killed it. And her husband always wondered about her because she would set there and wouldn't hardly talk.

One night he stepped out. It was in the wintertime and the snow was on the ground and the moon was shining. And he knew he saw his mother and he was scared and went back in the house and he was crying and felt real badly. And she asked him what was wrong with him, and he said, "I know I saw my mother."

And she said, "That's just your imagination. You didn't see your mother—you're just crazy—you know you didn't see your mother."

Every time she would set around the baby would be there in front of her. And her husband got to wondering about her. And when he would be sitting by the fire with her he would hear this horrible noise at the winders and everything and he didn't know what was going on and then he got so he seen the baby himself. And his wife wouldn't talk to him and she got worried and so they got divorced. She said, "I killed my baby," and said, "I can't kill my husband." But finally after they got divorced she did kill her husband and so she never was happy any more.

98a *Spirit of the Wreck*

UP IN NEW YORK they've got a road that is so bad there that they are building a road underground to keep from having so many wrecks. Well, not so long ago a man was passing away in the night, and he saw a girl—it was raining way in the night—and he saw a girl. He picked the girl up. He just opened the back door of the car. He had a lot of boxes and things in the front seat and he just let her in the back seat. He asked her why she was out so late at night. And so she said, "It's too long a story, but when we get home I'll tell ye." And she told him where to take her.

So he took her home. He backed his car up to the gate and reached back to open the door and the girl had done and gone out. So he got out of his car and walked up to the door and knocked on the door. An old gray-haired man come out and he told him his troubles, told him what had happened. And the old man said, "Why, that's nothing strange. That's happened three times here. That was my daughter that was killed there two years ago in an accident."

99 *Poor Man and His Witch Wife*

ONCE UPON A TIME there was a poor man, and he was brought up in a poor home. And when he got grown he wanted to marry a rich woman. So finally he fell in love with this woman and married. So when he was married to this woman she was very mean to him and she was always fighting him and he had to work hard every day. She made him work.

And on his way to work, this man had to pass by a grave-yard. And every night when he passed back by this place, why they'd be a woman come out and ask him to fight her. And he would always say, "No, I've worked hard all day. I don't want to fight you."

And this went on for a week or so. And he told his wife about it one night—about this woman coming out every night wanting to fight him. This woman said, "Next time you fight her."

And he said, "No, I don't want to fight the woman. I've always worked hard, and then again I don't want to fight no woman."

She said, "You be sure that you fight her next time."

So the next night when he come along from work, why this woman come out and asked him if he wanted to fight. And this man said, "Well, if nothing else will do you I'll fight you."

So the man and woman then started fighting. And the woman had big finger nails and she tore him up, and tore him apart and tore his guts apart and threw them up on some bushes.

The legend goes that the lady, the rich woman, was the one that killed the man. She was a witch.

Devil George 100a

WHEN I WAS a small girl there was an old man named George. The folks around home said he was a witch. The children were scared to death of him. I don't believe he was a witch, but here's my story.

One day I was in the barn milking when I suddenly heard a noise. I went to see what it was, of course. There stood George with his old crooked cane pointing at our old red cow.

She was fixing to butt him. But she turned around and walked right up the ladder into the barn loft. Well, we had a time getting her down from there.

A while after that my mother was churning but was not getting much butter to come. George came along and wanted to churn, so mother let him take the dasher. Well, he churned about five minutes and he had that churn full of butter. My mother was afraid to use the butter, so she gave it to our twelve hogs and they everyone died as dead as a wedge.

Old George used to tell people how he become a witch. He said he went to the top of the mountain before the sun rose and prayed to the Devil and cursed the Lord.

When the witch power in him was dying he broke out with big sores all over his legs. He got behind a log on the hill and took a razor from his pocket and cut them sores out of his legs. A week after that he was dead.

Now children, if Old George was a witch his power from the Devil was weaker than the Lord's.

100^b *The Bewitched Cow*

THIS STORY I AM about to tell you has been handed down for generations until at last it reached my ears. My great aunt whom I used to stay with tells it as follows.

"My father and mother were very poor people. We children were only very small when this happened, but I can remember every little bitty detail. Dad had a big spotted cow that we loved very much. We called her Bossy.

"Now there was an old woman in the neighborhood whom we called Aunt Elizy because she was powerful old. One day, unexpected, Aunt Elizy, who always got milk at our house, come for it, but mother didn't have any to give her right then. This made Aunt Elizy very angry at my mother, so she left hastily, slammed the door behind her.

"We had a small paling fence around our house, and as she left she tore off several small splinters and taken the short cut through the pasture where Bossy was grazing along. After this was done she went on her way home.

"That night dad was troubled at the old cow for not eating her fodder. The next morning he went to see about her again and she was lying down and wouldn't raise up. Dad sent for the witch doctor in a hurry, and when he come he told us little yerkers to get in the house and not to peep out anytime. We was very anxious to see what went on and when we went to the house we peeped through the cracks of the door. The doctor only slapped the cow on her back three times real hard, and the cow raised up and was as well as ever before. Then he told dad how to find out who bewitched old Bossy. This is what he told him to do.

" 'In the morning two old women on their way to pick blackberries will come to the fence and try to cross. One of them cannot cross until the other helps her. This is the one that done this awful thing to your cow.'

"Sure enough everything happened as it had been told to dad by the doctor. Old Aunt Elizy and a neighbor of her'n come along and went through our field. The other woman got over the little bit of a fence up there above the barn without no trouble, but Aunt Elizy couldn't get over it a-tall. The woman helped her and she finally made it. But dad was there by that time and he fussed with the women and when he told what happened to our cow and how she was well Aunt Elizy flew mad again but it wa'n't no use. Dad made them come back over the fence and sent them to the big road. And he told Aunt Elizy never to trespass on his land again. She went on and maybe got some blackberries sommers else. But I never saw that old woman again till she was carried to the point.

"Now children, if you ever see a witch don't be scared just because I have told you this story."

193

101 *Traveler's Dream*

ONCE THEY WAS an old man and his wife, and they was mighty wealthy people. An' the old man says, "Old worman," said, "I'll have to go off and be gone tonight." And says, "I don't know whether I'll get back before the next night or not." And he says, "You go ahead and get someone to stay with you tonight if you can, and I'll be back."

Well, he goes along ahead on his journey and he got out there and he taken up to stay all night at a man's home. Well, after a while it come to be bedtime. They got to bed. And on the bed where he was a-lyin' he dreamed that they was some two fellers at his place and killed his wife, and the baby a-layin' there with her on the bed a-suckin' her titty.

And he said to this man where he was at, he says, "Mister," he says, "I have dreamed a nawful bad dream." He says, "I don't know what to think about it."

This man says to him, says, "Well, mister," says, "you are just a-thinkin' about home. Why, they hain't nothin' like that." Says, "Go ahead and lay back down. You won't dream that any more."

Well, he laid back down and he dreamed the same dream over. That some two people at his home had killed his wife, and layin' on the bed the baby a-suckin' her bloody titty. An' those two men which was there at his place had a big stand table out in the floor. They had this man's money all on this table and was countin' it out to see how much it was.

Well, this man says to him, says, "Mister, you go ahead and go back to bed and if you dream this again," says, "I'll get up and go with you."

Well, he gets back in the bed and he lays down and he dreams the same dream over. Well, he waked up and he says, "I'm goin' home."

This man says, "I'll go with you."

They get out and they catch a couple of good horses, and they pull out, and run these horses ever' bit they could and they got near the house. And they looked and they saw a light through the winder. And they was two men around the table a-standin' there. One of these gentlemen went to one door and the other the other. And whenever they got to the door these men was countin' the money. They shot them both down right there in the man's house. Wife a-layin' on the bed and the baby a-suckin' her bloody titty. That's all, I reckon.

Watching Bulldog 102

WELL, ONE TIME they was an awful wealthy man—and wife. And this old man he says, "Old worman," he says, "I have to go off on a trip and be gone some time and I can't get back tonight." Says, "This evenin' you can go up here to this first house, and have someone to come down and stay all night with you."

Well, evening come. She goes ahead; she goes up there to this house and went in. She went in and she says, "Well," says, "I want you folkses to go down and stay all night with me tonight."

Well, the master says, "I'll tell ye—we can't go."

"Well," she says, "I want some of you to go. I'd druther you would all go down and stay with me. But I sure want some one of those kids to go down and stay all night with me. I've had a dread on me all day today, and I don't want to stay by myself tonight."

" 'Ell, we shore can't go. But I'll tell ye what I will do." Says, "I'll let you take my bulldog home with you and keep him. And if you will do what I tell you to do this bulldog will take care of you."

"Well, I'll take the bulldog, but I'd druther some of you would go."

"Well, we can't go. You take this bulldog up there. And

whenever you set down to eat," says, "you tell this bulldog to come and git in the chur by you. Ever' time you take a bite you give this bulldog a bite. Whenever you git ready to go to bed now, you fix your bed and you tell the bulldog to come and git in the bed with you. Ever' time you turn over tell him to turn over."

Well, she done this way. 'Rectly she heared a noise around her house. And from that they went to the winder and went and scratching around on the winder, like they was a-goin' to tear the winder out. And the bulldog begin growlin'—right low. She raises the winder up and she says, "Take him, bull!"

'Ell, the bulldog he goes out. He never did come back in the house again at all any more.

Well, whenever daylight come she opened the door back, and she taken her kid in her arms and away she went down to this man's house, where the bulldog belonged. She got down there. They was all a-cryin' together—down at that place. [The master had been gone all night and had never come back.]

Well, the lady that lived in that house says, "Well, we will have to git in a crowd of people and go back up there and see what the bulldog has done."

Well, they starts on their way back up there, and this lady of the house says, "Now missus, you will have to go in front and tell the bulldog to behave, or he will kill us."

Went on back up there, and there the bulldog lie, and the bulldog's master, right there on the ground dead. And a big butcher knife in this master's hand. And that is all.

103 *Old Buttermilk John*

ONCE IN THE HILLS somewhere around Cumberland, Kentucky, there lived an old man by the name of Buttermilk John. He got his name because he liked buttermilk so well. One day old Buttermilk John was out raisin' cane. He saw an old feller comin' up the road and he said, "Well, I reckon I'll go after that old feller 'cause I'm rather lazy anyway. I don't want to work around here."

So he follers the old feller for a while and catches up with him. And then he walks on. The old feller don't say anything and old Buttermilk John he says, "Where are you goin', old feller?"

He says, "Oh, just over the hill a piece, and I'd be mighty glad if you'd go along with me." Says, "It's mighty dangerous in these here hills, and they's a lot of robbers around here. They're liable to rob you when you're alone."

So old Buttermilk John he goes along with him. Well, they go over this hill and then go down through a valley and up another hill and down another valley and through a meader and half way up another hill. Old Buttermilk John he was gettin' very thirsty and he says, "How much further is it?" Said, "You told me it was just over the hill."

He says, "Well, we've got a little piece further."

So they go up another hill and down through a valley. About half way up another hill they come to his house. It was settin' on the hillside. A cozy little old place. Well, the old feller he goes in and he says, "I want to thank you, old Buttermilk John, for helpin' me home." Says, "What would you want most?"

Old Buttermilk John he was rather thirsty and says, "Well, I'll tell you now. I'd like to have all the buttermilk I could drink."

The old feller says, "Well, I reckon I could help you with that."

So he takes him out back and shows him an open place back in the ground. Old Buttermilk John goes in this cave of a place and there is a whole river of buttermilk. Old Buttermilk John he gets down on his hands and knees and drinks all he can hold. And what do you think he did? Well, he drank that much more. He drank till he couldn't drink any more. Then he got up—tried to get up rather—and he couldn't get up. And he laid there till he died.

They started to bury him and couldn't lift him. So a bunch

of men got together and they pumped all the buttermilk out of him and it measured 650 gallons of buttermilk.

Old Buttermilk John is dead, but his legend lives on in the minds of the folks around Harlan County.

104a *Skeletons in the Basement*

ONCE THERE WAS a man who drove a herd of cattle off and sold them. People knew that he would have a lot of money when he come back through the country. He stopped at a place to stay all night. They offered him supper, and while he was eating supper he saw about seven big hairy men pass by the window and look in at him, wondering if he would be there for the night.

Well, after supper the old man said, "When you're ready I'll take you over to a building where you are to sleep. We don't have room over here, so I'll take you over there."

So, after supper he took him over to the place and showed him the bed, and after he showed him the bed, he went out and locked the door. So this man begin to look around and he saw a window that had a piece of roofing nailed over it, so he took his big hawkbill knife and cut a piece out of the roofing, pulled it off. And so he threw his clothes out the window and out he jumped and took off up the road. He hid to see what they done when they come back after him. They come back down and went up and broke the door down and went in, and when they found nobody there, they come back out of there in a hurry. He stayed hid under an old wagon bed. He went up the road the next morning and got the law, and they come back down there, and they found about a thousand skeletons in this man's house, where they had killed people and robbed them and threw them down in there so that they wouldn't be found.

Guest Robbery 104ᵇ

MY GRANDFATHER WAS coming through from Virginia to Kentucky one time. Had an old hog rifle with him. He stopped to stay all night. He had a lot of money—had sold a farm down there and was coming into Kentucky to buy another. They put him upstairs and he got restless. And they's a little auger hole in the floor, and he peeped down, and they's whispering down there, and he saw 'em take the load out of his gun and pour it full of ashes and pour water in it. He just set on the side of the bed and never slept a wink that night.

Along before daylight he went down and they eat breakfast. The man of the house was gone. So the first thing he done he cleaned his gun. He had tow and stuff. He cleaned that gun out, loaded her up, put him a dry cap on it. He got out his hoss, got on it and started out. As he went down through an ivy thicket, out walked a man with a big knife in his hand. He walked up, took his hoss by the bridle, and said, "You give up your money or I'll kill ye."

He said, "You turn my hoss loose or I'll shoot you!"

He said, "Your old gun's full of ashes—it won't shoot."

He said, "You turn my hoss loose or I'll show you."

The feller wouldn't turn him loose, and he shot the man right th'ough the heart and killed him. He rode back up to the house and told 'em he'd killed a man down there. They went down there and got the man and washed him off, and he turned out to be the man of the house. Had his face blacked, you know, and he was the man of the house.

104C   *The Disguised Robber*

BACK IN ANCIENT days the people used to come th'ough here from Virginia to Kentucky hossback and settle in here. One time they's a feller comin' th'ough a long piny ridge ridin' a big black stallion-horse. It was claimed people got robbed th'ough there. He was ridin' along the road and there set a woman, dressed in black, settin' there a-cryin', with a satchel in her hand. She told him she wanted to ride a piece, she was give out. He got her up behind him, and when he got her up behind him he seed a big dirk knife slip out her shirt sleeve, you know, and that scared him. Well, he run under a limb a-purpose, knocked his hat off, and told her to jump down and get his hat. And when she jumped down to get it, he put the spurs to the hoss and away he went out of the pine country. She commenced to hollerin', "Throw off the budget, throw off the satchel, throw off the satchel."

But he kept it. He went across the river and got over into a town, stopped at a hotel, and told them what happened to him. They told him to open that satchel and look what was in it. He opened the satchel and it was full of money. She had been killin' and robbin' people. That was a man, instead of a woman, dressed in woman's clothes.

105   *The Fireproof Safe Business*

WELL, I DECIDED to go into the money safe business. I went out to sell fireproof money safes. I run into a pardner and he said, "What are you selling, Bud?"

I said, "Fireproof money safes."

He said, "Well, that's exactly my business. I sell fireproof money safes."

I said, "Well, I've got a little talk I use in my business, selling safes." I said, "Do you have a talk?"

He said, "Yes, sir."

I said, "Go ahead."

He got up and he said, "Ladies and gentlemen, I'm selling a fireproof money safe. The fireproof safe I'm selling has been tested and tried." He said, "This safe has been put in a ten-room building and fire was set to the building. The building burnt six hours, and after the safe got cool so we could handle it we unlocked it and the money was as bright as ever."

Well, it was my time, you see. I raised up and said, "Well, ladies and gentlemen, I'm selling a money safe, and I want to tell you what we have experienced with this money safe. We put this safe in a ten-story building. We put a rooster instead of money in this safe and locked him up. We set this building afire and it burnt twelve hours. The safe got red hot. After the building burnt down, the safe cooled off, we opened the door of the money safe, and what do you think happened? There stood that rooster with icicles to his tail feathers and he was froze to death."

Conclusion

THE PRECEDING STORIES are from a society that is swiftly passing from this continent. Transcribed faithfully from sound tapes and from scraps of paper, they come fresh from the folk mouth and show a primitive way of life. In these stories I hope the reader has seen a few visions and heard a few echoes of the far away and the long ago. In them is the flame of the hearth fire and the smell of cornbread browning in the ashes. In them one may envision a large family circle, warmed outside by the leaping flames and inside by heroes and heroines who ventured into danger and returned to the fireside to live happily ever after. Here are the Irishman anecdotes and other more realistic jokes that have sent up laughter from the throats of young and old for centuries. Here are stories that place emotional value upon home and family, respect for the dead and the living, love of children and old people, dogs and cats, hogs and wild animals.

I would like to tell two true stories of the hills that will reveal the people and the land more clearly than any words of mine. The love and enjoyment of children in the hills could be illustrated with countless incidents, but I shall let one suffice. Once we lived near my aunt, who had eleven children. One of her sons, a twelve-year-old, died of burns resulting from an explosion. Sundays for years afterward the mother climbed to the cemetery above our church carrying flowers and shrubs. After planting them she would kneel by the boy's grave and mourn for an hour. Other times, when she had to pass along the road, she would make her way to the grave. We children at school would see her there alone and whisper the fact to one another.

Shortly after the burial the mother did a curious thing. She sent an older son with roofing to waterproof the grave carefully. Most of us thought she wanted to conceal the fresh yellow earth. But at a later date I understood the mystery of it: She did not want any water to reach her boy and drive the fire deeper into his wounds.

My other story shows the love of home and the land. Once upon a time, in the very home where I grew up, there was an old Irishman by the name of Mike Roar. As I trotted about the old log house and its little village of outbuildings, I often heard about the Mike Roar Rocks on top of the hill. One day my older brother took me hunting with him. We stopped on a castle of rock that went down sheer for a hundred feet. Gnarled old oaks clung to the rocky cliff and twisted up toward the sun. The wind swept over the point and rolled the rattling leaves into the crevices. We kicked the leaves away until we uncovered a basin chiseled in the level portion of the rock. My brother said, "That's Mike Roar's grave. He never finished it. The lid to the coffin is on up here." We walked along the narrow path on the barrow until we came to a mossy lid—a block of stone seven feet long, four feet wide, and perhaps eight inches thick. It might have weighed a half ton.

Perhaps my brother told me more of the legend, but I remember my mother telling the tale this way:

"Why, this old feller lived here, back when they wa'n't nobody else in here, and he built all these old log houses here and then some that's been tore down. He had a big family—

I believe he had seven girls and some boys. Why Lin, some of his girls lives right over here on Island Creek, where he went when he left here. You can go over there and talk to 'em. But he wanted to be buried on his farm and went up there on the point and started makin' his grave. He worked at it, off and on, for years—that's when I's just a little girl and I used to hear my mother talk about it. She'd allas call him quare. But he never finished it. He got him a place over here in Pike County and never come back here but a time or two."

"Why did he want to be buried up there, do you reckon?"

"Now he told people here and there, the preacher maybe, that he wanted to be buried up there on his land. And he told 'em he wanted a barrel of salt under his corpse and two barrel on him. And he was goin' to have the lid ready to be bolted on with six big bolts so the devil couldn't carry him off before the Day of Judgment."

The people of the hills have the simple belief that at death the body sleeps in its place until the Judgment, a day that may not be long off. When Gabriel blows his horn all the graves will give up their bodies, God will breathe the breath of life into them, and they will be ready to live on here eternally. My aunt did not want the soul in her son's body to suffer, nor the body to receive water and dissolve away. Mike Roar felt that the hills and the coves that he loved would stand until he came again, perhaps visualizing his coming soon, when his sturdy houses and barns would be below him, and he would then descend the hill and live on with his family.

Now days have passed and nights have passed. The Judgment Day has been postponed. The old houses of the mountain people have crumbled and fallen to logs. The slopes have been cleared and the soil has been swept into the floods below. Timber is scarcer and of poorer quality. The oil and gas of the area have been leased by those with money and equipment to market them. The area's resources are going fast, and very few industries can replace them in the winding valleys and the rough places. The mountain people are now stuck with the poorest acres in one of the most isolated regions of

204

the nation. Their transition from a pioneering to an atomic age is full of problems and calls for sympathy and understanding.

Fortunately for the hill people some of their cultural traditions need not change. Before looming, spinning, basket- and chair-making died in the memories of the people, the cultural and economic value of products made by hand increased. The old handicrafts have survived and are reviving over Appalachia. The rich harvests of ballads and songs, plays and dances are now being used to keep alive the tradition of wholesome entertainment. Only a few volumes of the great store of tales have been gleaned from the valleys and the glens, and they too are becoming a part of the people's recreation again.

It is my hope that this collection of stories may be used not only to tell others of the people's precious heritage, but also to prolong the life of that heritage.

Notes

Abbreviations, short titles, and exact editions referred to in the notes are identified below. Titles infrequently used are not entered in this table, but are cited in full with the first reference and are shortened thereafter. To avoid varying number systems used by collectors, I have used Arabic numerals for stories that have, or may be given, numbers.

Addy, *Household Tales:* Sidney Odall Addy, *Household Tales with Other Traditional Remains Collected in the Counties of York, Lincoln, Derby, and Nottingham.* London, 1895.

Béal.: Béaloideas, The Journal of the Folklore of Ireland Society. Dublin, 1928–

Beckwith, *Jamaica:* Martha Warren Beckwith, *Jamaica Anansi Stories. MAFLS,* Vol. XVII. New York, 1924.

BP: Johannes Bolte und Georg Polívka, *Anmerkungen zu den Kinder- und Hausmärchen der Brüder Grimm.* 5 vols. Leipzig, 1913-1932.

Botkin, *Treasury of American:* Benjamin A. Botkin, *A Treasury of American Folklore.* New York, 1944.

Botkin, *Treasury of Southern:* Benjamin A. Botkin, *A Treasury of Southern Folklore.* New York, 1949.

Campbell, *West Highlands:* John Francis Campbell, *Popular Tales from the West Highlands.* New ed. 4 vols. London and Sheffield, 1890-1893.

Carrière, *Missouri:* Joseph Médard Carrière, *Tales from the French Folk-Lore of Missouri.* Evanston, Illinois, 1937.

Chase, *Grandfather Tales:* Richard Chase, *Grandfather Tales.* Boston, 1948.

Chase, *Jack Tales:* Richard Chase, *The Jack Tales.* With an appendix compiled by Herbert Halpert. Cambridge, Massachusetts, 1943.

C. Coll.: Stith Thompson, *European Tales among the North American Indians. Colorado College Publication,* No. 34. Colorado Springs, 1919.

Dasent, *Norse:* Sir George Webb Dasent, *Popular Tales from the Norse.* New ed. New York, 1904.

Fauset, *Nova Scotia:* Arthur Huff Fauset, *Folklore from Nova Scotia. MAFLS,* Vol. XXIV. New York, 1931.

FFC: FF Communications. Edited for the Folklore Fellows. Helsinki, 1907–

Gardner, *Schoharie Hills:* Emelyn Elizabeth Gardner, *Folklore from the Schoharie Hills, New York.* Ann Arbor, Michigan, 1937.

Grimm: *Grimm's Fairy Tales.* Trans. by Margaret Hunt, rev. by James Sterne. New York, 1944.

Halpert, "Southern New Jersey": Herbert Halpert, "Folktales and Legends from Southern New Jersey." Unpublished Ph. D. Dissertation, Indiana University, 1947.

Hazlitt, *Jest-Books:* W. Carew Hazlitt, *Shakespeare Jest-Books.* 3 vols. London, 1864.

Hurston, *Mules and Men:* Zora Neale Hurston, *Mules and Men.* Philadelphia, 1935.

Hyde, *Beside the Fire:* Douglas Hyde, *Beside the Fire.* London, 1910.

Jacobs, *Celtic:* Joseph Jacobs, *Celtic Fairy Tales.* New York, 1892.

Jacobs, *English:* Joseph Jacobs, *English Fairy Tales.* New York, 1890.

Jacobs, *More Celtic:* Joseph Jacobs, *More Celtic Fairy Tales.* New York, 1894.

Jacobs, *More English:* Joseph Jacobs, *More English Fairy Tales.* New York, 1895.

JAFL: Journal of American Folklore. Organ of the American Folklore Society. Boston, New York, and Philadelphia, 1888–

Kennedy, *Fireside Stories:* Patrick Kennedy, *Fireside Stories of Ireland.* Dublin, 1875.

Kennedy, *Legendary Fictions:* Patrick Kennedy, *Legendary Fictions of the Irish Celts.* 2nd ed. London, 1891.

208

MAFLS: Memoirs of the American Folklore Society. Boston, New York, and Philadelphia, various dates from 1894.

Motif: Stith Thompson, *Motif-Index of Folk-Literature. Indiana University Studies,* Nos. 96-97, 100, 101, 105-106, 108-110, 111-112. Bloomington, Indiana, 1932-1936.

MLW: Mountain Life and Work. Published by the Council of Southern Mountain Workers. Berea, Kentucky, 1924–

Münchausen: R. E. Raspe and others, *Singular Travels, Campaigns, and Adventures of Baron Münchausen.* Ed. by John Carswell. London, 1948.

Parsons, *Sea Islands:* Elsie Clews Parsons, *Folk-Lore of the Sea Islands, South Carolina. MAFLS,* Vol. XVI. New York, 1923.

Parsons, *Bahamas:* Elsie Clews Parsons, *The Folk-Tales of Andros Island, Bahamas. MAFLS,* Vol. XIII. New York, 1918.

Randolph, *Who Blowed Up:* Vance Randolph, *Who Blowed Up the Church House? and Other Ozark Folk Tales.* With notes by Herbert Halpert. New York, 1952.

Thompson, *Folktale:* Stith Thompson, *The Folktale.* New York, 1946.

Type: Stith Thompson, *The Types of the Folk-Tale:* Antti Aarne's *Verzeichnis der Märchentypen,* trans. and enlarged. *FFC,* No. 74. Helsinki, 1928.

White, *N. C. Folklore:* Newman I. White and others, *The Frank C. Brown Collection of North Carolina Folklore.* Vol. I. Durham, North Carolina, 1952.

1

Source: Clarence Day, age about 12, Paul's Creek, Leslie County. I had a Sunday morning recording session in Mitchell Joseph's house where about fifteen children and adults assembled and told some twenty stories. Some of the children reported hearing their stories from an old woman, but I refrained from visiting her on the Sabbath. Hereafter referred to as Paul's Creek session.

Type 130, The Animals in Night Quarters.

Motifs: B296, Animals go a-journeying together; K335.1.4, Animals climb on one another's back and cry out: frighten robbers; K1161, Animals hidden in various parts of house drive away intruders.

Study: Antti Aarne, *Die Tiere auf der Wanderschaft. FFC,* No. 11 (Hamina, Finland, 1913).

Parallels: BP, I, 237-59 (Grimm, No. 27); G. W. Dasent, *Tales from the Fjeld* (London, 1896), 283-88; Jacobs, *English,* No. 5 (taken from *JAFL,* I (1888), 227-33); Jacobs, *Celtic,* No. 14 (taken from Kennedy, *Legendary Fictions,* 4-11); Campbell, *West Highlands,* No. 11; *Béal.,* I, 94.

JAFL, I (1888), 227-33 (three texts, one with Jack as leader); XL (1927), 258; XLVII (1934), 294; Parsons, *Bahamas,* No. 83; Chase, *Jack Tales,* No. 4 (Halpert gives many British-American references, p. 191); Carrière, *Missouri,* No. 1.

Remarks: This is an animal tale having two forms stemming from the Reynard cycle that flourished in the Middle Ages. One form, that having objects such as sticks and beans on a journey, is widespread in India and in the East. The form from which this text came, usually featuring animals on adventures, is popular over Europe, especially in the Baltic states, and rather thinly distributed in western Europe, from whence it seems to have been first carred to the West Indies and then to continental America. See Thompson, *Folktale,* 219-24, for summary remarks on animal tales. Halpert in his notes reports not having a single text of the tale collected in England, but in his additional parallels to Chase, *Jack Tales,* in *Midwest Folklore,* II (1952), 66, he reports a discovery in *Folk-Lore,* XX (1909), 75-76. The original source of the tale then is continental Europe; however, the Appalachian versions may well have been carried to the American frontier by the Highland Scottish or Irish.

2

Source: Don Saylor, age 18, Bledsoe, Leslie County. He had heard his grandmother, who had been dead for a decade, tell many stories, of which he could recall only two (the other is No. 9a). A teacher, Lige Gay, of the Hyden School invited me to his seventh grade class for an all-day story session. The result was some 35 stories, and the session ended only with the school bus call, the children still eager to record their stories. Hereafter referred to as the Hyden School session.

Type 301A, The Three Stolen Princesses.

Motifs: G475.1, Ogre (old man) attacks intruders in house in woods; K1111.1, Ogre's beard caught fast; F92, Pit entrance to lower world; R11.1, Princess (girl) abducted by monster (old man); G512.1.2*, Ogre killed with his own weapon; K1935, Imposters (brothers) steal rescued princess (girls); K1931.2, Imposters (brothers) abandon hero in lower world; B325.1, Animal (bird) bribed with food; B542.1.1, Eagle carries man to safety; L161, Lowly hero marries princess (girl).

Study: F. Panzer, *Beowulf. Studien zur germanischen Sagengeschichte*, No. 1 (Munich, 1910), I, 1-246.

Parallels: BP, II, 300-18 (Grimm, No. 91); Jeremiah Curtin, *Hero Tales of Ireland* (London, 1894), 262-82; Kennedy, *Legendary Fictions*, 39-48; Campbell, *West Highlands*, Nos. 16 and 57; Addy, *Household Tales*, No. 52.

Isobel Gordon Carter, "Mountain White Folk-Lore: Tales from the Southern Blue Ridge," *JAFL*, XXXVIII (1925), 341-43; Parsons, *Bahamas*, No. 93; *C. Coll.*, Ch. II; Stith Thompson, *Tales of the North American Indians* (Cambridge, Mass., 1929), No. 79; Carrière, *Missouri*, Nos. 10 and 11; Chase, *Jack Tales*, No. 12; Randolph, *Who Blowed Up*, 82-83 (only motif K1111.1) and 148-50.

Remarks: This is a short version of the "Bear's Son" tale, thought by Panzer to have been used by the author of *Beowulf;* however, Thompson in his *Folktale* (33, n. 4a) says, "His conclusions are dubious." Although the tale is told over the whole world, its original home seems to have been northern Europe. Two of the Appalachian texts are from one German teller. Carter took down fifteen stories from a descendant of Council Harmon, of German extraction, who was the original teller of most of *The Jack Tales.* However, I have recently recorded a version of the tale from a family of Irish background.

The tale has been given some attention recently in *JAFL:* LXIV (1952), 409-13, reprints the story from J. Frank Dobie's *Tongues of the Monte* (Garden City, N. Y., 1935); LXVI (1953), 143-54, gives a Mexican text collected in Chicago; in LXV (1952), 187, Aurelio M. Espiñosa reports his listing of 47 versions of this tale from the Western Hemisphere in his *Cuentos populares españoles* (Stanford, Calif., 1923-1926), II, 498-99. The complete "Bear's Son" tale opens with the abduction of a woman by a bear, and

5

Source: Told by Patsy Ann Stacy, age about 13, Hyden, Leslie County, during the Hyden School session. She stated that she had heard the story from her nurse, meaning, though I didn't ask, that she had had a protracted illness either in a hospital or at home where a neighbor stayed and waited on her.

Type 310, The Maiden in the Tower.

Motifs: P234, Father and daughter; S222, Man promises child in order to save himself from danger or death; F848.1, Girl's long hair as ladder into tower; S165, Mutilation: putting out eyes; F952.1, Blindness cured by tears.

Parallels: BP, I, 97 ff. (Grimm, No. 12); G. Basile, *Il Pentamerone* (Naples, 1634-1636), 2nd Day, 1, and 3rd Day, 3.

Fauset, *Nova Scotia*, No. 3.

Remarks: There is only a slight change here from the German text, that of blinding, which in the latter is effected by throwing the prince into the thorns. Although the story has had greatest popularity in Italy, the present version must have come from the widely distributed German story.

6

Sources: 6a was told by Jimmy Pennington, age 17, Leslie County, from his grandmother. He also recorded No. 30a below and mentioned others, including "Bull-of-a-Horn" (see 15a, b for versions found in the region). A version of No. 6 not printed is 6b, "The Girl in the Robbers' Cave," told by Bill McDaniel, Big Leatherwood Creek, Perry County, heard from his grandmother, Nancy McDaniel, from whom I collected items given below. The girl in the story is mistreated by her stepmother. She follows a red ball into a robbers' cave and hides upon seeing men come in with a bloody corpse without a head. They discover her, tie her up, and gag her. She is found by a prince, rescued, and taken to his castle. The prince returns with men and kills the robbers.

Type 311, Three Sisters Rescued from the Mountain.

Motifs: P252, Sisters; G423, Ball falling into water (den) puts person into ogre's power; Q325, Disobedience punished; Q86, Reward for industry; S31, Cruel stepmother; R111.1.2, Rescue of princess (girl) from robbers.

Parallels: BP, I, 398 ff. (Grimm, Nos. 46 and 66); Campbell, *West Highlands*, No. 13; Addy, *Household Tales*, No. 52.

Beckwith, *Jamaica*, No. 115; Randolph, *Who Blowed Up*, No. 59 (list of parallels by Halpert in his notes, p. 197).

Remarks: The stories from Type 311 to 328 have elements in common and have been interwoven by the folk in various ways. In them a varying number of boys or girls, or both, leave home, come into the power of ogres or robbers, perform tasks, and make various escapes. Dr. Halpert in the notes to Types 311 and 312 in Randolph's collection calls for a study and a clearer number arrangement for some of these stories. Although Type 311 has been most popular in the Baltic states and in Norway, the parallels given here point to a British source.

No. 6a was published in *MLW*, XXVIII (1952), Spring, 21-22.

7

Sources: Number 7a, "Bluebeard," was told by Opal Roberts, McCreary County. By the name and contents of the story it seems to be close to the French text of Perrault. In it an old man entices pretty girls to his castle and does away with them. The last girl to go with him is given all the keys to the many rooms, but is forbidden to look into a certain room. She looks into it and finds many murdered women. She drops the key and gets blood on it. The man pursues her into the tower and throws a spear at her, just before the girl's brothers come and kill him. Number 7b was told by Wilgus Neace, age about 17, Perry County. Number 7c was told by Rose Sizemore, age 18, Leslie County. These last two versions seem to be in oral tradition and both have faint interpolations from the previous rescue story, Type 311.

Type 312, The Giant-Killer and His Dog (Bluebeard).

Motifs: T121, Unequal marriage; C611, Forbidden chamber; D1654.3, Indelible blood; C921, Death (threatened) for breaking tabu; C913, Bloody key as sign of disobedience; R211, Escape from prison; P251, Brothers; B391, Animal (bird) grateful for food; Q87*, Reward for obedience; G423, Ball falling into water (den)

Hainted House," was told by Kathleen Mills, Knox County, age about 20. In her version the hero is a preacher and he scares away the ghosts by using the name of God and passing a collection plate; 9h, "The Hainted House," was told by Bobby Abrams, age 14, Madison County; 9i, "Irishman in the Hainted House," was told by Charles Halcomb, age about 30, during one of my Big Leatherwood trips. His version is slighter than the others. The Irishman is chased from the house by the ghost and he runs till he is tired. Ghost comes up and says, "We're havin' a race, ain't we?" Irishman said, "Just give me time to rest and we'll have another'n too." Number 9j, "The Colored Man's Revenge," was told by Bobby Ambrose, age 13, Madison County. Colored man with head cut off jumps out of coffin with a big corn knife and says to the hero, "You killed me ten years ago and I'm going to kill you! Boo!" Number 9k was told by Anse Howard. The corpse in this version falls piecemeal down from the loft, jumps together, and reveals treasure; 9m, "The Mysterious White Horse," was told by Pearlie Adams, Leslie County. In it a mother kills her baby and is exposed by the ghost of her mother-in-law, in the form of a white horse; 9n was told by Harold Caudill, age 16, Letcher County. It was the only story he knew. He had heard it from an old man in his community.

Type 326, The Youth Who Wanted to Learn What Fear Is.

Motifs: H1376.2, Quest: learning what fear is; E281, Ghosts haunt house; H1411, Fear test: staying in haunted house; E467, Revenants (of animals) fight each other; F852.5*, Moving coffin; E422.1.1, Headless revenant; E545, The dead speak; E451.4, Ghost laid when living man speaks to it; E371, Return from dead to reveal hidden treasure; E451.5, Ghost laid when treasure is unearthed; P233, Father and son; K2321, Corpse set up to frighten people; K2152, Unresponsive corpse; E423.1.2, Revenant as cat; E261, Ghost makes attack; C946, Arm shortened for breaking tabu; E402, Mysterious ghostlike noises heard; E391*, Ghost responds when spoken to in the name of God; E592.3*, Ghost carries own head; E441.2*, Ghost laid when head is buried with body; H1411.1, Fear test: staying in haunted house where corpse drops piecemeal down chimney; E31, Limbs of dead voluntarily reassemble and revive; E423.1.3, Revenant as (white) horse; H1441.1, Fearless hero frightened by being awakened by eels (fish) put down his back.

Studies: Montague Summers, *The Vampire in Europe* (New

York, 1929); Louis C. Jones, "The Ghosts of New York: An Analytical Study," *JAFL*, LVI (1944), 237-54.

Parallels: BP, I, 22 ff. (Grimm, No. 4); Campbell, *West Highlands*, No. 52; Kennedy, *Legendary Fiction*, 137-40, 154-56; Hyde, *Beside the Fire*, 154-61; Addy, *Household Tales*, Nos. 4 and 22.

JAFL, X (1897), 240-41; XII (1899), 64-65, 146-47; XLII (1930), 19; XLVII (1934), 45-63; L (1937), 106-107; LXII (1949), 188-89; LXIV (1951), 371-82. Parsons, *Sea Islands*, Nos. 62, 136, 138, and 169; Fauset, *Nova Scotia*, No. 119; Gardner, *Schoharie Hills*, 88-89, 185-87, 191-93; Carrière, *Missouri*, No. 19; White, *N. C. Folklore*, I, 680-81.

Remarks: This is the most common and the most richly varied type that I have collected in the mountains. Two or three of these versions have all of the long and detailed episodes of the German story. But not all of the parallels listed have the entire type; in fact, many of them contain only a ghost motif or two and will be cited again under witch and ghost stories, below.

No. 9b published in *MLW*, XXVI (1950), Summer, 15-17.

10

Sources: 10a was told by Jane Muncy, age 11, Hyden, Leslie County, during the Hyden School session. Jane was living with a grandmother, from whom she had heard a goodly number of excellent stories. Number 10b, "Mother's Gold Knife and Fork," was told by John McDaniel during one of my Big Leatherwood trips. In the story the youngest girl escapes from the dangers imposed on her by saying the words of the title. She later saves her half-sisters by the exchange of caps. There is no obstacle flight as in the printed version. Number 10c was told by Gene Felty, age about 16, Clay County. He heard the story and a few others from an old woman in his rural community. Number 10d, "Hope o' My Thumb," was told by Henry Pennington, age about 65, Cutshin Creek, Leslie County. Henry had such a loud and harsh voice that I heard how he used to scare children before I caught up with him. He had forgotten, or would not tell me, his most frightful one, "Rawhead and Bloodybones." His Hope o' My Thumb is the familiar little man who leads his older brothers and sisters back out of the forest,

12

Sources: No. 12a was written by Claude Sturgill, age 16, Floyd County. He had heard a number of stories from his grandmother but, recalling them imperfectly, was prone to fill in when he wrote them out for my collection (see also No. 29). No. 12b, "Jack's Stepmother Returns," was told by an informant already described above, Anse Howard. In the story the ghost of the woman comes and asks for her hair and her leg and finally, "Where's my false teeth—I'm going to eat you up with 'em!" No. 12c was told by Bill McDaniel on one of my Big Leatherwood trips; No. 12d, "The Big Toe," was told by Wilgus Neace, age about 17, Perry County. The story is similar to 12c except it lacks the last motif of burning with stove wood; No. 12e, "The Hairy Toe," was told by Rose Sizemore, age 18, Leslie County. She had heard her stories from her mother and grandmother. I visited the home on Cutshin Creek, talked with the two older people, but found them too shy and apparently too religious to tell the stories to me. The story is like all of these versions except that it has interpolated the motif of killing and cooking the little boy (found in Nos. 27 and 30, below). No. 12f, "The Big Toe," was told by Harold Valentine, age about 13, Leslie County, at the Hyden School session; No. 12g, "The Big Toe," was told by Anse Howard; No. 12h, "Mary and the Devil," was told by Burley Barger, age 17, Perry County.

Type 366, The Man from the Gallows.

Motifs: E235.4.1, Return from the dead to punish theft of golden arm from grave; S31, Cruel stepmother; E235.4, Return of dead to punish theft of part of corpse; S12, Cruel mother; G61, Relative's flesh eaten unwittingly; S10, Cruel parents.

Parallels: BP, III, 478 ff. (Grimm, No. 211); Jacobs, *English*, Nos. 12, 24, and 32.

JAFL, XLVII (1934), 341-42 (reprinted by Botkin, *Treasury of American*, 679-80); Fauset, *Nova Scotia*, No. 130 and pp. 138-39; Mark Twain, *How to Tell a Story* (Hartford, Conn., 1900), 14-15 (reprinted by Botkin, *Treasury of American*, 502-503); Botkin, *Treasury of Southern*, 516-17; Chase, *Grandfather Tales*, No. 25 (Halpert's notes in *Midwest Folklore*, II (1952), 69, cite *Hoosier Folklore Bulletin*, I (1942), 11); White, *N. C. Folklore*, I, 676.

Remarks: This type of story has many versions, all apparently for the purpose of frightening children. Even the German fragment has BOO at the end and is very popular in Denmark and France. Mark Twain used "The Golden Arm" for making someone in the audience yell out. If the haunted house story is the most common long tale in eastern Kentucky, "The Big Toe" is the most widespread short *Märchen*, I having heard dozens of versions and parodies of it. In 12h, for instance, Mary, sent for whiskey, gives some away and is beaten by her father and visited by the devil at night for being stingy with it. The screams of the child bring the father, who sees the devil and swears off drinking any more.

13

No. 13a was told by Jane Muncy, age 11, Hyden, during the Hyden School session. No. 13b, same name, was told by Patsy McCoy, Wootens Creek, Leslie County, age about 18. The version is so close to 13a that I suspect a common source for the two, although the girls did not know each other. No. 13c, "Toads and Diamonds," was told by Irene Calmes, age 16, Beattyville, Lee County. In it good and bad half-sisters are working in the field and a fairy godmother comes and asks the good girl for a drink. The water is brought from a magic spring and the girl is to spit up pearls every time she talks. The cruel girl is sent, disobeys, and she spits up toads and frogs.

Type 403, The Black and the White Bride.

Motifs: S31, Cruel stepmother; G284, Witch as helper; G263.2*, Witch enchants wild horses; G263.3*, Witch enchants gate and makes poisonous; H1321.2, Quest for healing water; H1371.1.1*, Quest for well at world's end; Q2, Kind and unkind; Q42.1.1, Child divides last loaf with fairy (dwarf); D1381, Magic object protects from attack; D1383, Magic object protects from poison; E341.4*, Heads of the well grateful for bath; D1454.1.1, Gold and silver combed from hair; Q280, Unkindness punished; M431.2, Curse: toads from mouth (hair); F311.1, Fairy godmother; D1454.2, Treasure falls from mouth.

Study: P. Arfert, *Das Motiv von der unterschobenen Braut* (Rostock, Germany, 1897).

Parallels: BP, I, 99 ff. (Grimm, No. 13; cp. Grimm, No. 1, having enchanted frog in well); Dasent, *Norse,* No. 45; Campbell, *West Highlands,* Nos. 9 and 33; Addy, *Household Tales,* No. 28; Jacobs, *English,* No. 41 and 43; Hyde, *Beside the Fire,* 129-41; MacManus, *Donegal,* 97-133; Andrew Lang, *The Blue Fairy Book* (London, 1889), 196-99 ("Toads and Diamonds" from Perrault).

Remarks: The story in its three forms is well known over the world. Nos. 13a and b are well preserved versions of form 403A, The Wishes, a form familiar in England since it can be made out in the maze of tales making up Peele's *Old Wives' Tale,* written in the 1580's. It is also in the Jacobs volume, but has broken into two parts: No. 41, "The Well at the World's End," and No. 43, "The Three Heads of the Well." My two texts, coming from the same community and having the same erroneous title, are probably from the same family source. "Rawhead and Bloodybones" is one of those skits for frightening children that I have long been on the trail of but have not yet succeeded in recording. I have recorded recently another version of 403A; else I would have surmised that the form was rare in the American white population. My third text is close to Perrault's and suggests a distant written source.

No. 13b was published in *MLW,* XXVII (1951), Winter, 25-28.

14

Source: Margaret Stacy, age about 14, Hyden, Leslie County, told during the Hyden School session.

Type 410, Sleeping Beauty.

Motifs: F316, Fairy lays curse on child; M341.2.13, Prophecy: death through spindle wound; F316.1, Curse of fairy partially overcome by another fairy's amendment; D1364.17, Spindle causes magic sleep; D945, Magic hedge; D1978.5, Waking from magic sleep by kiss.

Study: P. Saintyves, *Les Contes de Perrault et les recits parallèles* (Paris, 1923).

Parallels: BP, I, 434 ff. (Grimm, No. 50); Basile, *Il Pentamerone;* Perrault, "La Belle au Boix Dormante."

Remarks: The story has been so widely distributed by the printed page, from Naples in 1634 and Paris in 1697, that it "has never become a real part of oral folklore," says Thompson, *Folktale,* 97. The girl stated that she had heard it from a nurse (meaning either a hospital worker or a neighbor who attended her during an illness), placing it rather close to a printed source. I give it here to show how easily a source is forgotten and a story made one's own.

15

Sources: No. 15a was told by Jane Muncy, age 11, Hyden, during the Hyden School session. She has been introduced as the teller of story 10a. No. 15b was told by Bill McDaniel during one of the Big Leatherwood trips. He is the student who took me to his valley and helped me to collect the material from the McDaniel-Halcomb family.

Type 425, The Search for the Lost Husband.

Motifs: P252, Sisters; D1470.1.36*, Magic wishing chair; N201, Wish for exalted husband realized; P210, Husband and wife; H461, Test of wife's patience; D1654.3, Indelible blood; D1364.7, Sleeping potion; K1843.2, Wife takes mistress's place in husband's bed; S31, Cruel stepmother; G402, Pursuit of bird (butterfly) leads to ogre's house (cat's den); D621.1, Animal by day, man by night; D721.3, Disenchantment by destroying skin; S111.7*, Murder by poisoned needle.

Study: Ernst Tegethoff, *Studien zum Märchentypus von Amor und Psyche* (Bonn, 1922).

Parallels: BP, II, 229 ff., III, 37 ff. (Grimm, Nos. 88 and 127); Dasent, *Norse*, No. 4; Perrault, "Beauty and the Beast"; Campbell, *West Highlands*, Nos. 3 and 12; Jacobs, *More English*, Nos. 48 and 50; Jacobs, *Celtic*, No. 11; Addy, *Household Tales*, No. 1; Kennedy, *Legendary Fictions*, 52-60; Curtin, *Myths*, 50-63.

JAFL, XXXV (1922), 66; Carter, *JAFL*, XXXVIII (1925), 357-59; Parsons, *Bahamas*, No. 76; Beckwith, *Jamaica*, No. 101; Gardner, *Schoharie Hills*, 112-18; Carrière, *Missouri*, Nos. 25 and 26; Chase, *Grandfather Tales*, No. 5; Randolph, *Who Blowed Up*, 173-75.

Remarks: This story of Cupid and Psyche has been popular in oral and in literary form for two thousand years. Says Thompson, *The Folktale*, 99: "It is told in every part of Europe, but it is especially popular in the western half, where several countries have already reported more than fifty versions. The sixty-one Italian oral variants are of especial interest in connection with the appearance of the tale in Apuleius and Basile." The type has taken three forms—425A, The Monster (animal) as Bridegroom (humanized in my first text); 425B, the same introduced by guessing animal by the skin (cp. Type 621, The Louse-Skin, and No. 25, "The Flea Skin," below); 425C, The Girl as the Bear's Wife (second text here). My two texts and that of Gardner are close to the story by Kennedy, suggesting an Irish source. The texts of Gardner, Randolph, and No. 15a have the new wishing-chair motif not found in European versions.

16

Sources: No. 16a, "Mother Golden," was told by Martha Joseph, age about 18, daughter of Mitchell and sister to Harold, who are introduced elsewhere. Martha performed during the Paul's Creek session. No. 16b, "The Gold in the Chimley," was told by John McDaniel, younger brother of Bill. John had stayed with his great-grandmother and in this story had a slightly different variant from that of his grandmother Nancy. No. 16c was told by Nancy McDaniel, age about 75, during the Big Leatherwood trips. She had heard a great number of stories from her mother and other contemporaries in the valley and had been a good storyteller down until almost the time of my visits.

Type 480, The Spinning-Women by the Spring.

Motifs: S31, Cruel stepmother; P284, Stepsister; S33*, Cruel stepsister; F92, Pit (well) entrance to lower world; Q2, Kind and unkind; D1658.1.7*, Loaves (cake) grateful for removal from oven; B395*, Sheep grateful for being sheared; D1658.1.5, Apple-tree grateful for being shaken; A1135.1, Snow from feathers; H511.1, The three caskets (boxes); Q111.2*, Shower of gold as reward; Q415.4*, Punishment: eaten by reptiles; C328*, Tabu: looking into chimney; D231, Transformation: man (woman) into stone; B394, Cow grateful for being milked; B396*, Horse grateful for being ridden; Q469.3, Punishment: grinding up in a mill; D1658.1.6*, Fence grateful for being laid up.

Study: R. T. Christiansen, *Norske Eventyr* (Oslo, 1921).

Parallels: BP, I, 207 ff. (Grimm, No. 24); Basile, *Il Pentamerone;* Perrault, "Toads and Diamonds"; Dasent, *Norse,* No. 17; Jacobs, *More English,* No. 64; Addy, *Household Tales,* Nos. 10 and 18; MacManus, *Donegal,* 233-56.

JAFL, VIII (1895), 143-44; Carter, *JAFL,* XXXVIII (1925), 68-70; Parsons, *Bahamas,* No. 14; Gardner, *Schoharie Hills,* 123-28; Chase, *Grandfather Tales,* No. 2 (Halpert's note in *Midwest Folklore,* II (1952), 68, mentions a text in the Murray State College Archive).

Remarks: This is another extremely popular tale, evidenced by about six hundred versions collected. Says Thompson, *The Folktale,* 126: "In the western hemisphere it occurs in three widely separated American Indian tribes; in the French folklore of Louisiana, Canada, the West Indies, and French Guiana; and in the Spanish tradition of Peru and the Portuguese of Brazil." My first text was so close to that of Grimm that I did not summarize it. The second and third texts have many details, including the *cante fable* verses, close to the English story. A stanza of verse from John's text is as follows:

> Sheep o' mine, sheep o' mine,
> Have you ever seen a maid o' mine,
> With a wig and a wag and a long leather bag,
> Who stold all the money I ever had?

I have collected another text, without *cante fable* verses, from Leslie County recently.

No. 16b (titled "Bag o' Gold") was published in *MLW,* XXVIII (1952), Autumn, 24-28.

17

Source: Told by Mrs. Marilyn Baker, age about 20, during the Paul's Creek session. She is the older daughter of Mitchell Joseph.

Type 507A, The Monster's Bride.

Motifs: Q42.3, Generosity to saint (grateful dead) in disguise rewarded; T172.0.1, All husbands (suitors) have perished on bridal night; D23*, Transformation: princess to witch; H524, Test: guessing person's thoughts; D1980, Magic invisibility; D766.1, Disenchantment by bathing (immersing) in water; L161, Lowly hero marries princess.

Studies: G. H. Gerould, *The Grateful Dead* (London, 1908); Sven Liljeblad, *Die Tobiasgeschichte und andere Märchen von toten Helfren* (Lund, 1927).

a close parallelism with the preceding Cinderella type. The motifs that distinguish this type are the girls unusual as to eyes and the helpful animal. It is rather thinly distributed over Europe and I really have seen no close parallels in the British-American tradition. Most of the stories cited have a mistreated boy and a helpful bull (see next story). My first text may have been derived from the German printed story, but the second version seems to be traditional, or at least adapted to modern reason. The girls are normal as to eyes and are acting almost normally in mistreating the ugly and handicapped one.

20

Sources: No. 20a, "Bill and His Bull," was told by Bug Cornett, age about 15, during one of the Big Leatherwood trips. The boy had been in school until this year and may have heard this story told or read. It is the fullest text I have of this type, but it is also closest to a printed source. No. 20b was told by Bill McDaniel; No. 20c, "Jack and the Bull Stripes," was told by Bill's younger brother John, who had his version from the great-grandmother. His version leaves off after the first giant, who makes the boy rich. No. 20d was told by Jane Muncy, the 11-year-old girl already mentioned. Her story, the first of the type that I collected, is given here because of its modernistic ending. No. 20e, "Jack and His Bull," was told by a man of forty years, Will Witt, from Paul's Creek. He was referred to me as a good storyteller by his two small boys, who came to a neighbor's house where I was recording. His story is still shorter, leaving off at the death of the bull.

Type 511*, The Little Red Bull (type number suggested by Thompson, *Folktale*, 129, since it was not given a number in the Index).

Motifs: S12, Cruel mother; B335, Helpful animal (to be) killed by hero's enemy; B115.1, Ear-cornucopia; D1472.1.8, Magic tablecloth (napkin) supplies food and drink; D1335.14*, Magic stick gives strength; D1344.11*, Magic bull stripe gives invulnerability; B11.11, Fight with dragon; H36.1, Slipper (shoe) test; S31, Cruel stepmother; D1812.3.3, Future revealed in dream(s); D1081, Magic sword; T91.7, Rich girl in love with poor boy; R41.3, Captivity in dungeon; K1915, Substitute bridegroom; K1917, Penniless bridegroom pretends to wealth; S11, Cruel father.

Parallels: Dasent, *Norse*, No. 50; Jacobs, *More English*, Nos. 48 and 79; Curtin, *Myths*, 114-28; Seumas MacManus, *In Chimney Corners* (New York, 1908), No. 1.

JAFL, XXX (1917), 198; Parsons, *Bahamas*, No. 16; Fauset, *Nova Scotia*, 41-43; Chase, *Jack Tales*, No. 2; Randolph, *Who Blowed Up*, 133-35 (Halpert's notes, pp. 215-16, are in addition to those he compiled in Chase, *Jack Tales*, 189-90).

Remarks: This is the story so rarely found in Europe that it did not receive a type number. The Norse story and the English No. 48 have the One-Eye development and the girl riding away on a helpful bull, while other European versions include either a boy or a girl character without the Type 511 framework. The recent collecting in Ireland has brought to light at least 50 versions of this Little Red Bull story, and I find it rather popular, with 7 texts so far. Says Thompson, *Folktale*, 129, "Its wide distribution . . . and its relative uniformity would seem to indicate that we have here an autonomous tale and not a mere variation of some more popular story." Note that the story is absent from the Harman-Ward tradition of North Carolina (Carter and Chase, collectors), whose earliest performer was of German stock. My latest text came from a man of Irish descent. Although this evidence strongly suggests an Irish home for the tale, it needs a study and a type number to place it properly in folk tale tradition.

21

Source: Told by Norma Fay Reedy, age about 13, Leslie County. This odd story came up during the Hyden School session, and I was obliged to record it, not knowing whether it was something authentic or not.

Type 520, People of the Big Feet.

Motifs: F517.1, Person unusual as to his feet; Q482, Punishment: noble person must do menial service; F261, Fairies dance; D1242.1, Magic water.

Remarks: I have found no parallels to this story. I place it here among ordinary folk tales because of the magic and fairy elements.

Parallels: Christiansen, *Norske Eventyr*, 87; Jacobs, *English*, No. 23 (water in sieve only); Jacobs, *Celtic*, No. 4 (water in sieve only); Dasent, *Norse*, No. 46.

Fauset, *Nova Scotia*, No. 18.

Remarks: In the Norse texts the king assigns tasks to suitors for his daughter. The youngest son, through kindness or curiosity, receives magic objects and succeeds where the older boys fail. No story that I have seen is a complete parallel to either the Norse stories or to mine. This story and the others from my informant came from an old woman about whom I have not received any more information, but a few of her stories seem to have come directly from northern Europe. Without considerably more study on this story I cannot determine whether this is the correct type number or not (see 11c and 25 for two other unusual stories).

25

Source: Told by Martha Roark, who heard it from the old woman discussed in the preceding story.

Type 621, The Louse-Skin.

Motifs: S12, Cruel mother; Q321, Laziness punished; B874.1, Giant louse (flea); H522.1.1, Test: guessing nature of certain skin—louse (flea) skin; H511, Princess (girl) offered to correct guesser; N475, Secret name overheard by eavesdropper; B211.12, Speaking frog; R111.1.5.1*, Rescue of woman from frog-husband; T96, Lovers reunited after many adventures.

Parallels: BP, III, 483 ff. (Grimm, No. 212; cp. No. 1); Basile, *Il Pentamerone*, 1st Day, 5.

Carter, *JAFL*, XXXVIII (1925), 372; Vance Randolph, "Folktales from Arkansas," *JAFL*, LXV (1952), 164.

Remarks: The Italian story of 1634 has a flea skin for guessing, the Appalachian text of Carter's has a louse skin, and the Ozark text has no guessing at all, just an enchanted frog. Although these two American regions are dominantly British in background, we have here a story rare in British tradition. Says Thompson, *Folktale*, 155, "Within Europe, the overwhelming majority of the variants are from four east Baltic countries." Unless this story was once in British tradition and then lost (or still uncollected), we have another story apparently from an east European source.

26

Source: Told by Dewey Adams, age 40, Perry County, during one of the Big Leatherwood trips. He was a truck driver and timber cutter, told his stories well, and in a session at the crossroads country store he delighted the crowd with several excellent tall tales and jokes.

Type 654, The Three Brothers.

Motifs: P251, Brothers; F660.1, Brothers acquire extraordinary skill; H504, Test of skill in handiwork; F675, Ingenious carpenter.

Parallels: BP, III, 10 ff. (Grimm, No. 124).

Remarks: There are three Types (653, 654, and 660) in European circulation having motifs of extraordinary skill. There is almost no other evidence that they came as units to America, but their motifs may be among our frontier exaggerations. Thompson thinks that the three types belong to literature. He says of Type 654, "A version . . . is found in the *Scala Celi* of Johannes Gobii, Junior, composed in France at the beginning of the fourteenth century. It has been used in jestbooks . . . and has been collected orally, though not frequently, from most parts of the European continent. It does not seem to have travelled beyond." (*Folktale*, 82).

27

Sources: No. 27a was told by Lige Cay, age 40, teacher of the seventh grade where I set up the recorder for the Hyden School session. Lige had heard this story and a few others from his mother. I visited her, found her, at the age of 82, still clever and alert but confined to her chair in her home on the Middle Fork below Hyden. She recalled the delightful evenings in her girlhood when folk came in to sit before the fire and tell stories, the sessions usually ending with ghost tales and candy-pullings. No. 27b, "Peewee under the Tub," was told by John McDaniel, during one of my Big Leatherwood trips. The story, learned from his great-grandmother, tells of a little girl murdered by her stepmother and buried under a big ivy stalk. A bird brings the death verses, and the girl's little dog leads the father to the spot. No. 27c, "The Silver Tree,"

Remarks: Claude reports quite frankly that this is a reconstruction of a tale about Jack that he once heard from his grandmother. There are no parallels close enough to include here, but I am inclined to believe that this item has fragments of a folk tale.

30

Sources: No. 30a was told by Jimmy Pennington, age 17, Leslie County, while a student at Berea. He had heard this story and No. 6a, above, from his grandmother. No. 30b, "The Rotten Pear," was told by Ruby Spencer, age 17, Letcher County, while a student at Berea. She had heard her stories (see 47a and 61) from her father, a coal miner. Her version is similar to No. 30a, except that the stepmother is killed for the murder by her husband, and the little girl miraculously comes to life.

Type 780, The Singing Bones.

Motifs: S12, Cruel mother; H1211, Quest assigned in order to get rid of hero (heroine); K1817.1, Disguise as beggar (old woman); K345.1, Sympathetic helper sent for remedy (fruit) and robbed (tricked); E632.1, Speaking bones (head) of murdered person reveal murder; E613.0.1, Reincarnation of murdered child as bird; Q412, Punishment: millstone dropped on guilty person; S31, Cruel stepmother; G61, Relative's flesh eaten unwittingly; E1, Person comes to life.

Study: Lutz Mackensen, *Der singende Knochen, FFC* No. 49 (Helsinki, 1923).

Parallels: BP, I, 260 ff. (Grimm, No. 28); Francis James Child, *English and Scottish Popular Ballads* (Boston, 1882-1898), No. 10; Jacobs, *English*, No. 9 (the ballad turned into prose); Addy, *Household Tales*, No. 43.

Alcée Fortier, *Louisiana Folk-Tales, MAFLS,* II (Boston, 1895), 61 (reprinted by Botkin, *Treasury of American,* 678-79); Parsons, *Bahamas*, No. 79; Parsons, *Sea Islands*, Nos. 133 and 134; Carrière, *Missouri*, No. 51.

Remarks: The ballad form of this type (usually containing only Motif E632.1) is more widely known than the prose form, having a vigorous tradition in Britain and in Europe, especially in Scandinavia. Perhaps 120 versions of the British song have been collected in Canada and in the United States. "The prose tale," says

Thompson (*Folktale*, 136), "as told throughout Europe, does seem to have a sufficient number of common details to constitute a definite narrative entity. Mackensen feels that this prose story probably originated in Belgium, but he recognizes the great difficulty of reaching conclusions that will give proper weight to the ballad tradition and to analogous tales which may have independently arisen in remote parts of the earth." In Addy's story the maid kills her little charge because the child is crying for its golden cup. Its spirit returns and reveals its murder. Closer texts to mine are those from the Bahamas and Sea Islands, in which there are motifs of the speaking head, and the eating of forbidden fruit from a fig tree, an apple tree, and, in one text, a peartree. Mrs. Parsons indicates French, British, and Spanish sources for the material in these two collections. Since mine are the only two texts yet reported from Appalachia, I can only suggest French as the most likely source for them.

31

Source: This story was told by Charles Halcomb, age 30, during a Big Leatherwood trip. The teller of thirteen stories for this collection, he has already been introduced with No. 9i.

Type 1535, The Rich and the Poor Peasant.

Motifs: K114.1, Alleged oracular (valuable) cow-hide sold; K941.1, Cows (horses) killed for their hides when large price is reported by trickster; K527, Escape by substituting another person; K2150, Innocent made to appear guilty; K526, Captor's bag filled with animals or objects; K842, Dupe persuaded to take prisoner's place in sack; K1051, Diving for sheep.

Parallels: BP, II, 1 ff. (Grimm, No. 61); Andersen, "Big Claus and Little Claus"; Dasent, *Norse*, No. 47; Campbell, *West Highlands*, No. 39; Jacobs, *Celtic*, No. 6; Kennedy, *Fireside Stories*, 98 ff.

JAFL, IV (1892), 248-49; XXIII (1910), 425-28; XXXIV (1921), 14; Carter, *JAFL*, XXXVIII (1925), 343-46; *JAFL*, XL (1931), 353-55; XLVII (1934), 308-309; and LXV (1952), 159-60 and 165-66; Fortier, *Louisiana*, 89; Charles L. Edwards, *Bahama Songs and Stories*, MAFLS, III (Boston, 1895), 95-96; Parsons, *Bahamas*, No. 18; Parsons, *Sea Islands*, Nos. 28 and 60; Beckwith, *Jamaica*, Nos. 107, 108, and 135; Fauset, *Nova Scotia*, Nos. 1 and 17; Hurston,

Mules and Men, 64-68; Gardner, *Schoharie Hills,* 177-82; Carrière, *Missouri,* No. 66; Chase, *Jack Tales,* No. 17.

Remarks: Since this story contains two rather popular types, I am compiling notes separately for them. Little more need be said for Type 1535 in showing that it is a story of universal interest. Clever cheating and cunning tricks, especially by the poor at the expense of the rich, tickle the human imagination. Says Thompson (*Folktale,* 165-66), "Type 1535 has been told in European literature since its appearance in the Latin poem *Unibos* in the tenth century and has seldom been omitted from any collection where it was at all appropriate. But it is also immensely popular as an oral tale. A hasty survey of easily available versions shows 875." This version could have come to Appalachia directly from Europe or from Britain.

Type 853, The Hero Catches the Princess with Her Own Words.

Motif: H507.1.0.1, Princess (girl) defeated in repartee by means of objects accidentally picked up.

Parallels: Under Type 853 are nine east European parallels; Jacobs, *More English,* No. 87.

JAFL, XXXV (1922), 74; Parsons, *Bahamas,* No. 77; *C. Coll.,* Ch. XVII; Randolph, *Who Blowed Up,* 6-7.

Remarks: This obscene text (not printed) leaves off two episodes. After the hero has caught the princess with her own words, he is thrown into prison, but he escapes with the help of magic objects. He then captures her again and will not release her until she answers "No" to three questions. He so phrases the questions that he gets her into his bed and later marries her. In the English text foolish Jack catches the girl and is assigned the task of sitting up with her all night without sleeping. It has no obscenity. In the Parsons version, dirty, stinking Jack makes the princess laugh by producing objects, the last "a lump of stool." The Ozarks story makes the girl answer "No" and "they was as good as married then and there." Thompson (*Folktale,* 157) traces the whole story to a Middle High German poem and in both French poetry and English ballads. Says he, "As a part of folklore, it is most popular in states around the Baltic, though it is known in all parts of Europe." Because of the obscene parts, the story is probably more in tradition than is revealed by these scattered references.

Sources: No. 32a was written by Bill Baker, age 17, already mentioned under 28a. He had heard the story from his mother, who got it from her mother, Mrs. Ben Miniard. I was able to visit Mrs. Miniard's home deep in the isolated section of Greasy Creek, Leslie County, and to collect the story again from her—No. 32b, "Rich Tom of Ireland." It contains all of the motifs in her grandson's version. She was a spry and witty woman of 75 years, who kept her house and large garden tidy and cared for her sons and their children on adjoining acres. From her I received a number of riddles and short tales on a later visit.

Type 910B, The Servant's Good Counsels.

Motifs: J163.4, Good counsels bought (worked for); J21.5, "Do not leave the highway"; J21.3, "Do not go where an old man has a young wife"; P210, Husband and wife; J21.2, "Do not act when angry"; J21, Counsels proved wise by experience.

Parallels: Robert Hunt, *Popular Romances of the West of England* (London, 1871), 344-46 (Tom Trezidder gets one counsel—J21.5); Jacobs, *Celtic*, No. 22 (notes, pp. 268-69, trace the tale to *Blackwood's Magazine* of 1818, to the *Gesta Romanorum*, and to *Turkish Tales*); Kennedy, *Legendary Fictions*, 66-70 (none of the three counsels common to my story).

JAFL, XXIV (1911), 408-11; XXVII (1914), 213-14; Beckwith, *Jamaica*, No. 122.

Remarks: The type takes four forms, all containing counsels and proverbs that are given under varying conditions. The type as a whole, and similar counsel lore, is traced to the East. Says Thompson (*Folktale*, 164), "They appear in the older literary collections from India, in Arabia and Persian reworkings, and in most of the books of exempla and jests in the Middle Ages and Renaissance." His footnote 23 gives three studies of literary sources. The Jacobs story, from *Blackwood's Magazine*, would have been exactly parallel to mine had not the editor dropped the last counsel and used an Irish counsel, "honesty is the best policy." The Jamaican text has motifs J21.5 and J21.2. Miss Beckwith does not dwell on sources for her volume except to mention many African and English influences. My two texts are the only ones that I am aware of in the American white population and are of British origin, even Irish, as suggested by the titles.

33

Source: The story was told by Mitchell Joseph, age 40, Paul's Creek, Leslie County, during the Paul's Creek session. He was a storekeeper and miner, father of seven or eight children, all of whom knew and liked to record stories.

Type 935, The Prodigal's Return.

Motifs: P233, Father and son; H506.5*, Test of resourcefulness: using gift of money; L10, Victorious youngest son; H1411, Fear test: staying in haunted house; E281, Ghosts haunt house; D812.4, Magic objects received from ghost; D1602.11, Self-returning magic coin; D1051.1*, Magic handkerchief that makes owner welcome; H251, Test of truth by magic object.

Parallels: Under Type 935 are four east European references (not available to me).

Carter, *JAFL*, XXXVIII (1925), 373-74; Silas T. Rand, *Legends of the Micmacs* (New York, 1894), No. 80; Carrière, *Missouri*, No. 59.

Remarks: This story may not be correctly classified because of the many tales (Types 563-569) with magic objects in use by adventurers and because of the scarcity of texts in western tradition. One reason for this scarcity could be an obscene situation effected by the hero. My informant's wife left the room, begging her husband not to tell this vulgar story. He left the passages out and would not tell me what they were. Thompson says of it (*Folktale*, 130), "In Europe this story seems entirely confined to the Baltic states and Denmark. . . . But its presence in America among the Micmac Indians and among the Missouri French gives every indication that it was brought across the ocean by Frenchmen. In Missouri it has been skillfully combined with the tale of The Youth Who Wanted to Learn What Fear Is (Type 326)." He does not mention the text by Carter, collected in Tennessee, which, along with this one, also has most of Type 326. Since there were French settlers in East Tennessee as well as in eastern Kentucky, a French source is indicated until more British texts come to light.

34

Source: Told by Janis Morgan, age 12, Leslie County, during the Hyden School session; heard from her grandmother.

Type 955, The Robber Bridegroom.

Motifs: K1916, Robber bridegroom (neighbor); D1317, Magic objects warn of danger; C611, Forbidden chamber (blood-hole); K758*, Capture by giving evidence as feigned dream; H57.2.1, Severed finger as sign of crime.

Parallels: BP, I, 370 ff. (Grimm, No. 40); Dasent, *Tales from the Fjeld*, 247-53; Jacobs, *English*, No. 26.

JAFL, XXX (1917), 196-97; Carter, *JAFL*, XXXVIII (1925), 360-61, 372 (riddle); Parsons, *Sea Islands*, No. 145; Gardner, *Schoharie Hills*, 146-55; Randolph, *Midwest Folklore*, II (1952), 87-89 (riddle).

Remarks: The story seems to be well preserved in its many European versions, all containing the experiences of a girl with a robber, the persistent verses, "Be bold, be bold," and the feigned dream which traps the villain. Jacobs in his notes, p. 268, traces allusions to the story in *Much Ado About Nothing* and in the *Faerie Queene*. My text preserves the outline of the story well enough to indicate an English source. There is a riddle about Mr. Fox, common in the mountains, which may be the detached *cante fable* verses of this story. It is:

> Riddle to my left, riddle to my right,
> Where did I stay last Friday night?
> The wind did blow, my heart did ache
> To see the hole in the ground that Fox did make.

This narrative explanation, or solution, is always given: A girl promises to meet her lover in the woods. She arrives before him and climbs a tree. The lover and another man arrive and begin to dig a grave, remarking about robbing and murder. The girl keeps silent until they are gone. She later traps the robbers with the riddle.

37

Source: Told by Mrs. Ben Miniard, age 75, Leslie County. She has already been introduced as the direct and indirect source of many stories.

Type 979, Witch Steed.

Motifs: G241.2.1, Witch transforms man into horse and rides him; G211.1, Witch in form of horse; G211.1.2, Witch as horse shod with horseshoes; F551.1.2.1, Woman with horseshoes on feet (hands); G275.6*, Witch killed with silver bullet.

Studies: Kittredge, *Witchcraft*, especially Ch. XIII; Gardner, *Schoharie Hills*.

Parallels: Campbell, *West Highlands*, II, 69-71; William Henderson, *Notes on the Folk-Lore of the Northern Counties of England and the Borders* (New ed., London, 1879), 190-93.

Cox, *SFQ*, VII (1943), 203-209; Gardner, *Schoharie Hills*, 65 (note 88 gives several references and remarks on the magic bridle); White, *N. C. Folklore,* I, 649-50.

Remarks: In many of the citations given in the two stories above there are instances of transformation of calves and other animals into swift steeds. This number represents a special kind of magic—the power in a bridle to change any creature, including man, into a steed. The plot thus becomes more satisfying, since the man can obtain the bridle and "ride the witch." The texts by Henderson and Campbell are almost exact parallels to the story here, indicating a British source.

38

Sources: No. 38a was told by Charles Halcomb on one of my Big Leatherwood trips. No. 38b was told by Delbert McDaniel on the same trip. Both men have been introduced.

Type 1032, Clever Dividing Which Favors the Divider.

Motif: J1241, Clever dividing which favors the divider.

Parallel: Hurston, *Mules and Men*, 102; U. S. Congress, *House Executive Documents*, 30 Cong., 1 Sess., No. 502 (Serial No. 511), 501-502.

Remarks: The first text perhaps represents the origin of the saying, often heard in the mountains, "He never said turkey to me." In the Hurston reference two Negroes are joking about the white man versus the colored man, when one of them says:

> Aught's a aught, figger's a figger,
> All for de white man, none for de Nigger.

39

Source: No. 39 was told by Bill McDaniel on one of the Big Leatherwood trips.

Type 1030, The Crop Division; Type 1036, Hogs with Curly Tails.

Motifs: K171.1, Deceptive crop division: above the ground, below the ground; K171.4, Deceptive division of pigs: curly and straight tails.

Parallels: BP, II, 355 ff. (Grimm, No. 189).

JAFL, XXX (1918), 175; XLVII (1934), 292; Carrière, *Missouri*, Nos. 22 (motif K171.1) and 62; *C. Coll.*, Ch. XXIV; Chase, *Grandfather Tales*, No. 9.

Remarks: Stories from this point on through the type numbers are shorter than most of those preceding, and to each one that can and sometimes does stand alone the indexers have assigned a type number, although some items contain only a single motif. But very often these short episodes are combined into a running narrative, as in this story of "Bobtail and the Devil." Of the many parallels for Type 1030, seven are from eastern Europe. I have no evidence of either type in the British tradition. In the German story the partners raise turnips and wheat; in Chase's text the two raise corn and hogs, and then play "Pitching the Hammer." My story is more nearly related to this latter one, but there are too few texts to trace sources.

40

Source: Told by Robert Wolfe, age 77, Cutshin Creek, Leslie County, during the Paul's Creek session. Robert sat with his toes in the ashes, complaining, but came alive when we had in some

deal with mistaken identity; some strain for a laugh through absurd overcredulity; others have no more than grotesque or incongruent situations.

44

Source: Delbert McDaniel, during a Big Leatherwood trip.

Type 1317*, The Dungbeetle Is Mistaken for a Bee (in "Types not Included").

Motif: J1751, Dungbeetle thought to be bee (mulberry).

Parallels: Under the type entry are references to Esthonian and Finnish texts.

Remarks: I have collected several other texts on later trips to the region. It seems not to have been reported elsewhere.

45

Source: Told by Will Witt, on a Paul's Creek trip.

Type 1318*, Numskull Wanting to Fight Is Sent to Hornet's Nest (my suggested number, competing with another in "Types not Included").

Motif: J2131.2, Numskull stung.

Remarks: No parallels discovered. I remember vaguely hearing this anecdote in the mountains in boyhood, but this is the only text collected.

46

Source: Mahala Grigsby, age 55, Perry County. She has been introduced under No. 28b, above.

Type 1319, Pumpkin Sold as an Ass's Egg.

Motif: J1772.1, Pumpkin thought to be an ass's (mare's) egg.

Parallels: BP, I, 317 ff.; Jacobs, *More Celtic*, No. 35; Kennedy, *Fireside Stories*, 119 ff.; Clouston, *Noodles*, 36-38.

JAFL, XXXI (1918), 78; Halpert, "Southern New Jersey," No. 145; Randolph, *Who Blowed Up*, 144-45 (Halpert's note, p. 218, gives exhaustive parallels).

Remarks: Says Thompson, *Folktale*, 190, "This anecdote not only appears in Turkish jestbooks, but is told all over Europe, in much of

Asia, and among the mountain whites of Virginia." I heard it in boyhood from a playmate of distant Swedish descent and have collected other texts recently.

47

Sources: No. 47a was told by Ruby Spencer, age 17, daughter of a miner in Letcher County. She was introduced under story No. 30b. No. 47b was told by Will Witt, during a Paul's Creek trip. He has been mentioned several times.

Type 1321*, The Watch Mistaken for the Devil's Eye.

Motif: J1781.2, Watch mistaken for the devil's eye (reptile, bug).

Parallels: Under the type number are Esthonian and Finnish references.

Parsons, *Sea Islands*, Nos. 55 and 56; Fauset, *Nova Scotia*, No. 39; Hurston, *Mules and Men*, 115-16.

Remarks: The terrapin is a small box tortoise, very common in the mountains. Though edible they are never, to my knowledge, eaten for food. When they invade our waterholes and springs we know that "dog days" have set in.

48

Sources: No. 48a was told by Nancy McDaniel during a Big Leatherwood trip. No. 48b told by Gene Felty, age 16, Clay County. He was the teller of No. 10c.

Type 1322**, Hidden Man Falling from Attic Frightens Away Enemies (my suggested number, competing with two others in "Types not Included").

Motif: K335.0.4, Owner frightened from goods (food) by a bluff.

Remarks: References to pioneers and Indians will occur again and again in the remainder of these stories. The people still hold in memory their hardships with wild animals and Indians. I have a few fragments of the old John Swift silver legend that flourished in the first decades of settlement. Tales of Civil War skirmishes in the area are heard often, and anyone in the confidence of an old resident may hear the story of a county feud from beginning to end.

49

Source: Charles Halcomb, on a Big Leatherwood trip.
Type 1324*, Turtle Taken for Cowdung.
Motif: J1761.6*, Turtle thought to be cowdung.
Remarks: No references discovered. I heard the story in boyhood and in a different context. The Irishman was turned out of the church door for disturbance. He saw a terrapin coming with cowdung on its back. He ran to the church door and called out, "You damn fellers quit your foolishness in there and come out here and watch this cowpile walk!"

50

Sources: No. 50b was told by Charles Halcomb. No. 50a, "Irishman and the Trap," was told by John McDaniel, brother to Bill. In it the trap catches the man by another part of his body.
Type 1325*, Object Taken for Man.
Motif: J1771, Object thought to be animal (man).
Remarks: No parallels discovered or other texts collected.

51

Source: "The Irishmen and the Train," told by John McDaniel. Two dupes attempt to board a bull as they would a moving freight train. Resultant confusion is obscene.
Type 1327*, Bull Taken for Train.
Motif: J1761.7*, Bull thought to be train.
Remarks: No parallels discovered elsewhere, but the anecdote is fairly common in some parts of eastern Kentucky.

52

Source: Told by Charles Halcomb.

Type *1328**, Numskull Misunderstands.

Motifs: J1771.2*, Fiddle thought to be cat: player is torturing it; J1761.3, Glowworm thought to be fire (sparks).

Parallel: Hazlitt, *Jest-Books*, I, 67 (boy thinks lute player is tickling a goose and "making the sweetest music").

Remarks: I heard the second part of this anecdote from my Swedish playmate.

53

Source: Told by Charles Halcomb.

Type *1329**, Mounted Numskull Thinks Mule Wants to Ride.

Motif: J1874.2*, Mounted numskull thinks his bucking mule wants to ride.

Parallel: Clouston, *Noodles*, 119-120.

Remarks: Clouston's story is exactly like this one.

54

Source: Told by Delbert McDaniel during a Big Leatherwood trip.

Type *1332*, Lazy Numskull Takes Place of Man on Gallows; Type *1333*, Numskull Pays Preacher to Pray Dead Friend Back to Life.

Motifs: K841, Substitute for execution obtained by trickery; E63, Resuscitation (promised) by prayer.

Parallel: Harris, *Uncle Remus*, No. 23 (rabbit caught up in rope persuades bear to take his place and earn a dollar a minute).

55

Source: Told by Nancy McDaniel during a Big Leatherwood trip.

Type *1334*, One's Mule Shaved, Other's Horse Disfigured.

Motif: J1535*, One's mule shaved, other's horse tore its mouth laughing.

Parallels: Dasent, *Norse*, No. 6.

Richard M. Dorson, *Jonathan Draws the Long Bow* (Cambridge, Mass., 1946), 91-93 (from the *Spirit of the Times*, XVI (March 20, 1847), 38).

Remarks: In the Norse story a proud princess cuts the ears off a suitor's horse and slits the mouth of another. She explains that the wind blew the ears off the one and the other laughed until he tore his mouth. In the text by Dorson there are two quarreling Yankees; one hobbles (cuts the tendons of) his enemy's sheep and the other slits the mouth of his enemy's hog.

56

Source: Written by Burley Barger, age 17, Perry County, already mentioned under No. 12h; and John Hammons, age 17, Knox County. These two boys were in my class at Berea and did a natural thing regarding these short anecdotes—string them along together. I have other "chains" that include as many as eight short Irishman jokes.

Types: *1324**, Turtle Taken for Cowdung; *1336*, Numskulls Harvest Crop with Explosives; 1228, Shooting the Gun; *1323**, The Ticking of the Clock Thought to Be Gnawing of Mice; 1242, Loading the Wood; 1881, The Man Carried Through the Air by Geese (Ducks); 1882, The Man Who Fell Out of a Balloon; *1337*, Atlas; 1227, One Woman to Catch the Squirrel, Other to Get the Cooking Pot (No. 40, above); *1338*, Numskull Wants to Be Dead; 1889, Münchausen Tales.

Motifs: J1761.8*, Terrapin thought to be water dipper; J2131.1.2*, Numskull induced to sit on explosive; J2131.4.2*, Numskull, seeing if gun will fire, shoots companion; J1789.2, Clock ticking thought to be gnawing of mice (accusation); J2213.4, If horse can pull one load, he can pull two (tree); X916, Lie: man carried through air by geese (ducks); X917, Man falls and is buried in earth (rocks): goes for spade and digs self out; A842, Atlas; J2661.3, One woman to catch the squirrel, other to get the cooking pot; J2188.1*, Numskull wants to take place of well-dressed dead companion.

Parallels: *Münchausen*, 22 (Type 1882).

Fauset, *Nova Scotia*, No. 39 (Type 1323*); Chase, *Jack Tales*, No. 16, and *Grandfather Tales*, No. 20 (Type 1881); White, *N. C. Folklore*, I, 697 (Type 1323*).

Remarks: The Hammons boy had heard the first six stories told together, with the title given; the other boy brought the last four episodes into one; I typed the two papers as a connected story. A mountain man from whom I have been collecting recently tells a chain of eleven of these jokes in one, eight in another, five in another. He says that he never did like to tell just one little short joke.

57

Source: "Mush for Supper," told by I. J. Miniard, age 30, Greasy Creek, Leslie County, son of Mrs. Ben Miniard. A miner with a family of three children, he had not remembered many of the stories and riddles that his mother still held in mind.

Type 1363, The Cradle.

Motif: K1345, Tale of the cradle (mush).

Studies: F. N. Robinson, *Complete Works of Geoffrey Chaucer* (Boston, 1933), "Reeve's Tale," and notes, p. 790a; W. F. Bryan and Germaine Dempster, *Sources and Analogues of Chaucer's Canterbury Tales* (Chicago, 1941), "Reeve's Tale."

Parallels: *The Decameron of Giovanni Boccaccio* (Garden City, N. Y., 1930), Day the Tenth, No. 6; Joseph Bédier, *Les Fabliaux* (2d ed., Paris, 1893), 463 ff.

Carrière, *Missouri*, No. 70; Randolph, *Who Blowed Up*, 16.

Remarks: Mush, New England hasty pudding, is made by boiling corn meal in water and salting to taste. Mr. Carrière classifies his text as Type 1775, The Hungry Parson. My text comes closer to the Chaucer story by the presence of young women in the room and the other obscenities. It was suggested to Mr. Miniard by his wife, who knew the story and was in the room most of the time while he recorded it, and his mother and father sat through it all.

The women shyly and quietly smiled at its telling. I have heard an almost exact version of the Chaucer story in the mountains, as follows: A bull has been stolen and two young men set out to find it. They happen to stay the night in the cabin of the thief and his wife and daughter. One boy uses a string to guide him to the pantry, and while he is gone, the other boy ties the end of the clue to the daughter's bed. The wife stirs in the night and returns to the other boy's bed. When the first boy moves again he gets in with the old man and, thinking he is whispering to his companion, tells that he has found out where their bull went to. The old man begins to curse and disturb the household.

58

Source: Told by Betty Valentine, age 14, Hyden, Leslie County, during the Hyden School session.

Types: 1450, Clever Elsie; 1384, Husband Hunts Three Persons as Stupid as His Wife; 1210, The Cow Is Taken on the Roof to Graze; 1286, Jumping into the Breeches; 1335, The Eaten Moon.

Motifs: J2063, Distress over imagined troubles of unborn child; H1312.1, Quest for three persons as stupid as his wife; J1904.1, Cow (hog) taken to roof to graze; J2132.2, Numskull ties rope to leg (arm) as cow grazes on the roof; J2161.1, Jumping into the breeches; J1791.2, Rescuing the moon.

Parallels: BP, I, 335, and II, 440 (Grimm, Nos. 34 and 104); Clouston, *Noodles*, 55, 161, and 191; Jacobs, *English*, No. 2; Kennedy, *Fireside Stories*, 9; Campbell, *West Highlands*, No. 48.

JAFL, LXV (1952), 162; Parsons, *Bahamas*, No. 78; Gardner, *Schoharie Hills*, 163-72; Chase, *Jack and the Three Sillies* (Boston, 1950).

Remarks: This story is a good example of the clustering of related jokes to make a long, episodic tale. Says Thompson (*Folktale*, 193, speaking of Type 1450), "It is probably Oriental and literary in origin." This text is close enough to the Jacobs story to indicate an English source, and its frequent use in school readers may place it close to a printed text.

59

Source: Clarence Day, age 12, Leslie County, during the Paul's Creek session. He has been mentioned as the teller of No. 1.

Type 1535, The Rich and the Poor Peasant; Type 326, The Boy Who Wanted to Learn What Fear Is.

Motifs: D474, Transformation: object becomes bloody; R163, Rescue by grateful dead man (woman); E422.1.1, Headless revenant; E371, Return of dead to reveal hidden treasure; E451.5, Ghost laid when treasure is unearthed; K842, Dupe persuaded to take prisoner's place in a sack; K1051, Diving for sheep (cattle).

Parallels: For Type 326, see story No. 9, above; for Type 1535, see story No. 31, above; Campbell, *West Highlands*, No. 29.

Remarks: It is easy to see in this strange fragment the haunted house motifs and the diving for sheep trick. But how about the whole vague story? The West Highlands story is one of those ancient Irish hero tales—the story of Fionn on a hunting trip. I have recently collected a story that looks like Cuchullain being attacked by another giant, but I suspect that it is from some written source. But this tale was told to this boy by his grandmother and is beyond doubt in oral tradition. It could be the rarest in my collection.

60

Sources: No. 60a was told by Jane Muncy, age 11, during the Hyden School session. She has often been mentioned above. No. 60b, "Big Scare and Little Scare," was told by Carl Davis, age 16, Morgan County. He knew only one other story (No. 95) and gave me little information about his sources.

Type 1553, The Boy That Would Not Be Frightened.

Motif: K1682.1*, Disguised trickster is himself frightened.

Parallels: *JAFL*, XXXI (1918), 81; Carrière, *Missouri*, No. 19; Halpert, "Southern New Jersey," No. 230.

Remarks: This is the introduction to the Missouri story, leading into the story of the youth who wanted to learn what fear was (Type 326). I have heard it on a few other occasions during my boyhood in eastern Kentucky.

61

Source: Told by Ruby Spencer, age 17, Letcher County. She was the daughter of a miner and has been mentioned as the teller of Nos. 30b and 47a.

Type *1554*, The Graveyard Wager.

Motifs: H1416.1*, Fear test: visiting a graveyard at midnight; N334, Accidental fatal ending of game or joke.

Parallels: Randolph, *Midwest Folklore*, II (1952), 83-84; White, *N. C. Folklore*, I, 686.

Remarks: In the Missouri text a girl accepts the wager, takes along a croquet stake, and drives it through her skirt; in the North Carolina story a girl drives a fork through her skirt.

62

Sources: No. 62a, "The Little Brave Tailor," was told by Rose Sizemore, age 18, Leslie County, the teller of Nos. 7c, 12e, and other stories. No. 62b was told by Charles Halcomb during a Big Leatherwood trip.

Types: 1640, The Brave Tailor; 1060, Squeezing the (Supposed) Stone; 1062, Throwing the Stone (Bird); 1052, Hauling a Tree.

Motifs: P441, Tailor; K62, Contest in squeezing water from a stone; K18.3, Throwing contest: bird substituted for stone; K1951.1, Boastful flykiller: "seven at a blow"; K1082, Ogres duped into fighting each other; K731, Wild boar captured in church; K71, Deceptive contest in carrying a tree: riding; K912, Giants' (Robbers') heads cut off one by one as they enter house.

Parallels: BP, I, 148 ff. (Grimm, No. 20); Campbell, *West Highlands*, No. 45; Jacobs, *English*, No. 19; Jacobs, *More English*, No. 58; Hyde, *Beside the Fire*, 1-15.

JAFL, XXIX (1916), 23 ff.; Fansler, *Filipino*, 51; Parsons, *Bahamas*, No. 82; *C. Coll.*, Ch. II; Carrière, *Missouri*, No. 67; Chase, *Jack Tales*, Nos. 1 and 6.

Remarks: The story has a wide circulation of perhaps 350 texts, most of them following the outline of the German story. In tracing its history Thompson (*Folktale*, 144) says, "This form of the story

. . . seems to come from a jestbook of Montanus published in 1592, though the tale was mentioned several times in the century preceding. The story is probably of Oriental origin, for a fairly close analogue is found in the Buddhistic literature of China dating from about the third century after Christ." Though these two texts are near the German, I have a story recently from a man of 75 years, who heard it from his parents when he was a boy.

63

Source: Told by Nancy McDaniel, age 75, during a trip to Big Leatherwood.

Type 1641B, Sleepy Woman Counting Her Yawns. Compare Type 1641, Doctor Knowall.

Motif: N611.2, Criminal accidentally detected: "that is the first" —sleepy woman counting her yawns.

Parallels: BP, II, 412; cp. BP, II, 401 (Grimm, No. 98, "Doctor Knowall").

Chase, Grandfather Tales, No. 23.

Remarks: Doctor Knowall goes to a lord's castle to detect thieves among the servants. He says, "That is the first," when a servant brings a dish of food. This was the servant first to steal, etc. These two American texts are close to this German story. The woman actress, however, makes an interesting variant to the type, perhaps meriting the new number that I have suggested.

64

Source: Told by Mrs. Ben Miniard, age 75, Leslie County. She has often been mentioned in the above notes.

Types: 1685, The Foolish Bridegroom; 1006, Casting Eyes.

Motifs: J2462.2, Casting sheep's eyes at the bride (girl); K1442, Casting eyes: animal's eyes.

Parallels: BP, I, 311 (Grimm, No. 32); Hazlitt, Jest-Books, III, 18-19; Jacobs, Celtic, No. 20 (taken from Kennedy's Fireside Stories, 74-80); Clouston, Noodles, 41-42, 126-28.

Remarks: This small item is sometimes found in Type 1000, Bargain Not to Become Angry. It is absent from a close parallel to the Celtic story in Chase, *Jack Tales*, No. 7. As a droll story it is current in continental Europe, where Jacobs traces it in his notes, pp. 282-83.

65

Source: Written by Delilah Garrett, age 20, Pulaski County. She had heard it from her father.

Type 1687*, Fool Forgets the Word He Is to Remember.

Motifs: J2671.2, Fool keeps repeating instructions so as to remember them; D2004.5, Forgetting by stumbling.

Parallels: Clouston, *Noodles*, 133-41; Jacobs, *More English*, No. 84 (from *Folk-Lore Record*, III, 153-55; Jacobs' notes, p. 267, cite Denmark, Germany, and Kennedy's *Fireside Stories*, 30).

JAFL, III (1890), 292-95; Thompson, *Tales of the North American Indians*, No. 109g; Carrière, *Missouri*, No. 69; Chase, *Grandfather Tales*, No. 14 (Halpert, in his notes to this volume in *Midwest Folklore*, II (1952), 68-69, gives five other parallels).

Remarks: Although Halpert classifies Chase's story as Type 1696, "What Should I Have Said (Done)?" it appears to be a distinct type, with a wide distribution over Europe, Britain, and the United States. It merits a study and a type number.

66

Source: "Old Bill Jones," told by I. J. Miniard, age 30, Leslie County, son of Mrs. Ben Miniard. He told story No. 57, above.

Type 1698G, Misunderstood Words Lead to Comic Results.

Motif: X111.7, Misunderstood words lead to comic results.

Study: Antti Aarne, *Schwänke über schwerhörige Menschen*, *FFC* No. 20 (Hamina, Finland, 1914).

Parallel: Randolph, *Who Blowed Up*, 80-81.

Remarks: Thompson says about the Aarne study (*Folktale*, 211), "All of these he has traced back to literary sources." Some few others that I have heard from the lips of jesting men are very effective orally.

67

Sources: No. 67a was told by Martha Roark, age 18, Magoffin County. She has been mentioned as the teller of stories 11c, 24, etc. No. 67b, "Walnuts in the Graveyard," was told by Anse Howard, teller of many stories. No. 67c, "Counting the Potatoes," was told by Mary McCay, age 17, Clinton County; No. 67d, "Counting Walnuts in the Graveyard," was told by Lois McCollum, age 14, Madison County.

Type 1791, The Sexton Carries the Parson.

Motif: X424, The devil in the cemetery.

Parallels: Richard F. Burton (trans.), *The Book of the Thousand Nights and a Night; Supplemental Nights* (London? 1885-1888), I, 288-97; Hazlitt, *Jest-Books,* I, 31-36; Dasent, *Norse,* No. 33; Addy, *Household Tales,* No. 2.

JAFL, XXXI (1918), 80; XLVII (1935), 263; Parsons, *Sea Islands,* No. 58; Fauset, *Nova Scotia,* No. 168; Hurston, *Mules and Men,* 117-19 (reprinted by Botkin, *Treasury of American,* 444-45); Halpert, "Southern New Jersey," No. 228; Randolph, *Who Blowed Up,* 25-26, 83-84.

Remarks: As the citations indicate, this short anecdote has had a long and popular tradition. Says Thompson (*Folktale,* 214), "This anecdote is certainly as old as the *Thousand and One Nights,* and appears in nearly every medieval and Renaissance tale collection. But it is widely told by oral story-tellers all over Europe and, for some reason, is about the best known of all anecdotes collected in America." It may be found in every community in eastern Kentucky.

68

Source: Told by Bobby Tate, age 18, Woodford County.

Type *1833E,* "Let Gabriel Blow His Horn."

Motif: X435.6*, "Let Gabriel blow his horn"—boy obliges.

Parallels: Fauset, *Nova Scotia,* No. 143 (note cites two other related texts); Richard M. Dorson reports several parallels in his manuscript of Negro folk tales.

69

Sources: No. 69a was told by Dewey Baker, age 18, Leslie County, the teller of Nos. 3b and 4. No. 69b, "Peach-Rock Deer," was told by Judy Day, age 11, during the Paul's Creek session. No. 69c was told by Dewey Adams, age 40, during a Big Leatherwood trip.

Type 1889, Münchausen Tales.

Motif: X910, Münchausen tales.

Parallels: *Münchausen,* 12-14.

[H. E. Taliaferro], *Fisher's River (North Carolina) Scenes and Characters* (New York, 1859), 50 ff. (reprinted by Botkin, *Treasury of American,* 586-88); Percy Mackaye, *Tall Tales of the Kentucky Mountains* (New York, 1926), 25-33; Chase, *Jack Tales,* No. 16; Halpert, "Southern New Jersey," 356.

Remarks: An old man of the Pine Mountain area by the name of Sol Shell was the celebrated teller of the Mackaye stories. I have recently collected some of the tales in the community, and my informants still attribute "the big lies" to Sol.

70

Source: Told by Dewey Adams, age 40, Perry County, during a Big Leatherwood trip.

Types: 1894, The Man Shoots a Ramrod Full of Ducks; 1895, A Man Wading in Water Catches Many Fish in His Boots.

Motifs: X921.4, Man shoots a ramrod full (great flock) of ducks; X921.5, Catching fish in boots while wading.

Study: Arthur K. Moore, "Specimens of the Folktales from Some Antebellum Newspapers of Louisiana," *Louisiana Historical Quarterly,* XXXII (1949), 723-58.

Parallels: Parsons, *Sea Islands,* Nos. 85 and 86; William O. Bradley, *Stories and Speeches* (Lexington, Ky., 1916), 131 f. (reprinted by Botkin, *Treasury of American,* 604); Hurston, *Mules and Men,* 151-53 (reprinted by Botkin, *Treasury of American,* 618-19); Chase, *Jack Tales,* No. 16; Chase, *Grandfather Tales,* No. 20; Halpert, "Southern New Jersey," Nos. 112, 116, and 117.

Remarks: This is typical tall hunting lore that evolved on the frontier in the days of Boone, Fink, Crockett, and Jim Bridger. Dorson says of it (*Jonathan,* 111-12), "The American hunting classic, the big bag of game with one shot, frequently recurs in nineteenth century publications, and is still being gathered in current oral texts: we can trace its course in New England from the Old Farmer's Almanac of 1809 to a verbal rendering given the writer in 1942." I have recently collected a "Long Hunt" down the Mississippi River, and among the many adventures is the daring escape from the old one-eyed giant (Polyphemus).

No. 70 (titled "I Bought Me a Dog") was published in *MLW,* XXVII (1951), Spring, 32-34.

71

Sources: No. 71a was told by Charles Halcomb during a Big Leatherwood trip. No. 71b was told by the old man Robert Wolfe on a Paul's Creek visit.

Types: 1889, Münchausen Tales; 1900, How the Man Came Out of the Tree Stump.

Motifs: X910, Münchausen tales; X911.2, Man escapes from bee's nest (hollow tree) on bear's tail.

Parallels: *Münchausen,* 21-22.

Carter, *JAFL,* XXXVIII (1925), 374; [Taliaferro], *Fisher's River,* 50 ff. (reprinted by Botkin, *Treasury of American,* 585-86); Botkin, *Treasury of Southern,* 464; Chase, *Jack Tales,* No. 16.

Remarks: Münchausen loses his silver hatchet on the moon; he uses the horns of the moon to secure his beanstalk for ascending and for tying his rope when descending.

72

Source: Told by Dewey Adams during a Big Leatherwood trip.

Type 1920, Contest in Lying.

Motifs: X905, Lying contest; X1021.8*, The great bedbug; X945*, Rapid construction of building.

Parallel: Halpert, "Southern New Jersey," No. 127.

73

Source: Told by Felix Turner, age 60, Burning Springs, Clay County. He was known for miles around his rural home for his humor and his tall tales. See also story No. 86.

Type *1960L*, The Great Opossum.

Motif: X1021.9*, The great opossum.

Remarks: This kind of hunting exaggeration matches like tales from those living in fishing country.

74

Sources: No. 74a was told by Charles Halcomb. No. 74b was told by Margaret Wooten, age 20, Wooten's Creek, Leslie County. She had heard it from her father.

Type *1962*, The Poisoned Timber.

Motif: X929*, Timber bitten by snake swells to great size.

Parallels: Botkin, *Treasury of American*, 583-85, and *Treasury of Southern*, 447-48.

75

Source: Written by Ronald Dunn, age 17, Magoffin County. He knew no more folklore. He had picked this item up recently.

Type *1970*, Unnatural Natural History.

Motif: X946*, Lie: fish trained to live on land falls into water and drowns.

Parallels: Charles E. Goodspeed, *Angling in America* (Boston, 1939), 315-16 (reprinted by Botkin, *Treasury of American*, 624-25); Dorson, *Jonathan*, 120-21 (reprinted from *The Tame Trout and Other Backwoods Fairy Tales* (Farmington, Me., 1941)); *California Folklore Quarterly*, III (1944), 177-79 (reprinted from *The Tame Trout*).

Remarks: This story only recently migrated to Kentucky. Ronald heard it from a teacher who was reared in Minnesota and who had spent some time in Maine.

76

Source: Written by Talmadge Calmes, age 18, Lee County. He is a brother to Irene, teller of some good stories (Nos. 13c and 18); he seemed not to know any more folk tales.

Type 1977, Animals Go Up in the Air.

Motif: X947*, Lie: animals so evenly matched in fight they go up in the air.

Parallels: Mackaye, *Tall Tales*, 49-56; *Southern Workman*, XXVI (March, 1897), No. 3, 122-23.

Remarks: Although I have collected several of Mackaye's tales orally, I feel that this one came from his printed source.

77

Sources: No. 77a, "The Drunken Bear," was told by John Miniard, age 16, Perry County. No. 77b was told by John Hammons, age 17, Knox County, already introduced under No. 56. No. 77c was told by Harold Joseph, age 14, Leslie County, during the Paul's Creek session. He is the son of Mitchell Joseph. No. 77d, "The Greedy Bear," was told by Estill South, age 18, Perry County.

Type 2028, The Fat Troll (Wolf).

Motifs: Z31.3.4, The fat troll (wolf, bear, man); K891, Dupe (animal) induced to jump to his death; F913, Victims rescued from swallower's belly.

Study: Archer Taylor, "A Classification of Formula Tales," *JAFL*, XLVI (1934), 77-88.

Parallels: Chase, *Grandfather Tales*, No. 7; Dorson, manuscript of Negro folk tales.

Remarks: This formula story has a close and confusing companion, Type 2027, The Fat Cat. It concerns a cat that eats a bowl, the ladle, the mistress, etc. Thompson says of it (*Folktale*, 231), "This is essentially a Scandinavian tale, though one version has been reported from India. The other [Type 2028] is also well known in Scandinavia, but is found in Russia, and an analogue has been taken down in east Africa." These several versions in America indicate a vigorous tradition, apparently coming from Europe.

78

Sources: No. 78a was told by Charles Halcomb on a Big Leather-wood trip. He said he had heard this on a "talking machine" record when a boy. No. 78b, "Skoon Kin Huntin'," was told by Martin Ambrose, age 16, son of a teacher in Berea College, who had heard a student from Alabama tell the tale. No. 78c was told by Mitchell Joseph, age 40, Leslie County, during the Paul's Creek session. He was mentioned under No. 33.

Type 2225*, Scrambled Tale.

Motifs: X954*, Topsy-turvy talk; X917, Man falls and is buried in earth: goes for spade and digs self out.

Parallels: Jacobs, *More English*, No. 51.

Parsons, *Sea Islands*, No. 80; Harris, *Uncle Remus*, No. 27; Whitney and Bullock, *Maryland*, 179-80; Chase, *Grandfather Tales*, No. 15 (Chase takes this material, a long speech, from his No. 1, "Mummers' Play." His No. 15 was reprinted by Botkin, *Treasury of Southern*, 525-26).

Remarks: Early recordings may account for the wide distribution of this kind of material in the United States. Its history can be traced, however, to the English story and play. Jacobs so traces it in his notes (p. 245). He sees some marks of "considerable antiquity" in his story and mentions instances of *Lügenmärchen* in the collection of Grimm.

79

Source: Told by Nancy McDaniel during a Big Leatherwood trip.

Remarks: I have little information about this item other than two other texts collected. The "Bear's Son" story is extant in the region (No. 2, above), but it is without the introduction in which a bear carries a woman to his den and mates with her. This item could be that fragment, broken away from the main story.

80

Source: Little boy, age about 12, Leslie County, during the Paul's Creek session. I failed to get his name or the source of his story.

Motif: A2217.2, Chipmunk's back scratched: hence its stripes.

Remarks: Under the motif number are two references to Indian myths. This item could have come from a school reader.

81

Source: Told by Bill McDaniel, age 20, Perry County, during a Big Leatherwood trip. He told 81a and 81b on separate occasions and I have left them that way, although they are from the same Greek legend.

Type, Legend of Theseus.

Motifs: P10, Kings; H1562.2, Test of strength: lifting stone; P30, Princes; P233, Father and son; R121.5, Ariadne-thread; Z130.1, Color of flag (sails) as message of good or bad news; N344, Father kills self believing that son is dead.

Parallels: *Bulfinch's Mythology* (Modern Library ed.), 124-25; Curtin, *Myths*, 244-69 (motif Z130.1).

Remarks: I believe this legend to be in oral tradition, but it could have come from some simplified schoolbook selection.

82

Source: Told by Charles Halcomb on a Big Leatherwood trip.

Parallel: White, *N. C. Folklore*, I, 632 (Indians steal fire from witches; animals help them rush it home).

83

Source: Written by Bill Baker, age 17, Leslie County. He has been mentioned as the teller of Nos. 28a and 32a.

Remarks: This is a good example of the legends about Indian

troubles, still told by the fireside in the hills. Occasionally some vivid tales of this kind appeared in Kentucky histories and may have been handed down from these printed versions.

84

Source: Told by Paul Howard, age 16, Bell County, as heard from his grandmother. He gave the title in a loud chant as though it were an Indian call or signal. Perhaps the words (here spelled phonetically) mean something in an Indian language.

85

Source: Written by Walter Howard, age 18, Leslie County.
Motifs: A985, Cliff from lovers' leap; T211.3, Husband and wife (lovers) kill themselves so as not to be separated.
Study: Louise Pound, "Nebraska Legends of Lovers' Leaps," *Western Folklore Quarterly,* VIII (1949), 304-13.
Parallels: White, *N. C. Folklore,* I, 631-32; Dorson, *Jonathan,* 143 ff.

86

Source: Told by Felix Turner, age 60, Clay County. He has been introduced under No. 73.
Motif: D1766.1.1, Magic fountain produced by prayer.
Remarks: There is some faith healing, handling of poisonous snakes, and witch practice in the mountains. The healers and "witches" are almost always men.

87

Source: Told by Viola Couch, age 18, Viper, Perry County. She did not know any other stories and was uncertain of the source of this one.
Motifs: P233, Father and son; R153.3, Father rescues sons.
Parallels: Compare Grimm, No. 15, "Hansel and Gretel"; Bishop

Thomas Percy, *Reliques of Ancient English Poetry* (London, 1846), III, 169-76, "Children in the Wood" (reprinted by Jacobs, *More English*, No. 68).

Randolph, *JAFL*, LXV (1952), 165.

Remarks: I see no way to trace this version beyond the mountains.

88

Sources: No. 88a was written by Mamie Bailey, age 18, Mercer County, West Virginia. She had heard this and some other legends (Nos. 90, 92, 93, and 94) from an old woman in her community. No. 88b, "Grandma and the Bear," was told by Julia Farler, age 17, Perry County. She had heard it and No. 100 at her home.

Studies: Lewis Spence, *The Fairy Tradition in Britain* (London, 1948), 199; Spence cites an elaborate study by J. G. McKay, *The Tale of the Cauldron* (Dundee, Scotland, 1927).

Parallels: Campbell, *West Highlands*, No. 26 (woman goes for kettle, borrowed by fairies. It has scraps in it, and as she starts for home dogs are let loose after her. She throws out scraps to delay the fairy animals).

Dorson, *Jonathan*, 252.

Remarks: I have heard this legend often, first from my mother when I was a child.

89

Source: Told by Mrs. Robert Wolfe, age about 60, Leslie County, during the Paul's Creek session. She also told No. 27c.

Motif: B535, Animal nurse.

90

Source: Written by Mamie Bailey, Mercer County, West Virginia, from an old woman. See No. 88a, above.

Motifs: P210, Husband and wife; N271, Murder will out.

91

Source: Told by Lettie Felty, age 18, Clay County, sister to Gene, who told Nos. 10c and 48b.

92

Source: Written by Mamie Bailey.

Motifs: E275, Ghost haunts place of great accident or misfortune; D1654.3, Indelible blood; E434.9*, Ghost cannot come into lighted room; E451.6*, Ghost laid when bloodstains uncovered.

Parallels: *JAFL*, X (1897), 240-41; XLIII (1930), 19; Fauset, *Nova Scotia*, No. 116; Fred W. Allsopp, *Folklore of Romantic Arkansas* (New York, 1931), II, 252.

93

Source: Written by Mamie Bailey from West Virginia.

Remarks: For most of these local legends I have not seen versions sufficiently parallel to list.

94

Source: Written by Mamie Bailey from West Virginia.

95

Source: Written by Carl Davis, age 16, Morgan County. He is mentioned as the writer of No. 60b, above.

Motifs: E402, Mysterious ghostlike noises heard; E371, Return of dead to reveal hidden treasure; E451.5, Ghost laid when treasure is unearthed.

96

Source: Told by Anse Howard, age 18, Leslie County. He has been listed as the teller of several stories (Nos. 9c, 9k, 12b, 12g, 36a, etc.).

Motifs: P210, Husband and wife; E221.2, Dead wife returns to reprove husband's second wife; C500, Tabu: touching; C946, Arm shortened for breaking tabu.

Parallel: Hudson and McCartie, "The Bell Witch of Tennessee and Mississippi," *JAFL*, LXVII (1934), 45-63.

97

Source: Told by Pearlie Adams, age 18, Leslie County. She knew only two stories (see No. 9m) and related them rather imperfectly.

Motifs: P230, Parents and children; S12, Cruel mother; E225, Ghost of murdered child.

98

Sources: No. 98a was told by Anse Howard. No. 98b, "Her Spirit Returns," was told by Barbara Rogers, age 14, Madison County. She did not know any more folklore.

Motifs: P230, Parents and children; E324, Dead child's friendly return to parents.

Studies: R. K. Beardsley and Rosalie Hankey, "The Vanishing Hitchhiker," and "A History of the Vanishing Hitchhiker," *California Folklore Quarterly*, I (1942), 303-35, and II (1943), 13-25; Louis C. Jones, "Hitchhiking Ghosts in New York," *CFQ*, III (1944), 284-92.

Parallels: Hundreds of texts collected and examined by the above writers; Randolph, *JAFL*, LXV (1952), 163-64.

Remarks: From a few texts in the 1920's until today this ghost story has spread all over the Western Hemisphere.

99

Source: Told by Bill McDaniel, Big Leatherwood, Perry County.
Motif: P210, Husband and wife.

100

Sources: No. 100a was told by Julia Farler, age 17, Perry County,
teller of No. 88b, above. No. 100b was written by Jewel Ballard,
age 17, Lincoln County. She did not know any other stories.
Parallel: Dorson, *Jonathan*, 35.

101

Source: Told by Henry Pennington, age about 65, Leslie County.
He had forgotten more tales than he told me, but see No. 10d,
above.
Motif: D1812.5.1.2, Bad dream as evil omen.

102

Source: Told by Henry Pennington. See preceding story.
Remarks: To clear up the story: The master had planned to rob
his neighbor while the man was away, but he had underestimated
the ferocity of his own dog. Another version, declared to be a "true
happening," was collected recently on the same creek (Cutshin).

103

Source: Told by James Blair, age 18, Harlan County. I failed
to get more information about this legend, but during a three-year
stay in this county I never heard the legend a second time.

104

Sources: No. 104a was told by Anse Howard, Greasy Creek, Leslie County. No. 104b was told by Ob King, age 65, Rockcastle County (lived most of his life in Clay County). He has been mentioned under No. 9f. No. 104c was also told by Ob King.

Parallels: Randolph, *Who Blowed Up*, 62-63; Dorson, manuscript of Negro folk tales.

Remarks: Reference has already been made to the struggles and hardships encountered on the Kentucky frontier. Men bought up herds of cattle, sheep, hogs, and even flocks of turkeys and geese, and drove them out of the winding hills to market, or they rafted their logs down the crooked rivers. These are a very few of the legends that evolved out of that way of life.

105

Source: Told by Dewey Adams, age 40, Perry County. See his other stories above (Nos. 26, 69c, 70, 72).

Informants

All informants were white. Places without state address are in Kentucky. All stories were recorded orally except those indicated as written.

Bobby Abrams, Madison County, age about 14. Story 9h, heard from his grandmother.

Dewey Adams, Perry County, age about 40. An excellent storyteller. Stories 26, 69c, 70, 72, and 105.

Pearlie Adams (girl), Leslie County, age 18. Stories 9m and 97.

Bobby Ambrose, Madison County, age 13. Story 9j.

Martin Ambrose, Madison County, age 16. No relation to Bobby. Story 78, learned from his father, a teacher at Berea College, who had heard it told by a student from Alabama.

Mamie Bailey, Mercer County, West Virginia, age 18. She had heard some of her stories from an older sister, a teacher who had collected stories, plays, and games for classroom use, and the others from an old woman in her neighborhood. Stories 88a, 90, 92, 93, and 94 (all written).

Bill Baker, Leslie County, age 17. He heard the stories from his mother and grandmother, Mrs. Ben Miniard (below). Stories 28a, 32a, and 83 (all written).

Dewey Baker, Leslie County, age 18. He heard the tales from his father. Stories 3b, 4, and 69a (first and third written).

Leona Baker, Leslie County, age 17. No relation to Dewey. Story 3a (written).

Mrs. Marilyn Joseph Baker, Leslie County, age 20. Daughter of Mitchell Joseph (below). Story 17.

Jewel Ballard, Lincoln County, age 17. Story 100b (written).

Burley Barger, Perry County, age 17. Stories 12h and part of 56 (both written).

James Blair, Harlan County, age 18. Story 103.

Irene Calmes, Lee County, age 16. Stories 13c and 18.

Talmadge Calmes, Lee County, age 18. Brother to Irene. Story 76 (written).

Type Numbers

These type numbers are taken from the Aarne-Thompson *The Types of the Folk-Tale* (*FFC* No. 74). Those numbers in italics mark the stories for which I have suggested new numbers and descriptions. The numbers after the type titles refer to the stories in this collection.

130. The Animals in Night Quarters, 1
301A. The Three Stolen Princesses, 2
303. The Twins or Blood-Brothers, 3
304. The Hunter, 4
310. The Maiden in the Tower, 5
311. Three Sisters Rescued from the Mountain, 6
312. The Giant-Killer and His Dog (Bluebeard), 7
313A. The Magic Flight, the Girl as Helper, 8
326. The Youth Who Wanted to Learn What Fear Is, 9, 59
327. The Children and the Ogre, 10
328. The Boy Steals the Giant's Treasure, 11
366. The Man from the Gallows, 12
403. The Black and the White Bride, 13
410. Sleeping Beauty, 14
425. The Search for the Lost Husband, 15
480. The Spinning-Women by the Well, 16
507A. The Monster's Bride, 17

510. Cinderella and Cap o' Rushes, 18
511. One - Eye, Two - Eyes, Three-Eyes, 19
511*. The Little Red Bull, 20
520. People of the Big Feet, 21
562. The Spirit in the Blue Light, 22
563. The Table, the Ass, and the Stick, 23
577. The King's Tasks, 24
621. The Louse-Skin, 25
654. The Three Brothers, 26
720. My Mother Slew Me; My Father Ate Me, 27
737*. Who Will Be Her Future Husband? 28
740. King of the Valley, 29
780. The Singing Bones, 30
853. The Hero Catches the Princess with Her Own Words, 31
910B. The Servant's Good Counsels, 32
935. The Prodigal's Return, 33
955. The Robber Bridegroom, 34
977. Fairy and Witch Magic, 35
978. Witch Transformation, 36
979. Witch Steed, 37

Harold Caudill, Letcher County, age 16. Story 9n.

Bug Cornett, Perry County, age 15. Stories 20a and 47c.

Viola Couch, Perry County, age 18. Story 87.

Carl Davis, Morgan County, age 16. Stories 60b and 95 (both written).

Clarence Day, Leslie County, age 12. He had heard his folklore from a grandmother. Stories 1 and 59.

Judy Day, Leslie County, age 11. Sister to Clarence. Story 69b.

Curt Duff, Hyden, Leslie County, age 57. A town official and storekeeper, who kept alive the local legends and personal anecdotes. Story 11b.

Ronald Dunn, Magoffin County, age 17. Story 75 (written).

Julia Farler, Perry County, age 17. Stories 88b and 100.

Gene Felty, Clay County, age 16. Good performer, who had heard a few stories from his grandparents. Stories 10c and 48b.

Lettie Felty, Clay County, age 18. Sister to Gene. Story 91.

Bertha Fields, Perry County, age 16. Story 19b.

Delilah Garrett, Pulaski County, age 20. She heard the tale from her father. Story 65.

Lige Gay, Hyden, Leslie County, age 40. He had heard some stories from his mother. Story 27a.

Mahala Grigsby, Perry County, age 55. She had heard many stories and short legends, but did not like to record them. Stories 28b and 46.

Charles Halcomb, Perry County, age 30. A grandson of Nancy McDaniel (below). He had heard many stories from a grandmother and a great-grandmother. Stories 9i, 31, 38a, 43, 49, 50b, 52, 53, 62b, 71a, 74a, 78a, and 82.

Earl Hamilton, Perry County, age 16. Story 23b (written).

John Hammons, Knox County, age 17. Stories 56 and 77b (both written).

Anse Howard, Leslie County, age 18. Stories 9c, 9k, 12b, 12g, 36a, 67b, 96, 98a, and 104a.

Paul Howard, Leslie County, age 11. Brother to Anse. He heard his stories from an elderly man living up the creek. Stories 9b and 35c.

Paul Howard, Bell County, age 16. Story 84.

Walter Howard, Leslie County, age 18. Story 85 (written).

Harold Joseph, Leslie County, age 14. Son of Mitchell. Story 77c.

Martha Joseph, Leslie County, age 18. Daughter of Mitchell. Story 10a.

Mitchell Joseph, Leslie County, age 40. Man with a large family, former coal miner. Stories 33 and 78c.

Ob King, Rockcastle County (lived most of his life in Clay County), age 65. Grandfather to Ronald Wyatt (below). Stories 9f, 104b, and 104c.

Mary McCay, Clinton County, age 17. Story 67c (written).

Lois McCollum, Madison County, age 14. Story 67d.

Patsy McCoy, Leslie County, age 18. Story 13b.

Bill McDaniel, Perry County, age 20. Grandson of Nancy McDaniel (below). Stories 6b, 8, 12c, 15b, 20b, 39, 81a, 81b, and 99.

Delbert McDaniel, Perry County, age 36. Son of Nancy, who lived with him. Stories 38b, 41a, 44, and 54.

John McDaniel, Perry County, age 17. Grandson of Nancy and brother to Bill. He had stayed with the great-grandmother and had learned slightly different versions of some of the tales, and he knew a few that the other boys had not heard. Stories 10b, 16b, 20c, 27b, 50a, and 51.

Nancy McDaniel, Perry County, age about 75. A sturdy, well-preserved old lady, who passed down to the younger generations many of the stories heard from her mother and others. Stories 16c, 48a, 55, 63, and 79.

Kathleen Mills, Knox County, age 20. Story 9g.

Mrs. Ben Miniard, Leslie County, age about 75. Grandmother to Bill Baker (above). Stories 32b, 35b, 36c, 37, and 64.

I. J. Miniard, Leslie County, age about 30. Son of Mrs. Ben Miniard. Stories 57 and 66.

John Miniard, Perry County, age 16. Story 77a.

Janis Morgan, Hyden, Leslie County, age 12. Story 34.

Jane Muncy, Hyden, Leslie County, age 11. An excellent performer, who learned her stories from her grandmother. Stories 10a, 13a, 15a, 20d, and 60a.

Wilgus Neace, Perry County, age 17. Stories 7b and 12d.

Henry Pennington, Leslie County, age about 65. Stories 10d, 101, and 102.

Jimmy Pennington, Leslie County, age 17. He related well stories that he had heard from his grandmother. Stories 6a and 30a.

Norma Fay Reedy, Hyden, Leslie County, age 13. Story 21.

Martha Roark, Magoffin County, age 18. Her stories, received from an old woman in her community, are well worn by a long oral tradition. Stories 11c, 24, 25, 35a, and 67a.

Opal Roberts, McCreary County, age 18. Story 7a.

Barbara Rogers, Madison County, age 14. Story 98b.

Don Saylor, Leslie County, age 18. He remembered only two of the many stories his grandmother once told around Bledsoe. Stories 2 and 9a.

Rose Sizemore, Leslie County, age 18. She learned these stories from her grandmother. Stories 7c, 12e, 19a, 23a, and 62a.

Estill South, Perry County, age 18. Story 77c.

Ruby Spencer, Letcher County, age 17. She learned her tales from her father. Stories 30b, 47a, and 61.

Margaret Stacy, Hyden, Leslie County, age 14. Story 14.

Patsy Ann Stacy, Hyden, Leslie County, age 13. Sister to Margaret. Story 5.

Claude Sturgill, Floyd County, age 16. He heard most of his folklore from his grandmother. Stories 12a and 29.

Bobby Tate, Woodford County, age 18. Story 68.

Felix Turner, Clay County, age 60. He had a local reputation as a teller of tall tales. Stories 73 and 86.

Betty Valentine, Hyden, Leslie County, age 14. Story 58.

Harold Valentine, Hyden, Leslie County, age 13. Brother to Betty. Story 12f.

Will Witt, Leslie County, age 40. I learned from his small children that he knew some tales, but found that he was almost too nervous to record. Stories 20e, 41b, 45, and 47b.

Robert Wolfe, Leslie County, age about 77. Stories 40, 42, and 71b.

Mrs. Robert Wolfe, Leslie County, age about 60. Stories 27c and 89.

Margaret Wooten, Leslie County, age 20. Story 74b.

Ronald Wyatt, Rockcastle County, age 18. Grandson of Ob King (above), from whom he had learned many legends. Story 9e (written).

Mrs. Luther York, Leslie County, age 50. Daughter of Mrs. Ben Miniard (above). She had heard many stories from her mother. Stories 9d and 36b.

Tommy York, Leslie County, age 16. Story 22.

Motif Numbers

The numbers are taken from Thompson's *Motif-Index*. When the narrative element in a story varies a word or two from the motif, the alternate words are enclosed in parentheses. Motifs marked with an asterisk are suggested new numbers. The number of the story where the motif is found follows the motif description.

A. *Mythological Motifs*

A842. Atlas, 56
A985. Cliff from lovers' leap, 85
A1135.1. Snow from feathers, 16a

A2217.2. Chipmunk's back scratched: hence its stripes, 80

B. *Animals*

B11.11. Fight with dragon, 20a
B13. Unicorn, 29
B113.1. Treasure-producing bird- (animal-) heart, 19b
B115.1. Ear-cornucopia, 20a, b, c, d
B131.1. Bird reveals murder, 27a, b
B134.2. Dog betrays murder, 27b
B211.12. Speaking frog, 25
B296. Animals go a-journeying together, 1
B300. Animal helpers, 10a
B325.1. Animal (bird) bribed with food, 2
B335. Helpful animal (to be) killed by hero's (heroine's) enemy, 19a, b; 20a, b, c, d
B391. Animal (bird) grateful for food, 7c

B394. Cow grateful for being milked, 16b, c
B395*. Sheep grateful for being sheared, 10a, b
B396*. Horse grateful for being ridden, 16b, c
B413. Helpful goat, 19a, b
B450. Helpful bird, 11a; 24
B505. Magic object received from animal (bird), 23a, b
B535. Animal nurse, 89
B542.1.1. Eagle carries man to safety, 2
B563.2. Birds point out road to hero, 10c
B601.1 Marriage to bear, 3a
B874.1. Giant louse (flea), 25

C. *Tabu*

C328*. Tabu: looking into chimney, 16b, c

C500. Tabu: touching, 7c; 96

C611. Forbidden chamber (blood-hole), 7a, c; 34

C913. Bloody key as sign of disobedience, 7a, b, c

C921. Death (threatened) for breaking tabu, 7a, b, c

C946. Arm shortened for breaking tabu, 9c; 96

D. *Magic*

D23*. Transformation: princess to witch, 17

D55.2.2. Devil (witch) makes self small, 35a, b, c

D231. Transformation: man (woman) into stone, 16b, c

D474. Transformation: object becomes bloody, 59

D621.1. Animal by day, man by night, 15b

D672. Obstacle flight, 8; 10a

D702.1.1 Cat's (Hog's) foot cut off: woman's hand missing, 36a, b

D721.3. Disenchantment by destroying skin, 15b

D766.1. Disenchantment by bathing (immersing) in water, 17

D812.4. Magic objects received from ghost, 33

D837. Magic object acquired through foolish bargain, 11b

D845. Magic object found in underground room (well), 22

D861.2. Magic object stolen by neighbor, 23a, b

D881.2. Recovery of magic object by use of magic cudgel (mannikins), 23a, b

D945. Magic hedge, 14

D1015.1. Magic heart of animal, 19a, b

D1019. Magic egg, 3a, b

D1051.1*. Magic handkerchief that makes owner welcome, 33

D1067.2. Magic cap, 35b, c

D1081. Magic sword, 20b

D1242.1. Magic water, 21

D1317. Magic objects warn of danger, 34

D1335.2. Magic strength-giving drink, 4

D1335.14*. Magic stick gives strength, 20a

D1344.11*. Magic bull stripe gives invulnerability, 20a, b, c, d, e

D1364.7. Sleeping potion, 15a

D1364.17. Spindle causes magic sleep, 14

D1381. Magic object protects from attack, 13a, b

D1383. Magic object protects from poison, 13a, b

D1401.2. Magic sack (light) furnishes mannikin who cudgels owner's enemies, 22; 23a, b

D1412.1. Magic sack draws person into it, 10a

D1421.1.4. Magic light summons genie, 22

D1454.1.1. Gold and silver combed from hair, 13a, b

D1454.2. Treasure falls from mouth, 13a, b, c

D1461.0.1. Tree with golden (wonderful) fruit, 19a, b

D1470.1.36*. Magic wishing chair, 15a

D1472.1.7. Magic table supplies food and drink, 19a, b

D1472.1.8. Magic tablecloth (napkin) supplies food and drink, 20a, b

D1472.1.22. Magic bag supplies food, 23a, b

D1521.1. Seven-league (nine-mile) boots, 8; 10a

D1581. Task performed by use of magic object, 24

D1602.11. Self-returning magic coin, 33
D1654.3. Indelible blood, 7a, b; 15a; 92
D1658.1.5. Apple-tree grateful for being shaken, 16a, b, c
D1658.1.6*. Fence grateful for being laid up, 16c
D1658.1.7*. Loaves (cake) grateful for removal from oven, 16a
D1681. Charm incorrectly uttered will not work, 35a, b
D1766.1.1. Magic fountain produced by prayer, 86

D1812.3.3. Future revealed in dream(s), 20b, c, e
D1812.3.4*. Fortune told by walking backward, 28a, b
D1812.5.1.2. Bad dream as evil omen, 101
D1962.2. Magic sleep by lousing, 8
D1978.5. Waking from magic sleep by kiss, 14
D1980. Magic invisibility, 17
D2004.5. Forgetting by stumbling, 65
D2165.1*. Escape by magic formula, 10b

E. *The Dead*

E1. Person comes to life, 30b
E31. Limbs of dead voluntarily reassemble and revive, 9k
E34. Resuscitation with misplaced head, 7c
E63. Resuscitation (promised) by prayer, 54
E221.2. Dead wife returns to reprove husband's second wife, 95
E225. Ghost of murdered child, 97
E235.4. Return of dead to punish theft of part of corpse, 12a, b, c, d, e, f, g
E235.4.1. Return from the dead to punish theft of golden arm from grave, 12a
E261. Ghost makes attack, 9b, i, j
E275. Ghost haunts place of great accident or misfortune, 92
E281. Ghosts haunt house, 9a, b, c, d, e, f, g, h, i, j, k, m, n; 33
E324. Dead child's friendly return to parents, 98a, b
E341.4*. Heads of the well grateful for bath, 13a, b
E371. Return of dead to reveal hidden treasure, 9a, c, d, e, f, h, k, m; 50; 95
E391*. Ghost responds when spoken to in the name of God, 9d, f, g
E402. Mysterious ghostlike noises heard, 9a, b, c, d, e, f, g, h, i, j, k, m; 95

E422.1.1. Headless revenant, 9a, b, e, f, h, i, j, n; 59
E423.1.2. Revenant as cat, 9b, c, d
E423.1.3. Revenant as (white) horse, 9m
E434.9*. Ghost cannot come into lighted room, 92
E441.2*. Ghost laid when head is buried with body, 9f
E451.4. Ghost laid when living man speaks to it, 9a, c, d, e, f, g
E451.5. Ghost laid when treasure is unearthed, 9a, c, d, h, k, m; 59; 95
E451.6*. Ghost laid when bloodstains uncovered, 92
E467. Revenants (of animals) fight each other, 9a, e, f
E545. The dead speak, 9a, c, d, f, h, j, k, m
E592.3*. Ghost carries own head, 9e, f
E607.1. Bones of dead collected and buried, return in another form directly from grave, 27a, b
E613.0.1. Reincarnation of murdered child as bird, 27a, b; 30a
E632.1. Speaking bones (head) of murdered person reveal murder, 30a, b
E761.1.1. Life token: water turns to blood, 3a, b
E761.2.1. Life token: staff (switch) stuck in ground shakes, 3a, b

F. *Marvels*

F54.2. Plant grows to sky, 11b

F92. Pit (well) entrance to lower world, 2; 16a

F261. Fairies dance, 21

F311.1. Fairy godmother, 13c; 18

F316. Fairy lays curse on child, 14

F316.1. Curse of fairy partially overcome by another fairy's amendment, 14

F343.5. Fairies (godmother) give beautiful clothes, 18

F512.1. Person with one eye, 19a

F512.2.1.1. Three-eyed person, 19a

F517.1. Person unusual as to his feet, 21

F551.1.2.1. Woman with horseshoes on feet (hands), 37

F660.1. Brothers acquire extraordinary skill, 26

F661.1. Skillful marksman shoots meat out of hands (forks) of giants, 4

F675. Ingenious carpenter, 26

F833.1. Sword so heavy that hero must take drink of strength before swinging it, 4

F848.1. Girl's long hair as ladder into tower, 5

F852.5*. Moving coffin, 9a, b, c, d, e, f, h, j; 28a

F913. Victims rescued from swallower's belly, 77a, b, c, d

F952.1. Blindness cured by tears, 5

G. *Ogres*

G61. Relative's flesh eaten unwittingly, 12e; 27a, c; 30b

G82. Cannibal (giant) fattens victim, 11a

G83. Cannibal (witch) sharpens knife to kill captive, 10a

G84. Fee-fi-fo-fum, 10c, d

G200.0*. Woman becomes witch by doing evil, 36a, b, c

G211.1. Witch in form of horse, 37

G211.1.2. Witch as horse shod with horseshoes, 37

G211.2. Witch in form of cat (hog), 36c

G211.3. Witch in form of dog, 3a, b

G211.14*. Witch in form of hog, 36a, b, c

G224.1. Witch's charm opposite of Christian, 36a, b

G224.2. Witch's salve, 35b

G241.1.5*. Witch rides bull, 35a, b

G241.2.1. Witch transforms man into horse and rides him, 37

G252. Witch in form of cat (hog) has hand cut off, 36a, b

G252.1*. Hog shot: woman has pain, 36c

G263.2*. Witch enchants wild horses, 13a, b

G263.3*. Witch enchants gate and makes poisonous, 13a, b

G263.4*. Witch transforms tail into ax and cuts tree hero is in, 3a, b

G275.2. Witch overcome by helpful dogs of hero, 3a, b

G275.6*. Witch killed with silver bullet, 37

G284. Witch as helper, 13a, b

G400. Person falls into ogre's power, 8

G401. Children wander into ogre's (witch's, giant's) house, 10a, b, d; 11a, b

G402. Pursuit of bird (butterfly) leads to ogre's house (cat's den), 15b

G423. Ball falling into water (den) puts person into ogre's power, 6a, b; 7c

G441. Ogre carries victim in bag (pocket), 10c

G442*. Witch adopts unpromising hero, 10a

H. Tests

J. The Wise and the Foolish

K. *Deceptions*

K731. Wild boar captured in church, 62a

K758*. Capture by giving evidence as feigned dream, 34

K841. Substitute for execution obtained by trickery, 54

K842. Dupe persuaded to take prisoner's place in a sack, 31; 59

K874. Deception by pretended lousing, 27a

K875*. Deception by pretended secret news, 27c

K891. Dupe (animal) induced to jump to his death, 77a, c, d

K912. Giants' (Robbers') heads cut off one by one as they enter house (yard), 4; 62h

K941.1. Cows (horses) killed for their hides when large price is reported by trickster, 31

K1043. Dupe induced to eat sharp (stinging, bitter) fruit (red pepper), 42

K1051. Diving for sheep (cattle), 31; 59

K1082. Ogres duped into fighting each other, 4; 62a

K1111.1. Ogre's beard caught fast, 2

K1161. Animals hidden in various parts of house drive away intruders, 1

K1336. Magic helper brings girl to hero's bed (room), 22

K1345. Tale of the cradle (mush), 57

K1347*. Person enters castle by being thrown on top of wall, 4

K1442. Casting eyes: animal's eyes, 64

K1611. Substituted caps (gold lockets) cause ogre (witch) to kill own children, 10a, c; 11a

K1682.1*. Disguised trickster is himself frightened, 60a, b

K1815. Humble disguise, 18

K1817.1. Disguise as beggar (old woman), 30a, b

K1843.2. Wife takes mistress's place in husband's bed, 15a

K1915. Substitute bridegroom, 20d

K1916. Robber bridegroom (neighbor), 34

K1917. Penniless bridegroom pretends to wealth, 20d

K1931.2. Imposters (brothers) abandon hero in lower world, 2

K1935. Imposters (brothers) steal rescued princess (girls), 2

K1951.1. Boastful flykiller: "seven at a blow," 62a, h

K2150. Innocent made to appear guilty, 31

K2152. Unresponsive corpse, 9b, c

K2321. Corpse set up to frighten people, 9b, c

L. Reversal of Fortune

L10. Victorious youngest son, 11a; 24; 33

L100. Unpromising hero (heroine), 10a, c, d

L161. Lowly hero marries princess (girl), 2; 17; 29

L162. Lowly heroine marries king (prince), 18; 19a

M. Ordaining the Future

M341.2.13. Prophecy: death through spindle wound, 14

M431.2. Curse: toads from mouth (hair), 13a, b, c

N. *Chance and Fate*

N201. Wish for exhalted husband realized, 15a

N271. Murder will out, 90

N334. Accidental fatal ending of game or joke, 61

N344. Father kills self believing that son is dead, 81b

N475. Secret name overheard by eavesdropper, 25

N611.2. Criminal accidentally detected: "that is the first"—sleepy woman counting her yawns, 63

N813. Helpful genie, 22

N825.3. Old woman helper, 19a

P. *Society*

P10. Kings, 81a

P30. Princes, 81b

P210. Husband and wife, 15a; 28a; 32a, b; 90; 96; 99

P230. Parents and children, 97; 98a, b

P233. Father and son, 9a, b; 33; 81a, b; 87

P234. Father and daughter, 5

P251. Brothers, 4; 7b; 10a; 11a; 24; 26

P252. Sisters, 6a; 10b; 15a; 19a, b

P253. Sister and brother, 3a

P284. Stepsister, 16a

P441. Tailor, 62a, b

Q. *Rewards and Punishments*

Q2. Kind and unkind, 13a, b, c; 16a, b, c

Q42.1.1. Child divides last loaf with fairy (dwarf), 13a, b

Q42.3. Generosity to saint (grateful dead) in disguise rewarded, 17

Q51. Kindness to animal (bird) rewarded, 23a, b; 27a, b

Q86. Reward for industry, 6a

Q87*. Reward for obedience, 7b

Q111.2*. Shower of gold as reward, 16a

Q280. Unkindness punished, 13a, b, c

Q321. Laziness punished, 25

Q325. Disobedience punished, 6a, b

Q412. Punishment: millstone dropped on guilty person, 27a, b; 30a

Q415.4*. Punishment: eaten by reptiles, 16a

Q469.3. Punishment: grinding up in a mill, 16b, c

Q482. Punishment: noble person must do menial service, 21

Q482.1. Princess serves as menial, 18

R. *Captives and Fugitives*

R11.1. Princess (girl) abducted by monster (old man), 2

R11.2.1. Devil carries off wicked people, 27c

R41.3. Captivity in dungeon, 20d

R111.1.2. Rescue of princess (girl) from robbers, 6b

R111.1.5.1*. Rescue of woman from frog-husband, 25

R121.5. Ariadne-thread, 81b

R135. Abandoned children find way back to clue, 10d

R153.3. Father rescues sons, 87

R155.1. Youngest brother rescues older brothers, 10a

R163. Rescue by grateful dead man (woman), 59

R211. Escape from prison, 7a, c, d

R225. Elopement, 29

S. *Unnatural Cruelty*

S10. Cruel parents, 12h; 19b

S11. Cruel father, 20e

S12. Cruel mother, 12a; 19a, b; 20a; 25; 27a, c; 30a; 97

S31. Cruel stepmother, 6b; 10b; 12b; 13a, b, c; 15b; 16a; 20b, c; 27b; 30b

S33*. Cruel stepsisters, 10b; 16a

S73*. Cruel sisters, 19a, b

S111.7*. Murder by poisoned needle, 15b

S115. Murder by stabbing, 28a

S165. Mutilation: putting out eyes, 5

S222. Man promises child in order to save himself from danger or death, 5

T. *Sex*

T22.3. Predestined husband, 28a, b

T68. Princess (daughter) offered as prize, 24

T91.7. Rich girl in love with poor boy, 20d

T96. Lovers reunited after many adventures, 25

T121. Unequal marriage, 7a

T172.0.1. All husbands (suitors) have perished on bridal night, 17

T211.3. Husband and wife (lovers) kill themselves so as not to be separated, 85

T251.2. Taming the shrew, 23a

T320. Escape from undesired lover, 18

X. *Humor*

X111.7. Misunderstood words lead to comic results, 66

X424. The devil in the cemetery, 67a, b, c, d

X435.6*. "Let Gabriel blow his horn" —boy obliges, 68

X905. Lying contest, 72

X910. Münchausen tales, 69b, c; 71a, b

X911.2. Man escapes from bee's nest (hollow tree) on bear's tail, 71a, b

X916. Lie: man carried through air by geese (ducks), 56

X917. Man falls and is buried in earth (rocks): goes for spade and digs self out, 56; 78

X921.4. Man shoots ramrod full (great flock) of ducks, 70

X921.5. Catching fish in boots while wading, 70

X929*. Timber bitten by snake swells to great size, 74a, b

X945*. Rapid construction of building, 72

X946*. Lie: fish trained to live on land falls into water and drowns, 75

X947*. Lie: animals so evenly matched in fight they go up in the air, 76

X954*. Topsy-turvy talk, 78a, b, c

X1021.8*. The great bedbug, 72

X1021.9*. The great opossum, 73

Z. *Miscellaneous Groups of Motifs*

Z31.3.4. The fat troll (wolf, bear, man), 77a, b, c, d

Z130.1. Color of flag (sails) as message of good or bad news, 81b